DEAD WEIGHT

CROSSROADS QUEEN
BOOK 5

ANNABEL CHASE

RED PALM PRESS LLC

Copyright © 2024 by Annabel Chase

All rights reserved.

No part of this book may be reproduced in any form or by any electronic or mechanical means, including information storage and retrieval systems, without written permission from the author, except for the use of brief quotations in a book review.

Cover by Trif Designs

❦ Created with Vellum

CHAPTER 1

The tiny hairs on my arm sizzled as puffs of smoke rose from my skin. I wrapped the bottom of my shirt around my arm to keep it from bursting into flames. My upgraded ward was no joke. It didn't reach the level of stop, drop, and roll, but I wouldn't mind a less intense physical response.

Resident ghost Ray Bauer glanced at me. "Couldn't you just have invested in one of those security camera systems? Seems like it does the same thing without the risk of injury."

"Cameras aren't as effective when dealing with supernaturals." I adjusted my shirt and strode toward the door. According to the scorched hairs on my arm, Kane Sullivan, the demon prince of hell himself, had arrived.

Nana Pratt, my other resident ghost, appeared beside me, wringing her hands.

"What's up?"

"There's a strange creature loping across the bridge. He looks...wrong."

Not a certain prince of hell then. A lot of things were wrong with Kane, but his looks weren't one of them.

I pulled a dagger from my boot, not bothering to ask for a

more detailed description. Nana Pratt had a tendency to focus on unhelpful features like, 'his hair seemed to be parted on the wrong side,' or 'he looks like he might pass the basket in church without donating.'

I opened the door and strolled outside to greet my unwelcome visitor.

Bulky frame, blank expression, and the stench of desperation. Textbook ghoul. Not the ideal way to kick off the day.

The ghoul wasn't loping as much as meandering. The creature seemed drawn to the cemetery yet distracted by whatever crossed its path. Right now, it leaned over the bridge and stared at the moat like water was a new and exciting invention. I'd never seen a stoned ghoul before. First time for everything.

I stood on the porch and leaned against a column, fingering the handle of my dagger. "Hey, buddy," I yelled.

The ghoul's deformed head jerked in my direction. It took the fool about twenty seconds to locate the source of the sound. Good grief. Never mind too stupid to live. This one was too stupid to kill.

The ghoul grunted angrily, like I'd interrupted a private conversation with its reflection.

"You're trespassing," I said. "You should move along."

The ghoul sniffed in the direction of the cemetery.

"Sorry, pal. No fresh meat in those graves. Nothing to see here."

What would've prompted it to explore my property in the first place? Unless somebody pointed the ghoul in my direction, it would have no reason to come here. There was also the curious fact that this ghoul seemed to be traveling alone. They rarely traveled solo, especially not in broad daylight.

"Where's your friend?" I asked. Maybe the friend had wandered off and this ghoul was trying to find its companion. Great. That meant two possible problems.

Saliva dripped from the ghoul's mouth and hissed as it hit the bridge.

Charming.

"Please don't drool on the bridge," I said. "I need a hole in the wood like I need a hole in my head."

It would be much easier to deal with the ghoul if I didn't have to get within stabbing distance of it.

I felt the presence of the ghosts behind me.

"What is that thing?" Ray asked.

"A ghoul."

"Why does it look like it downed half a bottle of Wild Turkey?"

As though to prove Ray's point, the ghoul staggered forward and nearly fell into the moat. The creature managed to catch itself in time and regain its balance.

"What does it want?" Nana Pratt asked.

"Fresh bodies from a grave, usually," I replied. "Not sure about this one, though. Seems to be in a stupor." I omitted the part about not traveling solo; I didn't want to worry them.

"Didn't you say this is no longer an active cemetery?" Ray asked.

"Correct." I'd made sure when I bought the house adjacent to it.

The ghoul wiped a dribble of saliva from its cheek.

"Aw. Reminds me of Steven when he was a toddler," Nana Pratt said. "I almost feel sorry for the poor creature."

"Me, too," I said quietly.

The ghoul stumbled forward, closing the gap between us. I continued to grip the dagger just in case I needed it for self-defense, but I had no intention of using it. This wasn't a fair fight.

Before the ghoul reached the porch step, it dropped to the walkway in a heap. I stared at the large lump of weirdness.

Nana Pratt peered over the edge of the porch. "Is it dead?"

"Probably sleeping it off," Ray offered.

I wasn't sure. I ventured forward for a closer look.

"Are you sure about that, Lorelei?" Nana Pratt's voice rose an octave. "Why not call one of your friends?"

"She can handle this fella," Ray said.

I crouched in front of the ghoul and listened for sounds of life. A soft grunt was all I needed.

"Alive," I called over my shoulder.

"I can't decide whether to be relieved or disappointed," Nana Pratt said.

"It can't hurt you, Ingrid," Ray reminded her.

"I know, but it can hurt Lorelei."

I was touched by her concern.

"You don't need to baby her. She's a grown goddess," Ray said.

I turned to look at them. "I appreciate the level of care I'm hearing, but can we save the chitchat for later? I'm trying to focus."

The ghosts proceeded to spend the next sixty seconds shushing each other while I examined the ghoul.

"Now might be a good time to use that dagger you're holding," a voice said.

I glanced up to see Kane Sullivan gliding toward the walkway. He must've flown over the gate in his blackbird form. Between the dark blond hair that circled his head in soft waves like an angelic halo and whisky-colored eyes that promised endless nights of devilish passion, the demon was a walking contradiction. Notably, my arm didn't catch on fire when the ward activated. Instead, a warm sensation flooded my body. Odd.

"There's something wrong with it," I told him.

"All the better to put the creature out of its misery." Kane leaned down to inspect the heap. "It's a ghoul, isn't it?"

"Yes."

He shot me a quizzical look. "Since when are you in the business of rescuing ghouls? They're disgusting scavengers."

I looked at him. "And you're a demon prince of hell. Should I put you out of your misery, too?"

He resumed an upright position. "Point taken."

"It stumbled in here like a drunken pirate in search of its next barrel of rum and then collapsed. I'm not sure what to do."

"I think that decision is now out of your hands." He lowered his gaze to the walkway, where black liquid oozed from beneath the creature.

I listened closely. The sounds of life had fallen silent. The ghoul's body began to fold in on itself and crumbled to dust. I scrambled backward to avoid the sticky goop, as well as taking a face full of ghoul debris.

"A puddle of ghoul," Kane said. "That will stain your pavement unless you treat it right away, you know."

I could practically feel the ghosts stiffen in response to that information.

"I'll get a bucket of water," Ray announced.

"And I'll find a sponge," Nana Pratt added. "You'll need to buy another 3-pack next time you go to the store. This one will need to be thrown away."

I mentally added 'sponges' to my grocery list.

"Any idea what happened?" Kane asked.

I tucked away my dagger. "None. And now I'm worried about the second one."

Kane's gaze swept the property. "There's a second one?"

"Not here, but it must be somewhere. They don't travel solo."

"I flew across town and didn't see anything out of the ordinary."

"Would you mind doing another quick circle overhead? If there's a sick ghoul nearby, I'd like to know." It was one thing to darken my doorstep; it was quite another to endanger the people of Fairhaven who didn't know about them.

"Do you think the creature knew you lived here?"

"No, but it's possible the ghoul was drawn to my energy." They were, after all, creatures partial to the dead. Although they didn't obey me in the way some did, they might sense my presence and gravitate to me without being aware of it. Ghouls weren't known for their brains, only that they feast on them.

Kane's six-foot-four frame spouted black wings as he morphed into a blackbird and flew away. I watched as he disappeared from view. Nope. Nothing wrong with the way he looked.

I heard a thunk and turned to see Ray slide through the door. "What happened?"

He winced. "I forgot the bucket can't go through solids like I can."

I hopped onto the porch and opened the door to liberate the bucket.

"You're very smiley for someone with a dead ghoul on her sidewalk," Ray observed.

I touched my cheeks. "Am I?"

"It's her gentleman caller," Nana Pratt said. "Brings out the sunshine in her."

"You're giving him too much credit," I replied. "I had bacon and eggs for breakfast."

Ray nodded sagely. "Bacon always puts you in a good mood."

"I wish it didn't. I have a fondness for pigs."

My gentleman caller returned a few minutes later, and the warm sensation in my body repeated. Interesting.

By now, Nana Pratt and Ray were hard at work on the puddle of ghoul, and I'd moved to the porch to avoid stepping in black goo.

"No sign of any ghouls." Kane observed the moving sponge and bucket. "They're like those two mice to your Cinderella."

"Jaq and Gus," I said.

"I heard that," Ray grumbled.

Kane gestured to the house. "Shall we divide and conquer your household chores?"

"Everything we need is out and ready." I looked at the ghosts. "Kane is here to help me hang a few picture frames."

"I could've done that," Ray mumbled.

"Oh, be quiet," Nana Pratt said. "It's only an excuse to spend time with him. Goodness knows she doesn't need to spend any more time with the likes of us."

I left them to their squabbling and retreated inside the house with my royal handyman.

I'd picked up a few framed pictures during a drive around town last week. One of many lessons I'd learned from my grandfather was the ability to scavenge household goods. Pops had been an expert upcycler. I hadn't reached his level of expertise, mainly because I lacked his creativity, but I knew a pretty picture when I spotted one from a stop sign across the street.

Kane halted at the edge of the drop cloth on the floor. "You need a drop cloth for hanging pictures?"

"Nana Pratt insisted. Apparently, making holes in the wall can result in debris on the floor."

Kane examined the first painting. "Gustav Klimt? Really?"

"What's wrong with Klimt?" I fell in love with *The Kiss* during a visit to the Vienna museum where it was on display. When I saw the reproduction, I knew I had to have it.

The demon cocked his head. "I feel like I'm in a sorority house."

"When were you ever in a sorority house?"

He cleared his throat. "Never mind."

I lifted the painting and held it in place. "Is it centered?"

"A little to the left."

I craned my neck to look at him and nearly dropped the painting in the process. "Your left or my left?"

Kane's sigh of exasperation was whisper quiet.

Still. "I heard that."

He moved to stand behind me. "I'm going to touch you now."

"Is that a threat or a promise?" I joked, but I knew the reason he'd given me advanced notice.

I steeled my mind as he snaked an arm along mine to guide my hand. "This left."

A pleasant sensation zinged down my spine as his body pressed gently against mine. The last time we were this close, we were on the floor trying to rip off each other's clothes. At the time we'd blamed a god-infested lust goat when, in fact, the goat had been of the normal sock-chewing variety.

"Think we could mimic their pose?" he asked, his voice as close and intimate as the picture in my hands. "Let life imitate art."

I brushed him aside, too caught off guard by his bid for closeness to accept it. "They're mythical figures. They're not meant to be imitated."

"Hmm. You told me you intend to move slowly with me. Now I'm beginning to think you meant it."

"Oh, I meant it. For both our sakes." Following the goat debacle, Kane and I agreed to move forward with our relationship, albeit at a glacial pace. He feared reverting to old hellish habits while under the influence of a goddess of nightmares.

I feared … everything.

I settled the wire of the frame on the hook. It immediately slid and tilted to the right.

Kane arched an eyebrow. "Didn't you tell me you were raised by someone handy? It appears a few basic skills are lacking."

"We didn't hang many picture frames together."

"We didn't hang many in hell either, at least not in the traditional sense."

I looked at him. "I don't think I want to know the details."

I'd gotten a glimpse of Kane's circle of hell thanks to one of his nightmares and I wasn't eager to repeat the experience.

He adjusted the frame so that it was perfectly straight. Show-off.

He pivoted to face me. "I do."

"You did do. Well done." I reached up and patted his head.

"Not the painting. You said you didn't want to know the details, but I'd like to know them about you. Consider this the vetting stage of our relationship."

I had so little experience answering questions about myself with honesty and clarity—the vetting stage sounded like my version of hell.

"All right then. Vet me."

"When did you discover you were different from the other kids?"

I shifted my attention back to the picture frame. "Don't we all grow up thinking we're different? It's part of childhood development."

"Except you really were different. You must've realized from an early age."

"This feels too much like an interrogation." I adjusted the frame a millimeter and stepped back to observe the change.

"That was already straight. You've thrown it off balance." He stepped forward and fixed it again. "It's hardly an interrogation. That would involve far more nails."

I cut him a sidelong glance. "You of all demons think that's funny?"

When Kane attempted to overthrow Lucifer, he was caught and tortured. The torment would've lasted for an eternity if the prince of hell hadn't been rescued by his loyal friend, Dantalion.

"What doesn't kill us makes us stronger."

"Bullshit," I said. "What doesn't kill us makes us lucky."

Kane picked up the hammer and drove another nail into

the spot I'd marked on the wall. "Speaking of lucky escapes, you should know Magnarella is making noise."

"Seems to be all he does."

"According to my sources, this claim has teeth."

"Don't you mean fangs?"

Kane grunted. "Watch your back, that's all I'm trying to say. He won't have forgotten you. Vampires hold more grudges than the gods."

Vincenzo Magnarella's grudge against me began when I ruined his blossoming business and destroyed his expensive laboratory. The vampire's lab had been devoted to developing an elixir that turned mundane humans into deities, which were then showcased in a fighting ring. As a favor to my friend, Gunther Saxon, I'd volunteered as tribute in his sister's stead and ended up fighting for my life in a pit of despair. I won the fight and destroyed their science experiment before they could clear my mind to make space for another goddess. Despite the target on my back, I had no regrets.

"What have you heard?" I asked.

"There's been movement at his compound. Trucks in and out, that sort of thing."

"The Corporation?"

"Not to my knowledge."

A wave of relief rippled through me. The Corporation was even bigger and badder than Magnarella. The vampire's lead scientist, Dr. Edmonds, had left their employ and brought his knowledge and expertise on avatars to Magnarella's lab.

Kane hung the next picture. "No word from Addison Gray, I take it?"

"No."

Addison Gray, an avatar of the goddess Aite, recently became aware of my deified status, as well as my ability to pull nightmares into reality. Although I didn't reveal my true name, it wouldn't take much for her to figure out my identity and use the information as leverage for some other purpose. From what I gathered, Aite had her own issues with The Corporation, and she seemed like the type willing to sacrifice me in order to regain their favor.

Kane met my gaze and held it. "Starting to regret your decision to move to Fairhaven?"

Truth be told, if I had realized Fairhaven housed a multi-realm crossroads that drew otherworldly beings to town, I wouldn't have bought Bluebeard's Castle and settled here. I wasn't sure what I'd been thinking when I hit the buy button on a house from the Gilded Age anyway. Despite its grand history, it was now an enormous money pit. No offense to its original owner, Joseph Edgar Blue III. The tycoon's heart and wallet were in the right place when he built this house.

"I miss the anonymity I had in London," I admitted.

"I can understand that, but for selfish reasons…" His phone buzzed, interrupting his statement. His face darkened as he scanned the message. "I'm sorry. I need to go."

"What's the problem, Batman? Is the Joker holding up the local bank?"

"Vaughn's in jail. I need to bail him out."

"Official business?" I asked. Vaughn worked as an assassin and was a member of the local guild overseen by Kane.

"No. That's why I'm curious to find out what happened."

I glanced at the third painting resting on the floor. I still had no clue where I wanted to hang this one. "I'll come with you. I've always wanted to spring somebody from jail."

His mouth twitched. "This isn't a jailbreak. It's perfectly legal."

"Okay, fine. I just can't face making this decision alone. I'd rather help you rescue a felon."

"A misdemeanor."

I draped the drop cloth across his broad shoulders and dusted the ends. "Not all heroes wear capes."

CHAPTER 2

February in Fairhaven meant bleak skies and frigid temperatures. I tried to ignore the downsides and focus on the fact that I was alive and, dare I say it, as close to thriving as I'd ever been, despite living in the shadow of fear and uncertainty.

Fairhaven Police Jail looked like a holdover from the Wild West. The small, nondescript building stood in the shadow of the modest police station. The inmates looked more hungover than hardened, except Vaughn who looked like he could slice you in half with the swipe of his impressive jawline.

He didn't appear remotely surprised to see Kane. "Took you long enough," the mage said, as the cell door opened.

"You're lucky I'm here at all," Kane replied. "I was otherwise engaged."

Vaughn's gaze slid to me. "I see. Are you two a package deal now?"

I shrugged. "I'm nosy."

"What happened?" Kane asked.

Vaughn's face turned stony. "Outside."

The mage retrieved his possessions from the lady at the

counter. "Is that sketch artist still around, Val? I'd like a copy of those pictures she drew."

Val's bushy eyebrows lifted. "So you can play vigilante again? I don't think so. Those sketches are for cops, not perps."

Vaughn blew her a kiss. "Love you, too."

Despite the roll of Val's eyes, I could tell she enjoyed the interaction. "See you next time, smooth operator."

I glanced at the assassin as we exited the building. "Not your first visit to the local slammer, I take it."

"Only murder is off the menu in this town."

"It isn't that simple, and you know it," Kane snapped. "Care to tell me what happened?"

Although the rest of Vaughn's face telegraphed 'you're not the boss of me,' his mouth said, "I rescued a damsel in distress."

"Any damsel I know?" Kane asked.

"I don't know her name. One of the Arrowhead wolves."

I swallowed laughter. "I don't think there's a single she-wolf in the pack you can refer to as a damsel."

"I don't know what to tell you. I was leaving Monk's when I saw two guys harassing her. I assumed it was unwanted sexual advances, not that I would know anything about that. She tried to get around them and they started kicking the absolute crap out of her."

"So you decided to intervene?" Kane queried.

Vaughn adjusted his collar with the quick flick of his fingers. "I didn't like her odds."

"She didn't shift?" I asked.

"None of them did until that new cop showed up, then the two cowards turned tail and ran into the woods."

"Why arrest you?" I asked.

"Disorderly conduct. I got a few good punches in before they fled. Pretty sure one of them has a broken nose."

"Can you describe the she-wolf?" Kane asked.

"Middle-aged brunette. Leather jacket. Permanent snarl. Major attitude." Vaughn smiled. "Which I would've appreciated more if it didn't end with her lip split open."

There was only one werewolf in town that fit that description. "Anna," I said. "Her name is Anna Dupree."

Kane's eyebrow quirked. "You know her?"

"We've crossed paths more than once. She and West are tight."

"Too bad he wasn't with her," Vaughn said. "I have no doubt the world would be short two werewolves this morning, and I don't mean Anna and West." He rubbed his jaw. "I would've done it myself if not for the rules."

Kane clapped Vaughn on the back. "The guild thanks you for your restraint."

"I'm sure Anna would offer her thanks as well," I said. "You still saved her, regardless of whether or not you killed her attackers."

"I gave the sketch artist a description of the two attackers, and she nailed it." He paused. "Speaking of which, if she weren't so young, I'd want to…"

I leveled him with a look. "Don't you dare finish that sentence." Val had been wise not to summon the sketch artist back to see Vaughn. The handsome assassin could charm the skin off a snake.

Vaughn directed his remarkable jaw at the demon prince. "Are you going to give me a demerit?"

I laughed. "You give demerits? You're assassins, not Boy Scouts."

"A well-run organization requires a system," Kane said. He glanced at the mage. "I'm undecided about the demerit. Give me a couple days."

"Am I free to go?" Vaughn asked. "I have work to do."

Kane nodded. "We'll drop you off at home."

Vaughn slid into the back seat without complaint. I'd half

expected him to yell "shotgun" and steal the passenger seat out from under me.

"Why do you think Anna didn't shift?" I asked. It seemed out of character for her to let two werewolves whale on her without reverting to her stronger form. And why would two werewolves be the ones attacking her? The pack had their squabbles, but they generally took them to West to be resolved rather than engage in physical combat in the parking lot of the local dive bar.

"Hell if I know," Vaughn said. "She seemed almost frozen, like she didn't know how to fight back."

That definitely didn't sound like the Anna I knew.

Kane pulled into the driveway of a beige house that looked like it had been built in the 1960s. If I had to choose a house for Vaughn, it would've been this one. I didn't need to peer inside to know the interior was full-on swank. It wouldn't surprise me to learn there was a rotating bed with a mirror on the ceiling, not that I had any intention of finding out. I'd leave that to my friend Camryn.

"See you at the next meeting," Kane said.

Vaughn left the car without another word.

"What?" Kane asked, as he reversed out of the driveway.

I looked at him askance. "What do you mean?"

"Something's bothering you. I can tell."

"It doesn't sound like Anna to shrink from a fight."

"Who knows? Maybe they were her brothers, and she didn't want to fight them."

"Do you believe Vaughn's version of events?"

Kane shot me a curious glance. "You think I shouldn't?"

"You know him better than I do."

Kane turned the wheel to the left.

"Um, my house is that way." I pointed to the right.

"You've got me thinking."

"You mean second guessing."

"I trust Vaughn, but I'd like more details about what happened last night."

"And you want to go right now?" I asked.

"No time like the present."

I stared out the window at the passing trees. "It's because I'm with you, isn't it?"

"West likes you. He'll be more willing to let me talk to one of his members if you're with me."

I barked a laugh. "West likes me the way little kids like broccoli. He tolerates me, but he wouldn't choose me."

"He tolerates you better than he tolerates me."

"It's my wit and charm."

"Yes," Kane said slowly. "Let's go with that."

The paved road turned to dirt as we drove northwest and entered pack territory.

Arrowhead trailer park was located in the wooded outskirts of town and consisted of about three dozen trailers in a horseshoe shape. The only way to reach the park on wheels was via dirt road. The pack had no interest in making visitation easy on outsiders. I didn't envy the local delivery carriers.

I encouraged Kane to park a reasonable distance from the trailers. The wolves could be a feisty bunch, and the last thing I wanted was to break up a fight because one of them decided to ding Kane's shiny car.

Despite West's alpha status, his trailer was indistinguishable from the others, except for a looped iron symbol affixed to the front door—the Greek symbol for alpha. As far as leaders went, West leaned more democratic than most. He'd made it clear that he didn't appreciate my presence in Fairhaven, not because he knew my real identity, but because he sensed I was dangerous.

His instincts were spot on.

West put the protection of his pack ahead of everything

else, including his personal life. I related to him more than he knew.

A familiar buff werewolf intercepted us as we approached the trailers on foot.

"Well, if it isn't the lady of the big pile of blue stones and her demon pet." The werewolf I'd dubbed Beefy Bert bowed in a sweeping gesture.

"Arise, Sir Bert," I said.

Kane gritted his teeth. "If you need help arising, I'd be happy to assist you."

I pictured Bert flying through the air and landing on the doorstep in a mangled heap. Not the outcome I wanted.

Before the interaction had time to escalate, Weston Davies rounded the corner of his trailer. He wore his trademark worn jeans paired with a long-sleeved black shirt beneath a black puffy vest. Black work boots and wraparound sunglasses made him look more like an off-duty Colorado ski instructor than a backwoods werewolf alpha. Still, the look suited him.

"Hey, West," I greeted him. I couldn't help but like him, regardless of his mixed feelings about me.

"Clay." His gaze slid to Kane. "Sullivan, what brings you to pack territory?"

"One of your members," Kane replied. "Anna."

West's brow furrowed. "What business do you have with Anna?"

"Have you seen her today?" I asked. "Or last night?"

West cast a quizzical look at Bert, who shrugged. "Is there a problem?"

"You know Anna," Bert interjected. "She probably mouthed off to the wrong supernatural, and now she's somewhere licking her wounds."

"Oh, I definitely think she's licking her wounds," Kane said. "From what I understand, there are many of them."

West growled. "And how'd she get these wounds?"

"I'd worry about that part later," Kane suggested. "In your position, I'd be more concerned with her well-being."

"It wasn't us," I added quickly. I wanted to make it clear that we were here to help, not apologize.

West flicked his chin at Bert, who made himself scarce.

"This way," West said.

He ambled to a trailer farther along the horseshoe shape, three doors down from his own. The only decoration in the compact front garden was a small Bigfoot statue carrying three gnomes.

West noticed my gaze. "Anna has a mild obsession with Bigfoot. You'll see."

"Everybody needs a hobby," I quipped.

He knocked on the front door, calling Anna's name. No answer. He pivoted to face us. "Stay here until I tell you otherwise." He turned back to the door. "Anna, this is West. I'm coming in."

The door was unlocked. He slipped inside the trailer, leaving the door ajar. I didn't pass up the opportunity to spy. I took a casual step closer to the inch-wide crack and leaned forward. The interior was too dark to see anything except the outline of furniture.

"Anything?" Kane prompted.

I shook my head.

"A blackbird can squeeze through that gap. Shall I sprout wings?"

I looked at him. "And have West fry you for lunch? I don't think that's a good idea."

"I'd have to agree," West said, startling both of us. "I don't have a taste for blackbird."

"How's Anna?" I asked.

"In rough shape and refusing to talk. I figure your presence in her home might loosen her lips." He pulled open the door, widening the gap. "Come on in."

I felt a twinge of guilt as I crossed the threshold, knowing

Anna would be furious. But something wasn't adding up and it seemed important to get to the bottom of it before anyone else landed in jail, or worse.

I noticed a Bigfoot clock on the kitchen wall as I passed by on the way to the bedroom.

Anna lay sprawled across the bed on her stomach. Her appearance matched Vaughn's description. Her face sported a gash on her cheek and a nasty bruise under her eye. Considering it was more than eight hours later and she hadn't fully healed, her injuries must've been extensive. Yet Anna had chosen to suffer alone and in silence.

"Hi, Anna," I said. "Can you tell us what happened last night at Monk's?"

She sneered. "What's the matter? Afraid you'll have to find a new dive bar to frequent?"

Kane glanced at me. "How often do you go to Monk's?"

I shrugged. "Your club is nice, but I'm not always in the mood for nice."

His lip curved slightly at the ends. "I see. I'll tuck that information away for future reference."

"I don't get why these two give a shit what happened to me," Anna said. Despite her harsh tone, her voice was surprisingly weak.

"Tell us what happened," West insisted, although I noticed his expression soften at the request. He knew she was hurting, and he didn't want to make it worse.

Anna made a point of swinging her legs off the side of the bed and switching to a seated position. Her pained grimace didn't escape my notice.

"I got into a fight. Nothing new there."

"This was no ordinary bar brawl," Kane pointed out. "You were attacked by two werewolves. And how bad must it have been that your wounds haven't healed?"

West's head snapped to attention. "You didn't tell me they were wolves. Which ones?"

"Doesn't matter," Anna muttered. "What's done is done. I'll heal eventually."

West stared at her intently. "Why are you protecting them?"

Her face radiated anger. "I'm not protecting anybody. This isn't a cause for concern. It was a heated moment and now it's over."

"One of my assassins ended up in jail trying to protect you," Kane said.

"That's on him," Anna shot back. "I didn't ask for help." A low growl escaped her. "I'd never ask for help from the guild."

Forget the Assassins Guild. She'd never ask for help from anyone outside the pack. Anna was more insular and stubborn than West when it came to pack politics.

I nudged Kane's arm. "We should go. Vaughn is fine, and Anna clearly doesn't want to involve us."

"I appreciate your concern," West said, in an effort to diffuse the tension. "Thanks for coming."

"No problem." I walked to the door and Kane reluctantly followed.

"She was hiding something," Kane said, once we were out of earshot.

"I'm sure she was, but there was no chance of her confiding in us. Her vault was locked up tight." Which I appreciated, given that she'd been served a taste of what I was capable of. My first night at Monk's, Anna had caused trouble. Sometimes weaker wolves cowered in my presence for reasons they didn't understand. Anna wasn't one of them. I'd slipped into her mind and triggered her worst nightmare in order to subdue her.

"Vaughn could've been killed by those wolves. He was lucky the cop scared them off."

"Anna probably doesn't want to get her friends in trouble with the alpha. Maybe they were drunk," I speculated.

Kane unlocked the car. "Werewolves or not, anyone who would pummel her like that isn't her friend."

I didn't disagree, but I also wasn't a werewolf. They had customs and dynamics that were beyond my expertise.

"Why don't you drop me off at the fork in the road?" I suggested. "There's no point in driving me home when you're much closer to yours."

"I don't mind."

"I could use the exercise." And the space. As drawn as I was to Kane, I was also mindful that this growing attraction between us had trouble written all over it, and I got myself into enough trouble without him. Besides, he had a nightclub to run and assassins to manage, and I had … an endless list of household chores. Hmm. One of us seemed to have a more interesting life than the other. Maybe it wasn't his charm and smoldering good looks I was drawn to. Maybe it was his colorful life. When you lived long enough in black and white, a speck of gold had to be blindingly appealing.

And by gods was he blindingly appealing.

Kane pulled to the side of the road. "If you're sure."

I wasn't sure about anything, but right now getting out of the car and putting distance between us seemed like the only sane move I could make.

"You look hungry," he commented. "I could cook us something at my place." His whisky-colored eyes fixed on me. "And, for the record, I always serve dessert."

No doubt.

I practically ripped the door off its hinges in an effort to escape from his close proximity.

"We'll talk later," I called over my shoulder.

I was fairly certain I heard laughter as he pulled away.

CHAPTER 3

Despite the cold and darkening sky, I didn't mind walking through the woods. There was beauty everywhere in Wild Acres, from the frosted tree branches to the icicles that hung from them like glittering pendants. I was glad to have worn my boots. The grippy soles kept me upright more than once.

Walking home had been the right decision. If I had taken Kane up on his offer of a meal followed by dessert… Well, we both knew the whipped cream wouldn't end up on the pudding.

And I wasn't ready for Kane's whipped cream.

I squeezed my eyes closed, trying to block the invading images that were so, so tempting.

Little hairs tickled the back of my neck and all thoughts of a cream-covered Kane dissipated. My eyes snapped open.

I wasn't alone.

That news wasn't necessarily bad. It could be a family of deer or scampering squirrels, but my increased heart rate suggested otherwise. Sometimes our bodies know before our minds do. I learned a long time ago it was foolish to ignore the warning signs.

Slowly, I lowered my hand to retrieve my dagger.

"I wouldn't move another inch if I were in your shoes," a lilting voice said from the gloaming. "Apologies, I meant boots." He paused. "Are you some sort of laborer? I suppose that makes sense."

Laborer? Who said laborer in this day and age?

Ignoring his warning, I slid the dagger from its hiding spot. "If you're looking for Little Red Riding Hood, I passed her about a mile back. Plucky little thing with a toothy grin and a red cape. Can't miss her."

"I can hear the mockery in your voice, but I do not understand the jest."

A visitor from the crossroads. Interesting.

"If you are here to deliver my package, then do so and move on. I have no quarrel with you," the voice demanded.

I pivoted in the direction of the voice. "Do I look like UPS to you? Trust me, brown is not my color."

A figure emerged from the shadows. He was tall and slender, with moon-kissed skin and ears slightly pointed at the ends. His eyes were his most remarkable feature—cat-shaped and greener than a blade of grass. He was the definition of a pretty boy.

"You're one of the fair folk," I said.

"And you are not, although I cannot determine any more than that." He glanced over my shoulder. "I do not see the package. Why would you come alone? Is this what your people refer to as a shakedown?"

Now it was my turn to be confused. "Why do you think I'm here to give you a package?"

He patted the nearest tree trunk. "Because this is the appointed meeting spot."

"I have no plans to meet anyone here. I'm walking home."

"I see." He paused, uncertain. "Have you seen anyone else?"

An idea occurred to me. "You're not looking for two werewolves, are you?"

His face scrunched in a ball. "Werewolves? There are werewolves in these woods?"

I folded my arms. "Let me get this straight. You made plans to meet someone in the woods and you don't know who they are or, evidently, where you are? What kind of package are you collecting?"

He sniffed with indignation. "None of your concern."

"If you want my help, I need more information. If not…" I turned to walk away.

"Wait," he said quickly. "Perhaps we got off to a bad start."

I spun back toward him. "I'm listening."

"My mother made the arrangements, but she is too unwell to travel and sent me in her stead. I would prefer not to return empty handed. Mother would be so disappointed."

"A mama's boy. Nice. You don't meet too many of those anymore."

He frowned. "Are you mocking me again?"

"No, it's my tone. I sound like I'm mocking everything."

He nodded. "I have an uncle like that. Leopold. I find him exhausting."

"Then I'm sure we'll get along swimmingly. Did you come through the crossroads?"

He blinked rapidly. "How did you know?"

"You're one set of green tights short of a Keebler elf. What's your name?"

He eyed me with distrust. "Why do you ask my name?"

"Because I want to steal your soul. Why do you think? We're having a conversation. It's polite." And, as my grandfather always said, *know with whom you're having the pleasure*.

His large eyes narrowed. "You know you speak to a fairy. Names hold great power."

"Only if we let them, but that's not what we're doing here, is it?" I asked matter-of-factly.

His tongue flicked across his upper lip. "No, I suppose not."

"Here. I'll start. My name is Lorelei Clay."

He recoiled slightly. "A bad omen. Both your names mean death."

"Well, I give you my word that I have no intention of killing you. I'm merely passing through on my way home."

He continued to regard me with suspicion. "My name is Sian," he finally said.

"A pleasure to meet you, Sian. Did you happen to encounter any werewolves when you came through the crossroads?"

"There were two men guarding the entrance to these woods. Are they the werewolves you referred to earlier?"

They weren't, but I ignored the question. "How did you get past them?"

"I did not hurt them if that is your question. I only tricked them into running the opposite direction to investigate a sound." He cupped his hands around his mouth and made a strange noise that seemed to emanate from behind me.

"What is that?" I asked.

He grinned. "The mating call of a whipper-crackle. I suspect your guardians did not know what to make of it."

"I highly doubt it, or they wouldn't have been so quick to investigate. Now, tell me what you expected to find here, and maybe I can help." As the self-appointed liminal deity of the crossroads, I felt a sense of obligation to preserve the peace.

He pressed his lips together. "I think I should wait here until my contact arrives."

Sian's nose glowed red. Poor guy wasn't dressed for this weather. He had to be numb by now.

"If you wait outside any longer, you'll be sent home as a fae-cicle. Come with me."

His gaze dropped to the dagger in my hand. "Why should I?"

"Because I'm going to take you to one of your kind and let you hash this out together."

He seemed taken aback. "My kind live here?"

"Not many, but yes."

He nodded slowly. "Then yes, I would appreciate the introduction. Perhaps I will even find what I seek there."

My stomach rumbled, and I began to regret turning down Kane's invitation. Sage and her grandmother didn't live too far from here. I could dump Robin Hood in their laps and still have enough time to cook a pot of chili when I got home.

"Right this way, Sian."

He maintained a safe distance from me as we walked. I got the distinct impression he'd been on the receiving end of many lectures about the treacheries of this world.

"How old are you, Sian?"

"Twenty-one in human years."

That explained the doe-eyed look. "What's wrong with your mom?"

The only sound was the crunch of a branch beneath my boot.

"I'm sorry she isn't well."

His gaze flicked to me, as though trying to discern the sincerity of the remark. "Thank you," he said.

A heavy grunt alerted me to someone's presence. I peered through the trees to see Sage outside chopping wood. Her blonde hair was tucked behind a green bandana that framed her round, cheerful face.

We stepped into the clearing. With another grunt, she split one more log before stopping to acknowledge us. "Lorelei, hi."

"How's it going, Savage?"

She smirked. "I stand by my claim."

When I first met Sage, she introduced her name as Savage, which her grandmother promptly denied.

"Sage, this is my new friend, Sian. There's a situation I hope you can help him with."

Her gaze skated to Sian. "You're one of us."

"He came through the crossroads," I explained. "He was supposed to meet someone to collect a package on behalf of his sick mother, but that's as much as he's willing to tell me. I thought you might be able to get more out of him before he froze to death."

Sage set aside the axe. "Right. Come inside then. Talking outside won't help matters."

Sian observed the exterior of the modest cabin. "This is your home?"

"Yes, I live here with Gran."

I couldn't tell whether he was horrified or impressed. I hadn't been to the fae realm, so I had no idea how their houses stacked up against ours.

"Peppermint tea?" Sage offered, once we were inside. The warmth of the roaring fire reached me within seconds, and I practically melted from comfort.

"Yes, please," I said.

Sian nodded vaguely, appearing distracted by the contents of the cabin. Every single object seemed to catch his attention.

Sage disappeared into the kitchen.

"This is how you live," he remarked.

Sage poked her head through the doorway to peer at him. "I can't decide if that's an insult."

He touched a framed photograph of Sage, her mother, and her grandmother that rested on top of a bookshelf. "All fae."

"Yes, for now."

I didn't miss the not-so-subtle hint that Sage had no desire to keep their line pure. It was clear to me that she and West had feelings for each other, although neither one seemed willing to upset their respective families by acting on them.

"Who's out there?" a grouchy voice scratched.

Sage emerged from the kitchen. "Nothing to worry about, Gran," she called. "Lorelei stopped by with a new friend."

"What does she want this time?" Gran asked.

"This time?" I mouthed to Sage. I was hardly Ray's granddaughter, Alicia. She may not be supernatural, but that kid had a sixth sense for whenever I picked up an extra treat at the store.

"Go back to sleep," Sage urged.

"Might I have a peppermint tea, too?" Gran's voice adopted a tender quality.

"Of course." Sage returned to the kitchen.

Sian sighed. "She is too old."

"I wouldn't say that loud enough for Sage to hear."

Sage reentered the room carrying a tray with four dainty floral cups on saucers. Their feminine design seemed at odds with the feisty fae's personality. I could see why West was sweet on her. Sage had proven herself to be a fiercely independent and highly competent woman. Takes one to know one.

Sage flopped into a bright yellow chair. "Drink up. The peppermint is fresh from the herb garden."

Sian didn't hesitate. He lifted one of the teacups to his lips and let the steam warm his face.

"You don't get winter in your realm, do you?" I asked.

"It is only ever spring where I live," Sian confirmed.

Sage reached for a cup and saucer. "Seelie court then."

"Yes."

"You can trust Sage," I told him. "Whatever this package is, she can help you get it."

Gran ambled into the room. "I thought I sensed someone of interest."

I smiled. "I'm flattered."

Her gaze skimmed over me. "Not you, Lorelei. I mean the handsome gentleman from the old world."

Right.

Sage passed her cup and saucer to her grandmother. The teacup clinked against the saucer as the old fairy's hand trembled.

"Our family emigrated from Faerie over a century ago," Gran said. "Came through the crossroads and liked the looks of Fairhaven, so they stayed."

Sian glanced at Sage. "And where are your parents?"

"Dead," Sage replied, in a tone that left no room for follow-up questions.

"It isn't every day we get a strapping young fairy like yourself in our neck of the woods," Gran said. "My beautiful granddaughter has been deprived of such company."

Sage's cheeks burned pink. "I have plenty of company, Gran."

Gran perched on the arm of Sian's chair. "Tell us about your family, young man."

"And then you can tell us why you're here," Sage added.

Sian sipped his tea. "As the stories are intertwined, I can do both at the same time."

Finally, we were getting somewhere. It was too late for chili, but I could bake salmon. That only took about twenty minutes in the oven. I calculated the time it would take to walk home on top of the prep time. My stomach would make it.

"I was supposed to meet someone at the place in the woods where Lorelei happened upon me. They had agreed to bring information for me."

"What kind of information?" Sage asked.

"About a child from many years ago," Sian said. He fiddled with the handle of his teacup.

Gran's eyes sharpened. "You mean a changeling?"

Sian's gaze lowered. "My younger sister, Rhiannon."

I swallowed a mouthful of tea and wished to the gods

Sage would bust out a Bundt cake or a lemon-poppyseed muffin. At this point, any baked good would do.

"Your sister was swapped with a human child?" Sage asked. "I thought that practice died out ages ago."

"I do not know the details. My mother has been unwell ever since my father's passing. I only learned of my sister's existence when I heard my mother crying out in her sleep. When I went to rouse her, I stopped to listen. She was lamenting the child she'd lost, the one she gave to a human family as a changeling. I long believed Rhiannon died in infancy."

"You said your mother made the arrangements to meet someone in the woods."

"I said I acted in her stead, which is true. The information was to be delivered at the appointed place and time. I was to learn whether my sister still lived and, if so, where she can be found."

"How did you find out the details?"

His head sank lower. "I found her account on the changeling forum and logged in as her."

"There's a forum for changelings?" Because of course there was.

"It's how many arrangements are made this century. My mother's login details were saved, so I was able to open her account. It was last active eighteen years ago."

Which would make Rhiannon about nineteen now.

"I found her messages to and from a woman named Sarah and arranged to meet her in Fairhaven, which is when I met you."

"But no Sarah," I said.

"Apparently not. I only wanted to see my mother smile again," Sian admitted. "Father's death was difficult for both of us. We should have leaned on each other, but my mother only turned inward."

"What happened to the other child?" I asked. "The human your mother took in exchange?"

He shook his head. "The records do not say."

"Sacrificed, most likely," Gran said without a trace of empathy.

Sage gasped. "Gran!"

"What? It's true. One of the old customs that our family rejected." She gave Sian a pointed look.

"Sian has no control over the behavior of his parents any more than I have control over you," Sage said.

I looked at Sian. "You mentioned you're a member of the Seelie court. Would a fairy from the Seelie court sacrifice a human child? Sounds more like the actions of the Unseelie."

"You know more than you let on," Sian said, almost admiringly.

Always.

"Why are you here?" Sage asked. "To reclaim your sister without any information about the human child she replaced?"

Gran snorted. "Sounds about right. An arrogant race, we are."

"I don't know what became of the human child," Sian said. "As I said, I found no information on any child except my sister."

"Why not ask your mother for the details?" I asked.

Sian set his empty teacup on the tray now balanced on the side table. "Because she might tell me to abandon my quest, but I know that finding her lost child will vastly improve her spirits. The way she cries at night…" He gazed absently at the wall. "I do not wish such feelings on my worst enemy."

Sage pinned me with a curious look. "Didn't you track heirs for a living in London?"

I knew where this was headed. "And?"

"And never mind us. You're the perfect person to help

Sian track down the changeling. Why ask another fairy when he's got someone with real experience finding lost relatives?"

Sian fidgeted with excitement. "I did not realize you had such expertise. Surely the Fates intended that you assist me with my quest."

Surely the Fates hate me.

Sian's eagerness was so pure, it distracted me from inventing an excuse to prevent my involvement.

"I did assist you. I brought you here, to the home of other fae."

"Lorelei, you're perfect for this," Sage insisted. "It'll take you far less time than it would take me."

"From your lips to the gods' ears." I leaned forward and knocked on the wooden coffee table.

"Do you know where the phrase 'knocking on wood' came from?" Sage asked. "It stems from the ancient belief that every tree is inhabited by a spirit."

"Like a dryad," I said.

"Or a hamadryad," Sian added.

"In ancient times, people would knock on a tree trunk to summon a spirit to come to their aid," Sage continued. "Sometimes to ward off evil and other times to request a wish be granted."

"My grandfather always believed that the forest protected us," I said.

"Maybe that's one of the reasons you left London for Pennsylvania," Sage suggested. "You missed the sanctuary of the forest."

I wasn't sure I'd ever truly felt safe. Even when I was too young to know the dangers attached to my existence, I recognized that I was somehow unsafe. That point was driven home time and time again as the loved ones around me were stripped away.

"I did not sense any spirits in the trees during my walk through the woods," Sian said.

"They've long since gone." Gran sounded regretful. "It's only the power of the supernaturals in Fairhaven that protect us now."

I ignored the hunger pains that tormented me. "Do you know the last name of the person you were supposed to meet? Are they the same person that raised your sister?"

"The only name on the forum is whom I believe to be the mother, Sarah, and she is also the one who agreed to meet me with information about my sister."

My only lead was the name Sarah. Terrific.

"You're welcome to stay with us while you search for your sister," Sage offered.

"You'll have to share a room with Sage," Gran added. "Quarters are tight in this home."

Sage swatted her grandmother's arm. "Don't be ridiculous. I'll bunk with you. Sian can have my room."

"Worth a try," Gran grumbled.

Sian stretched his arms over his head. "Might I rest my weary bones? The journey to the crossroads has been more arduous than I anticipated."

Sage pointed him in the direction of the bedroom. Gran took the opportunity to slide into his empty chair.

"He turned up like a lucky clover," Gran commented.

"Let's hope we can say the same about his sister," I shot back.

Gran waved a bony hand. "Fairhaven is a small town. If she's here, you'll find her in no time. I'd like to think if I ever went missing, a strapping young man like Sian would tear the world apart to find me."

"Except Rhiannon likely doesn't know she's fae," I pointed out. And she probably grew up feeling out of place but didn't know why. I felt a surge of compassion for the young fairy.

Sage's eyes blazed with light. "Kane would search for you,

Lorelei. He would turn the entire town upside down to find you."

"That's probably an overstatement." I wanted to tell Sage that West would do the same for her, but it seemed like a bad idea. I didn't know the particulars of their relationship, nor whether Sage's grandmother approved of the match, although I doubted it.

Gran laughed. "We should all be so fortunate to have a demon prince in our corner."

"You do. Kane would search for any of you. He protects this town as much as the police do. So does West." I caught the hint of a smile as it passed Sage's lips.

Gran scoffed. "The pack's priority is the pack. They wouldn't get involved unless one of their own was missing."

I waited to see whether Sage would rise to West's defense. She didn't. Instead, she busied herself collecting the empty cups and placing them on the tray. As someone with a lifetime of experience hiding facts and feelings, I recognized the signs of a woman with a secret. It was the small movements that gave her away, the casual avoidance and intent focus on nothing of consequence. Gran struck me as the opposite of her granddaughter. If I dipped into her mind, I had no doubt I'd find a distinct lack of shadows. What you see is what you get with Gran, for better or worse.

"I should head home before it's pitch dark," I said. "I'll be in touch."

"Thank you, Lorelei," Sage said. "You're a credit to the community. Fairhaven is lucky to have you."

I offered a polite smile, feeling a pang of guilt as I left the cabin. West's suspicions clearly hadn't rubbed off on her. If Sage knew what I truly was, she might not feel so fortunate.

CHAPTER 4

I started the next day with a quick trip downtown. The main priority was milk, which Nana Pratt managed to spill while trying to surprise me with French toast for breakfast. Although I mourned the loss of a quality breakfast, the absence of milk took precedence since it negatively impacted my consumption of Yorkshire tea. My strong preference was controversial in certain circles. My friend Matilda would rather walk across hot coals than add milk to her tea.

I whooped for joy when I snagged a parking spot right outside Five Beans, the local coffee shop. I debated adding a lottery ticket to my purchases today.

As I fed the meter, I spotted Chief of Police Elena Garcia walking toward me, yawning. Her choppy brown hair had grown into more of a shag haircut that made her appear older than her mid-thirties. The dark circles under her eyes didn't help.

"Hey, Lorelei. Heading inside?"

I glanced over my shoulder at the coffee shop. I had only planned on a quick trip to the store, but it occurred to me this could be an opportunity to get an update from the chief on the werewolves that attacked Anna. The little voice in my head warned me to leave the problem to the pack.

I ignored the little voice and joined the chief inside.

"What are you having?" she asked. "I'm torn between the new shaken espresso and my usual."

"What's new about the shaken espresso?"

"They infuse it with olive oil. It's called the Grand Italia."

I cooked with olive oil, but I wasn't so sure about adding it to my coffee. "I think I'll stick with a plain cappuccino." I skimmed the prices. "Make that a plain coffee with cream and sugar."

The chief laughed. "And I thought I was stuck in my ways. You're even less daring than I am."

I couldn't afford to spend five bucks on a drink only to decide I didn't like it. In fact, I shouldn't be spending money in Five Beans at all, except I wanted unfettered access to the chief. It was worth the price of a cup of coffee.

I waited until we'd exhausted all pleasantries and were seated at a table by the window to kick off my interrogation.

"Hey, did you manage to catch the two men who attacked Anna Dupree?"

The chief shook her head. "Not yet. I searched the woods myself after Leo took Vaughn into custody, but the only fresh prints I saw belonged to animals, and those were large enough to make me turn back."

Her survival instincts were appropriately placed. It seemed incredible to me that she was clueless as to the existence of werewolves in her own backyard. Then again, I'd grown up exclusively among humans, and if there was one thing I'd learned, they were masters at only seeing what they wanted to see. An affair. A troubled teen. A dwindling bank account. Humans were wired to overlook what was too difficult to acknowledge as a coping strategy to avoid pain.

"Have you ID'd them?" I asked.

"Nope."

"The sketches weren't helpful then?"

The chief's ears perked up. "You saw the sketches?"

"Not personally. Vaughn mentioned that the sketch artist did a good job drawing the attackers."

"That's Wendy. She's a wunderkind. I couldn't draw a decent stick figure at her age." The chief glanced out the window. "To be fair, I can't draw a decent stick figure now. My only concern is I think she's developed a crush on Leo."

The news didn't surprise me. Officer Leo was easy to adore. "Honestly, that could happen at any age."

The chief smiled. "Not to me."

"Fair enough." I sipped my coffee. "Vaughn seemed confident you'd be able to ID them from the sketches."

The chief sighed. "If only."

"Would it be possible to see them?"

"I'd love that, but it isn't possible. They were stolen before we were able to do anything with them."

I straightened. "Someone stole the police sketches from Wendy? Was she hurt?"

"They didn't take them from her directly. They swiped them from the counter at the station." She ducked her head. "Which I would ask that you not repeat since it doesn't exactly show the police department in a good light."

"Do you think it was the attackers?"

"Seems like the obvious answer. The weird thing is, I got a look at the sketches before they were taken, and I didn't recognize either one of the men, which begs the question—how would one or two strangers have been able to walk into the station unnoticed and steal the sketches?"

"You think because you didn't recognize them that they're from out of town?"

She shook the remaining ice in her cup. "I think it's likely. I may not remember names, but I remember faces."

"And yet they stayed behind to steal sketches instead of

leaving town, knowing they'd be arrested if they're caught. Curious, isn't it?"

The chief's eyes met mine. "It is. You sure you don't want a job with the police department?"

"I'm sure." As much as I needed money, a job with law enforcement wasn't in the cards for me. One slip of my hand and I'd end up torturing some poor soul who didn't deserve it. No, the cost of a mistake was too high.

"The fact that they're probably from out of town isn't out of the ordinary," the chief continued. "We get rowdy guys passing through the bars here all the time. Usually hikers and bikers. In their case, my money's on hikers, given that they took off on foot."

"Did you check the campsites?"

"Leo did." She tapped her half empty cup. "This shaken espresso is pretty good. You should try it next time."

"I'll consider it." *Once I buy that winning lottery ticket.* "What if they're camping in an undesignated area in Wild Acres?"

It occurred to me that, if they were camping at an unofficial site, the two werewolves might still be somewhere in the vicinity. Might be worth a hike through the woods, although it seemed unwise to search alone. I still didn't know who these werewolves were and why they attacked Anna.

The chief grunted. "Do you know how big the area is? We don't have the resources for that, certainly not for a bar brawl." Her eyes narrowed to slits. "Oh, boy. I see that glint in your eye. You want to form a search party." Her head fell forward. "It's cold and miserable, Lorelei. Do yourself a favor and find a good show to binge."

How did I tell the chief of police that I now wore the mantle of liminal deity for this town?

Right, I didn't.

The chief rubbed her cheeks. "Listen, if you take a volunteer search party, I won't stop you, but I'm giving you two rules. The first one is no vigilante justice. I don't need any additional paperwork. If you find them, call me. Don't do anything stupid."

No promises. "And the second?"

"Avoid Bone Lake."

"Where?" I'd come across a creek, a pond, and a river in Wild Acres, but no lake.

She sucked in a breath. "Nobody's warned you about it yet?" She clucked her tongue. "And here I thought you'd made friends in town. Of course, it's pure superstition as far as I'm concerned."

"Superstitions exist for a reason," I said. "What will happen if I stumble upon Bone Lake?"

"You could end up as another skeleton, that's what."

Another skeleton. "How many have there been?"

The chief scratched a small mole on her cheek. "Enough people have disappeared in its vicinity to make it a no-go zone. It's like the Bermuda Triangle of Fairhaven."

Consider my curiosity piqued. "How many people have disappeared there?"

"Dozens. The most popular theory is that they were killed as part of a ritual."

I thought of the Bridger witches, who'd attempted a ritual murder in their backyard pond. "If people have continued to disappear in that area, I doubt it was a ritual murder."

"Some people think it's because the lake is cursed."

"No monster sightings? No Bigfoot or Nessie?" Despite my teasing tone, an otherworldly creature seemed to be the most likely culprit. One that strayed through the crossroads years ago and never left, but the chief wouldn't believe that theory.

"If there was a monster living in there, it's probably dried off and migrated to some kid's closet by now," the chief said.

"When's the last time anyone disappeared there?"

She tipped back her head and blew out a breath. "About

two years ago, two hikers from out of state went missing. Their gear was found nearby."

"No bodies?"

She shook her head. "We tried to send divers down and drag the lake, but there were constant problems."

My supernatural sensors started buzzing like crazy. "What kind of problems?"

"Unexpected storms. Murky water. The grappling hooks kept breaking. You name it. Bone Lake was already considered one of the most haunted places in the county, so this only helped seal its reputation. From what we gathered, the hikers were there to see the lake for themselves."

And paid the ultimate price for their interest.

"How were any skeletons discovered before then? Did their divers not have issues?"

The chief hesitated. "Because they didn't find the skeletons *in* the lake. They found them scattered in pieces *around* the lake."

Delightful. "Now I get why you were surprised no one warned me about it."

And, even better, I now had a hunch where two werewolves from out of town might be hiding.

I was in and out of the grocery store in under five minutes. As I climbed into my truck, my thoughts were still fixated on Bone Lake. I knew I should share my theory with West and let the pack investigate, but something held me back.

I glanced at the grocery bag. It was twenty-seven degrees outside. No chance the milk would spoil if I took a quick trip. If the wolves were there, I'd sneak away and then decide whether to report my findings to West or the chief.

I searched on my phone and found what I assumed was Bone Lake on the map—a small blue dot located northwest of the Falls.

It was too dangerous to invite Officer Leo along. My best bet was someone with strong instincts and fighting skills, which basically encompassed every nonhuman I knew in Fairhaven.

I debated calling Kane, but I didn't want to become overly reliant on the demon. Just because he'd made it clear he was on my team didn't mean I had to include him in every potentially dangerous move I made. I'd been independent my entire adult life; I didn't want to send a message that I needed him.

Because I didn't. There was no needing of any kind.

In the end, I decided to stay within my comfort zone. I worked better alone. No risk of hurting anyone accidentally. No risk of discovery. I'd check for signs of a campsite, nothing more.

I turned off the main road and pointed Gary in the direction of Wild Acres.

It was a bumpy ride, and I was forced to abandon my truck before I was ready to brace myself against the cold. At least I was prepared. Thanks to Pops, I always kept spare clothes, a hat, and gloves in the emergency kit in the truck in case of a breakdown. I swaddled myself in layers and headed toward the most haunted lake in the county.

I hadn't ventured to this part of the forest before. An eerie silence blanketed my surroundings.

I crisscrossed between a tight-knit group of birch trees. No squirrels. No birds. Even the animals were too frightened to dwell here. The question was—did the two werewolves feel the same?

A subtle pressure began to build behind my eyes and across my shoulders. There were spirits nearby. Many of them.

Bits of light filtered through the trees. The spirits stirred in response to my presence. The number of dead here… I was beginning to think the locals had underestimated the dark history of the lake.

I emerged from the darkness of the trees and immediately shielded my eyes from the brightness of the light's reflection off the water.

I'd arrived.

I gave my eyes a moment to adjust. Twenty yards to my left, I spotted a flash of silver metal among the patches of brown and green. I ignored the call of the spirits and walked over to investigate.

Drops of dried blood darkened the ground as I approached the small metal object.

A lighter.

No sign of a bone or a full skeleton.

I fished a tissue from my pocket and wrapped the lighter inside.

My thought process was interrupted by a ripple of tiny waves across the lake. I watched the water and waited.

Desperate voices called to me, crowding my mind. This was overwhelming, much worse than when I arrived at the Castle cemetery and relocated the remaining ghosts. These people hadn't been laid to rest, and their spirits had been trapped in the lake for years, possibly even centuries for some.

I had to help them.

I approached the edge of the lake. The wind picked up, blowing back my hair. It seemed to be a warning, which didn't make sense. The spirits knew I could free them.

I closed my eyes and focused. I lost count of the number of voices I heard. So many lost souls begging for my attention. My skin began to crawl and the little hairs on my arms stood on end. I was the goddess of ghosts, not afraid of them. Yet my body seemed to know something that my mind failed to register.

My eyes snapped open just as the water parted to reveal

the creature—or three. Three scaled heads, each the size of a T-Rex skull, fixed their attention on me. The middle mouth gaped open, releasing a funnel of fire. I dodged the streak of flames and was relieved to see the fire failed to reach the trees. A forest fire in Wild Acres would be devastating.

I turned back to the water as the trio of heads submerged. A serpentine tail broke the surface and smacked the water, sending waves in my direction.

Three heads plus one tail equaled one megamonster.

I had no doubt this creature was the reason for the skeletons. With three massive mouths to feed, the monster likely ate them whole and spat out their bones.

I remained a couple yards from the edge of the water. Now that the threat had passed, I became acutely aware of the spirits again. I tried to concentrate with my eyes open. I'd be a fool to close them again with a three-headed dragon lurking nearby.

The grey sky darkened as storm clouds formed overhead. A bolt of lightning hit directly behind me, and I jumped forward to avoid it, landing in the water.

The creature was there to greet me with the whack of its serpentine tail. I flew halfway across the lake and landed with a splash.

Any one of those heads could swallow me in one gulp, Jonah and the whale style, which was likely its plan. If there was no food left in the lake, the creature had to get clever. But why not leave in search of food? The forest was filled with tasty treats and the creature's body was built for land as much as water.

I put my thoughts on hold as I swam for shore. I felt the creature's presence below me, like a shark awaiting the right moment to attack its prey. The spirits began to crowd me, clinging to my body like barnacles. If the monster didn't drown me, the weight of their despair would.

The shoreline was only ten yards away. My arms and legs pumped furiously. Nine yards.

The spirits grew heavier as more clung to me. Their terror seeped into my pores.

Below me, the monster sliced through the water. It was toying with me, letting me believe I had a chance to make it out alive.

Maybe the game had been a winner in the past, but that was all about to change.

I connected with the spirits and asked them to come to my aid. I'd intended to help them cross over; instead, I needed them to help me survive. The irony wasn't lost on me.

My arms and legs grew weaker. I had to shed the spirits before they drowned me.

I could command them to help me, of course, but it was against my personal code of ethics. It was better if they came to the decision on their own.

You'll be okay, I told them. *The monster can't hurt you anymore.*

I didn't need them to attack the creature; I only needed them to distract it long enough for me to flee.

Seven yards.

Something scraped against my shin. The creature was preparing to make its move.

Help me so I can help you. I could no longer keep the panic from my tone. The situation was critical.

One by one, the spirits peeled away from me. Their courage seemed to grow by the second as more spirits let go. A wave rolled past me, and I realized they were trying to manipulate the water to propel me forward.

Clever ghosts.

Another wave rolled toward me as a giant jaw unhinged below. The wave crested, bringing me with it. The jaws snapped closed and missed, but not before one of the scales tore open my shin. My adrenaline kicked in, numbing the pain. The force of the spirits' wave launched me to shore. I didn't look back. I dragged myself from the water and clawed my way across the mud.

I remained on the ground until my heartbeat slowed to a normal rate. When I finally rolled onto my back, the creature had retreated underwater. Playtime was over, it seemed.

I struggled to my feet and limped away, ignoring the pain that bit into my bone with each excruciating step. I'd heal, but not quickly enough.

The spirits would have to wait.

CHAPTER 5

"Gary, you're a sight for sore eyes." I'd never been happier to see the inside of my truck. There was no tourniquet in the first aid kit, so I grabbed a spare shirt and wrapped it around my lower leg to stop the bleeding. Then I reversed the truck out of the dirt lane and hit the gas. Chief Garcia was right about Bone Lake; it was a no-go zone.

In light of my impromptu meetup with the three-headed monster, my first call was to West. If that creature devoured Anna's attackers, this wasn't a case for the police.

The sound of a gruff female voice on the end of the line caught me off guard. "Anna?"

"That's right. Who's this?"

"Lorelei Clay. I thought I called West."

"You did. The alpha is otherwise engaged at the moment. He asked me to screen his calls."

"Does he usually ask you to do that?"

"No, but he's waiting for a call from his lawyer, and he doesn't want to miss it."

"How are you feeling?"

"Why do you care?"

I could practically hear her scowl. "You weren't in great shape when I saw you. It seemed polite to ask."

"I'm fine. Only a few scratches."

"I guess it's a good thing you answered. I have news for you. I think your assailants might've been eaten by a monster."

A long stretch of silence greeted my declaration.

"Hello?" I prompted.

"What makes you say that?" Her voice was uncharacteristically quiet.

"I went to Bone Lake today to see if your attackers were camping there. I found a lighter, and there was evidence of a fight."

"What kind of evidence?"

"Blood, and a giant three-headed dragon monster."

"Right." She didn't sound particularly surprised.

"Do you know about the monster?"

"I know about Bone Lake, and you're right. The wolves were there, but not anymore."

Something in her tone unsettled me. "Because you tossed them in the water?"

"No, because they ran off. The lighter is mine."

Okay, I didn't see that coming. "Yours?"

"Didn't you see my initials? They're engraved on the side."

I dug the lighter from my pocket and flipped it over. Sure enough, the initials A.D. were etched in the metal. Some fake detective I was.

"Your blood, too?"

"Not this time."

Now it was my turn to hesitate. "Who are they?"

"Mind your own business, Clay."

An uncomfortable truth jumped up and bit me on the nose. "You're the one who stole the sketch."

"How do you know about that?"

"Who are they, Anna?"

"I told you to stay out of it and leave West alone. He has enough on his plate. He doesn't need to be bothered with this."

I glanced at the phone to see that she'd disconnected the call. So much for getting to be the bearer of good news.

My leg throbbed by the time I hobbled up the steps of my front porch, carrying my grocery bag.

"Ray, Lorelei's home," Nana Pratt said.

I pulled my hair into a ponytail and squeezed out the excess water. Then I removed my boots and set them on the porch.

Ray joined his ghostly cohort. "What happened? Did someone accuse you of being a witch and try to drown you?"

"No need to kick a girl when she's down." I strode into the house, dreaming of a hot shower.

"May we come in?" Nana Pratt called from the threshold.

I continued my painful walk to the staircase. "You may."

"What happened to your leg?" Ray asked, finally noticing my blood-soaked bandage.

I stopped at the bottom step, summoning the strength to lift my leg. "There was a monster in a lake."

"Which lake?" he asked.

"Bone Lake."

"What kind of monster?" Nana Pratt asked.

"The monster is TBD," I said.

Nana Pratt frowned. "Tiny But Deadly?"

"To Be Determined," Ray answered for me.

"I thought you knew all there is to know about these creatures," Nana Pratt said.

"I haven't seen all of them up close and personal. Sometimes they require a little research."

Ray lit up like the sky at sunrise. "I can help with that."

"Can the description wait? I am desperate to wash off the dirt and grime."

Nana Pratt folded her arms. "Yes, you're tracking it through the house, and I only cleaned the floors this morning."

"You cleaned the floors?"

"You've been so busy. They needed a little elbow grease."

I was touched by the kind gesture. "Thank you. You know you don't have to do that."

"I wouldn't do it unless I wanted to," she insisted.

"We'll reconvene in the kitchen in twenty minutes."

"Good," Nana Pratt said, "because we also need to discuss your budget."

My stomach churned at the mention of my precarious financial situation. "Okay."

"Problems don't go away just because you ignore them, Lorelei," the elderly ghost counseled me.

"I'm well aware of that, thank you."

"Would you like ibuprofen when you come down?" Nana Pratt asked.

"Yes, please."

Nana Pratt looked at Ray. "You'll have to manage the bottle. I can't undo the childproof caps."

"Here," Ray said. "I think I can handle the groceries. The bag looks light."

I let him take the bag and dragged myself upstairs before Nana Pratt could tell me the pitiful amount circling the drain of my bank account. I needed twenty more minutes of blissful ignorance, thank you very much.

I let the water run until it was piping hot and stepped inside. I scrubbed my body, rinsed the wound, and washed my hair twice, all the while trying to identify the monster from the deep. As much knowledge as I'd garnered over the years, I couldn't always name a species on sight. What bothered me more than my ignorance, however, was the knowledge that the spirits had been trapped in Bone Lake with their killer for gods knew how long. That was a special kind of torture I didn't wish on anyone.

Ray was hovering outside the kitchen when I finally descended the stairs. With clean hair, warm, dry clothes, and a fresh bandage, I felt like a new person, ready to tackle the problem I'd uncovered.

"Was it a kelpie?" he blurted.

"Nope." I blew straight past him, heading for the stovetop to put on the kettle.

"No need, Lorelei," Nana Pratt said. "I've already prepared a cup of tea for you while you were in the shower. The pills are next to the cup."

I spotted the steaming cup on the table. "Thanks. I appreciate it."

"I enjoy putting my poltergeist skills to work," the elderly ghost said.

"Same," Ray chimed in. He drifted over to the computer. "Which is why I started searching for your monster as soon as you went upstairs."

"It's definitely not a kelpie," I told him. "That I would recognize."

I'd once had the displeasure of encountering a kelpie in a lake and managed to escape with a broken ankle and more bruises than I could count. Not the first time I'd been grateful for rapid healing abilities.

Ray tapped the keyboard. "I left a few tabs open, so I wouldn't forget what I found."

I sipped my tea and was delighted to taste the burst of turmeric and lemon. I wouldn't have chosen an herbal tea, but Nana Pratt made the right call. It was exactly what I needed right now.

"How about a relative of Nessie?" Ray asked. "Did it have a long neck?"

I offered a small shake of my head. "The Loch Ness

monster doesn't have a cousin in Bone Lake. Anyway, this monster didn't have one neck. It had three."

"Hydra?" Nana Pratt queried.

Ray and I turned in unison to regard her.

"What?" she asked. "I've read the tales of Hercules. He defeats a hydra."

"It wasn't a hydra either. I think the heads were female and she was shaped like a serpentine dragon." Similar to Bruce Huang, although he didn't have multiple heads.

"How do you know the heads were female?" Nana Pratt asked. "Did they have long eyelashes?"

I stared at her.

Nana Pratt blinked in response. "What? That's how they differentiate in cartoons."

"I felt feminine energy."

"Perfect." Ray turned back to the ancient computer. "That gives me more to go on."

An odd sensation washed over me as I observed the ghost hunched over the keyboard. It had to take all his energy and focus to make contact with each key. He could've opted to float aimlessly around the cemetery and simply wait for his daughter and granddaughter to make the occasional appearance; instead, he chose to help me. Ray was one of the good ones. Nana Pratt, too.

I cleared my throat awkwardly. The words wouldn't come easily, but I felt they were too important to keep inside. "Can I just take a second to say how amazing you both are?"

Ray glanced at Nana Pratt. "Did you put something extra in the tea?"

"Of course not. I wouldn't even know what to add."

"As much as I appreciate everything you've been doing for me, though," I continued, "I'm starting to feel like you work for me, and that makes me very uncomfortable."

"That would make us your minions," Ray remarked.

"Minions are for villains," Nana Pratt interjected. "Lorelei isn't a baddie."

"I guess it depends on your definition," I replied. I certainly wasn't as pure as a Disney princess.

"Either way, as I told you before," Nana Pratt said with a hint of indignation, "I'm doing it because I want to, not out of a sense of obligation."

"I enjoy it," Ray added. "I feel like I still have a life, even though it takes a different form from the one I had before."

"Therein lies the problem," I insisted. "You shouldn't have lives. This is your afterlife. You should be frolicking in the Elysium Fields, or whatever spirits do once they cross over to the next plane. Instead, you're attached to my property, doomscrolling on the internet like everybody else." I waved a hand at the computer that, to be fair, only sporadically managed to connect to the internet.

Ray sucked in an imaginary breath. "I am *not* doomscrolling. It's called research."

"I don't know what doomscrolling is," Nana Pratt said.

"I only know from Alicia," Ray said.

I rapped my knuckles on the table. "Can we please stay on topic?"

"There is no topic," Nana Pratt said. "You're overthinking it." With those words, she dissipated. If only I had the luxury of exiting an uncomfortable conversation so easily.

"I'm going to keep researching, if you don't mind," Ray said. "And maybe you could stop at the library and see if you can find any books to bring home. Even if they don't have the details, sometimes they'll give enough information that allows me to find more online."

"I can do that." I paused. "I mean it, Ray. I never want you to feel like you owe me anything."

He wore a tender smile. "Is that your way of saying you're not the boss of me?"

I could so easily become the boss of him. I had to exercise

caution when it came to my two houseguests, or they'd end up the Renfield to my Count Dracula. None of us wanted that outcome. I'd sooner ship them off to the afterlife.

"I'm going to have a snack and then head to the library."

At the mention of food, Nana Pratt reentered the chat.

"Don't forget you have dinner at your vampire friend's house tonight," she said with a hint of disapproval.

"His name is Otto," I reminded her for what seemed like the fiftieth time.

"I'm not sure it's a good idea to go over there if you're dripping blood." She angled her head toward my wounded leg.

"Otto doesn't drink blood." I doublechecked the bandage anyway, not wanting to drip on my beautiful hardwood floors. The bandage was spotless. I was already on the mend.

"What kind of vampire doesn't drink blood?" she asked.

"He's cursed. I'm sure you already knew that." Sometimes I suspected Nana Pratt was being willfully obtuse.

"I'm an old woman. I can't be expected to remember every detail of your life."

"Fair enough. I can hardly keep up with myself."

That reminded me, I also wanted to research changelings while I was at the library. Maybe I'd find information that would help me locate Sian's sister. The fact that there was a changeling forum and phones in Faerie meant that, as much as I already knew, there was still plenty to learn.

I found the librarian hiding in the janitorial closet.

"Hailey? What are you doing in here?"

Hailey Jones peered out from behind a tower of buckets. "What are you doing opening the closet door?"

"It was ajar, and I couldn't find you. Why are you hiding?"

"I'm not hiding. I'm taking a quiet moment for myself."

"You do realize libraries are meant to be quiet spaces, right? Maybe you could institute old-school policies and start shushing people."

Hailey grimaced. "I don't think I could hush anybody. I'm too polite."

"You'd rather hide in the closet than shush someone? That seems like the kind of thing you ought to work on."

Hailey struggled to get out from behind the buckets without knocking them over. I offered her a hand, which she accepted with a profuse apology.

"No need to be sorry," I said. "We all have our issues." And Hailey's issue seemed to be a misalignment between her career choice and her personality needs.

"If it weren't for my family, I'm not sure I would've gone down this route. I love books. People, not so much."

Hailey's mother Ida had been the librarian before her. Her grandfather apparently had had the Sight but refused to talk about it. I got the impression he'd viewed it as more of a curse than a gift.

"Never mind people," I said. "Can we focus on your love of books? Because I need help with a research project."

The sparkle returned to Hailey's eyes. "Is this more mythology?"

"Yes. I'm hunting for a creature with three heads that's built like a serpentine dragon. Can breathe fire and might have the ability to cause localized storms."

Hailey pondered me for a moment. "That sounds very specific. I'm surprised you haven't found anything online."

I shrugged. "You know what the internet is like. Too noisy and crowded."

Hailey's lips formed a thin line. "Sounds a lot like the library."

"If now isn't a good time, I can come back."

She nearly wrenched my arm out of its socket. "No, no. Stay. Please." She cast a furtive glance around the corner.

"Looks like a clear run to the mythology section. We can make a break for it."

I trailed behind her as she bolted across the library.

"I'd also like to see what you have on changelings," I said, once we were within the safety of the stacks.

Hailey started pulling books from the shelf. "Changelings I've heard of. Fae, right?"

"Yes. I'd like to know if there are any telltale signs for identifying them."

"Other than pointy ears and a lilting voice?" She snorted at what she thought was a joke.

"Pointy ears are easily hidden by hair, and I suspect the lilting voice is more nurture than nature, like an accent."

Hailey started to flip through the books in her arms. "There's a good book on fae written by a local. You should start with that."

Yes, I definitely should. "What's the title?"

"I forget, but I can tell you exactly where it is. Third case down from here, second shelf, fifth book from the left, unless somebody moved it, in which case I will hunt them down and…" She stopped.

"Hunt them down and what?"

"I don't know. The worst thing I could think of was to make them pay a fine, but that's not too horrible, is it?"

"It is to me." I followed her instructions and located the book, entitled *The Fae Among Us* by Lesley P. Grant. I checked the author's biography. Lesley's slender, hypnotic face smiled back at me. Definitely fae blood in her family. According to the bio, Lesley died five years ago. The book would have to do as a primary source.

I returned to Hailey, who was now seated at a nearby table with the books spread out in front of her.

"Did you find it?" she asked.

I held up the book. "Exactly where you said."

"Phew." She tapped the book on Albanian mythology

directly in front of her. "I don't think this one has ever been checked out. It's in perfect condition." She frowned as she inspected the inside back cover. "Wait, I stand corrected. It was checked out once. Bridger. How about that? I didn't think anyone from the Bridger family ever used the library. I heard they have their own."

I peered at the faded library card. "Well, according to the date, it was a long time ago." Fifty years ago, in fact.

I'd had the misfortune of meeting the Bridger witches when I first moved to Fairhaven. Phaedra was the only one left of their coven, and it was no coincidence that she was the only one I liked. Witches and I generally mixed like citrus and milk. So far, Phaedra had proven to be the exception to the rule, which worked in my favor, given my need for her services.

A piercing scream filled the air. Hailey sat perfectly still and closed her eyes. "I'm in my happy place. I'm in my happy place," she chanted quietly.

I looked across the room just as a child lofted a book over his head with both hands and chucked it on the floor. Based on the pinched, red face and balled hands, this was gearing up to become a level five tantrum.

Time to go.

I patted Lesley's book. "I think I'll take this one. Any others you'd recommend?"

"Save yourself." Hailey loaded two books into my waiting arms. "Mount Toby is about to blow. I'll check them out for you."

"Thanks, Hailey. You're the best."

I sprinted to the exit just as a wailing cry erupted. Some dangers weren't worth the risk.

CHAPTER 6

I parked outside the house on Walden Lane. Well, it wasn't so much a house as it was a testament to a bygone era of extravagance. Twin columns supported three massive floors, the second and third each boasting its own generous balcony. Black shutters, chalky white paint, and glossy red double doors completed the look.

I rang the bell, lamenting my casual attire. Never mind that he was blind; my host had a sixth sense when it came to my appearance. Unfortunately, I hadn't allotted enough time to change between the library and dinner. At least the bandage on my leg was dry.

Otto Visconti was a little vampire who lived in a very big house, although I also lived in a very big house.

But I was taller.

On the other hand, his ego probably took up more space.

Heidi, his housekeeper, answered the door with a gruff nod. Although she wasn't the friendliest person in the world, she seemed good at her job. Despite the number of times I'd visited, I still couldn't quite determine whether she liked me or merely tolerated me. Not that it mattered. I was fine with being disliked. West and Josie could attest to that.

"How are you?" I asked, as we walked along the corridor toward the rear of the house.

Her gaze flitted to me. "Fine. Why do you ask?"

I shrugged. "This is the extent of my polite conversation skills."

Heidi snorted. "They need work."

She directed me to a different room than the one I expected. "Aren't we going to the study?" I asked.

"Not yet. I need to dust first." She rolled her eyes. "Mr. Visconti became aware of a dust bunny that was not to his liking."

"Would any dust bunnies be to his liking?"

Her lips stretched thin. "No." She halted at the door. "In here. I will let you know when the study is available." She turned on her heel and stalked off like an ornery teenager asked to do chores for the first time in a month.

I entered the darkened space and let my eyes adjust to the lack of light. Otto sat in an upholstered chair by the fireplace. The miniature vampire was one cigar and a velvet robe short of a Hugh Hefner parody.

"Good evening, Lorelei. So nice of you to dress for the occasion."

"I'm wearing silk."

He chortled. "And here I thought I heard the sound of cheap polyester."

"Is there an expensive kind?"

He smiled, displaying two stunted fangs. "How are you?"

"Busier than I'd like. What's with Heidi? Her nose seems a little out of joint."

"Ah, well. That's to do with Monique."

"Who's Monique? New housekeeper?"

"A recent guest. She departed this afternoon, but not before identifying a layer of dust that Heidi missed the last time she cleaned. I felt inclined to mention it."

"Got it." To be fair, I'd be miffed, too, if I was suddenly receiving criticism from a random woman who appeared out of nowhere with bedhead and smeared lipstick.

"Granted, Monique might be a tad overprotective. She seemed concerned I was being taken advantage of because of my blindness."

"Because Heidi missed a little dust?"

Otto turned his face toward the fire. "I felt pressure to address the situation."

"Because you want to see Monique again? If I were you, I'd be more concerned with retaining Heidi. Moniques come and go, but good help is hard to find."

Otto offered a tiny smile. "They do come and go, I assure you." He motioned to the empty chair beside him. "Come in. We'll chat here until the study is ready for us."

I surveyed the ornate room with its brocade drapes and gilded mirrors. "This is an interesting space."

"I call it the Collections Room."

"I didn't realize you collected anything aside from expensive cars and inappropriate women." I crossed the room to examine a large display case on the wall. "Holy shitballs. Is this a Stradivarius cello?"

"From his golden period, yes."

"I thought the family only made violins."

"The cellos are even rarer than the violins."

Of course they were.

"The case is temperature and humidity-controlled," he continued.

My gaze swept the room. "Where are the Beanie Boos? The Barbies in boxes? None of these things look related to each other."

"I collect rare items. That's the only connection between them, and their incredible value, naturally."

The next item on display nearly brought me to my knees.

The sword wasn't a weapon but a work of art. "Pinch me, I'm dreaming. That's the Honjō Masamune."

"Yes, the lost sword of the samurai. I'm surprised you know it."

"My grandfather said this was taken by the US Army after World War II to be destroyed. How did you get it?"

"A story for another time."

"The Japanese consider this a national treasure. Have you considered returning it?"

"I'm under no obligation to return a valuable item just because somebody wants it."

I glanced at the other display cases. "What's the last item you added to the collection?"

"I appreciate your curiosity. One of the many qualities I like about you."

"Does that mean you don't want to tell me?"

"No, I trust you. It's a Fabergé egg, but quite some time has passed since I obtained it. I grew bored with acquisitions. It's the main reason this room is underutilized. I'm much more interested in games and music these days."

I scanned the cases for the Fabergé egg. "That's too bad because you've got some cool things here. You should open this room to the locals as a mini museum. They'd be fascinated."

"I'd draw too much unwanted attention. A talented thief could easily bypass my security system."

"Then maybe you should consider an upgrade. I know a talented witch you could hire."

He chuckled softly. "Yes, I know you do.

"You said yourself you've lost interest in your collection. Imagine all the people who would benefit from your good deed if you returned the sword."

"I occasionally lend the cello to worthy musicians in the city. Does that count?"

"Better than nothing."

He sighed. "I'm glad you're here. I've missed your company, Lorelei."

"I'm sure Monique has kept you occupied."

"She'll do for now."

"Not a keeper?"

"No."

"Why not?"

"She leaves her makeup all around the sink. I reached for my toothbrush this morning and nearly shoved a tube of mascara in my mouth."

"You could ask her not to do that. Problem solved."

Otto sat in silence for a moment, as though the idea hadn't occurred to him.

An unsmiling Heidi appeared in the doorway. "The study is ready, Mr. Visconti. Dinner will be ready shortly. I apologize for the delay."

"Thank you, Heidi. No need to apologize. We'll be there in a moment." He paused. "I hope I didn't embarrass you in front of my guest earlier. You're excellent at your job, and I appreciate your hard work. If my request suggested otherwise, I sincerely apologize."

Heidi's mouth dropped open. "Thank you, sir. I take my duties very seriously."

"I know you do, and Lorelei was kind enough to remind me of that."

Heidi's gaze darted to me. "I will bring you hot cocoa after dinner. I have a new caramel drizzle for the whipped cream."

"Sounds wonderful," Otto said.

Heidi withdrew.

Otto pushed himself to a standing position. "You scored brownie points."

"More like caramel drizzle points." And now I was thinking about caramel drizzle on a brownie. Great.

Otto and I walked the short distance to the study.

"How did you meet Monique?"

"Online."

"Dating app?"

"Actually, a gaming site. We started with online chess. Luckily for me, she enjoys all sorts of games."

I wouldn't touch that statement with a ten-inch pole while wearing a hazmat suit.

"Is she local?"

"No, she lives in the city, but she works from home, which leaves her schedule more flexible." His fangs popped out as we entered the study.

"You're thinking about her flexibility now, aren't you?"

"Is it that obvious?"

I shuddered. "Let's stop talking about Monique. I want to enjoy my caramel drizzle later."

Otto seated himself on the piano bench. "Very well then. What's new with you?"

I leaned my forearms on top of the piano. Not a dust bunny in sight. "I need to find a fairy."

"You're a detective now?"

"Not officially, but I told this guy I'd help him out."

"What's in it for you? A matching inflatable swan for your boyfriend?"

"Kane isn't my boyfriend. And one swan is enough for my moat."

"Are you certain? It's a big moat."

"If I added a second swan, he'd call dibs on the black one, but I wouldn't feel comfortable on the white one. One swan is better."

His fingertips tapped a few piano keys. "You've already given this some thought."

"No," I said, quickly enough to recognize that maybe I had.

"Do you like each other?"

"We get along."

"Are you attracted to each other?" he asked.

The muscle next to my eye twitched. "That's none of your business."

"You like each other. You're attracted to each other. You spend time together. Face it, Lorelei, you have yourself a boyfriend."

"We're too old for that word."

"Paramour? Inamorato? Leman? Will any of those suffice?"

"Now you're just practicing Scrabble words. Speaking of which, should we play?"

"After dinner. Perhaps I'm leaning too archaic. Sweetums?"

"Does the prince of hell strike you as a sweetums?"

"I don't judge. Terms of affection are a nice way to connect to a loved one."

"You assume he's a loved one."

"I understand. You've yet to have the discussion. Why delay the inevitable?"

I bristled. "What's the rush? We haven't known each other very long."

"You've been alone a long time, my friend, and so has he. Wouldn't it be nice to be in a relationship?"

"I could say the same to you." I'd only known Otto since I moved to Fairhaven, but the curmudgeonly vampire had become one of my closest friends. Life was full of surprises.

"Are you afraid?" Otto asked.

"Afraid of what?"

"Of getting involved with a prince of hell. I can understand your trepidation. You try to keep a tight lid on your abilities, whatever they may be, and someone like Kane Sullivan could make you lose control. You might descend into darkness together."

His assessment was uncomfortably accurate. "I'm not sure I'm capable of going full darkness."

"Of course you are," Otto said. "In fact, I'd argue it's what you fear the most."

I glanced at him. "What makes you say that?"

"Come now, Lorelei. You're smarter than that. You're the one who told me you won't touch a piano or sing those pitch-perfect notes."

"Because they remind me of the loved ones I've lost."

"And?" he prompted.

"And what? That's not enough for you?"

"We've all suffered losses. Every living being on the planet. You think a vampire who's been alive as long as I have hasn't suffered loss? I lost my vision due to a curse, or have you forgotten?"

Years ago, Otto was cursed to die if he drinks even a drop of human blood. Blindness was an unexpected side effect.

"Maybe you've found a way of dealing with it that works for you. Some of us prefer to avoid emotional pain by not engaging in the activities that would allow those feelings to surface."

"Nonsense," he scoffed.

"I don't criticize the way you choose to live. Why are you criticizing me?"

"Because you aren't being honest with me or yourself. What are you afraid would happen if you opened yourself up to that pain?"

"That it will hurt, obviously." Duh.

"And then what?"

"Pain isn't enough? There has to be more?"

"You're no stranger to pain, Lorelei, both physical and emotional. You're injured now, although I'm not sure where."

"That doesn't mean I enjoy it and want to entertain it."

"You fear your own power," he continued. "You fear that

if you tap into that emotional pain, you'll lose control and unleash hell on earth."

For someone who didn't know my identity, he was awfully astute. "I'm perfectly in control, but thanks for the warning."

Otto smacked the keys, producing an unpleasant sound. "You cannot change what you refuse to acknowledge."

I pushed away from the piano. "If I'd known this was going to be a therapy session led by a vampire who can't even tell a woman her makeup needs to stay in a bag, I would've stayed home."

"Please don't go, Lorelei."

I strode toward the doorway. "I'm not interested in hearing anything else you have to say. Not today anyway."

"Is this why you left London? Did someone share an opinion you disliked, and so you ran?"

I stopped, turning slowly to look at him. "I'm not a coward, Otto. I never run from a fight."

"Maybe not the kind that involves swords, but you certainly are quick to flee the scene when feelings are involved."

"Let's reschedule dinner. I've lost my appetite. Have a good evening, Otto."

I left the house before I said something I'd regret. I hastily buttoned my coat as I entered the cold darkness. It was my grandfather who'd taught me to run. The moment anyone caught a whiff of my uniqueness, I was out the door of one school and into another. He'd been trying to protect me, and after he died, I learned to leave places I felt threatened to protect myself.

On the other hand, Otto had a point. And I really wanted that caramel drizzle.

I turned back toward the house and pulled out my phone to text him that I was coming back. Two hulking silhouettes appeared in front of me.

"Excuse me," I said.

"Your presence has been requested," a gruff voice said.

"I don't need Otto to send anyone for me. I was coming back of my own accord." I attempted to sidestep their brawny frames.

They moved in unison to block my path.

I glanced up at their faces and noticed the fangs. Strange. Otto didn't mix with his kind.

A light went on in my head. "You work for Magnarella."

"What gave it away?" His voice was a deep rumble, like the start of an avalanche miles away.

"Your cheap jacket and worn shoes. I figured it had to be someone who doesn't pay his employees a living wage."

The goon looked down at his shoes as though to verify my claim. I seized the opportunity and clocked him in the back of the head.

I sprinted for my truck. One of them grabbed the strap of my purse and yanked me backward. I heard the dreaded sound of a crack as my phone hit the sidewalk.

"I do not have insurance on that phone," I seethed.

Something hard cracked my skull. My teeth rattled, and I sank to the ground, giving in to the pain.

Otto would approve.

I awoke blanketed in darkness. Well, not quite a blanket but a hood. My wrists and ankles were bound to a chair.

"Hello? Anybody there?"

"Finally. I was beginning to think we should douse you with water."

Someone tore the hood from my head. I squinted at the unwelcome bright light.

Vincenzo Magnarella's face came into focus, only inches from mine. His fangs were longer than I remembered, or maybe because I hadn't seen them this close.

"There she is," he sang.

I resisted the urge to spit. The moon-sized bullseye was too easy anyway. "You sound unreasonably happy to see me. I thought I was public enemy numero uno for you."

"Perhaps I'm happy because I'm about to get my revenge."

I peered at him. "No, that's not it. If you wanted me dead, your goons would've done it and left me in the street so it couldn't be traced back to you."

"Very well." He resumed an upright position and swiped a hand through his dark hair. His custom suit was impeccable. He and Kane had that in common, but that was about it. "I'd like to offer a truce."

"You kidnapped me and held me prisoner to offer a truce?"

"I assumed it was the only way I could get you here for the conversation."

"Well, I'm here. Care to untie me? As you can see, there's a bandage on my leg. I don't want to sit too long and develop a blood clot."

He snapped his fingers, and an unseen hand removed the bindings from my wrists and ankles from behind the chair. "Now that your hands are free, can I offer you light fare and a beverage?"

"Oh, I'll take a prosecco and a cheeseboard, please." I glared at him. "But what I really want is to get the hell out of here." I rubbed my wrists and stretched my legs.

"Not yet, Miss Clay. Business first. Please."

It was the 'please' that kept me from bolting for the door. Magnarella's manners had always been beyond reproach, but this version of 'please' hinted at mild desperation. My curiosity got the better of me, so I stayed put.

"I'm listening."

"I'm hosting a gala next week, entertaining potential

investors for my new venture. I'd like you to attend with Mr. Sullivan, or another guest of your choosing."

"You'd like me to attend your fancy party? Are you kidding? Have you forgotten the threatening messages and the assassin you sent to kill me?" Thankfully, Brody had decided to put his nature mage skills to use on my behalf rather than against me.

The vampire waved a dismissive hand. "Water under your moat, Miss Clay. I'd like you to attend the gala as the first step in our new partnership."

"Partnership? You want me to be your corporate partner in crime? Why would you need me?"

"Like all good things, my previous professional relationships have come to an end. I seek new blood."

I cocked an eyebrow. "Why do I get the sense you mean that literally?"

"Only a metaphor, I assure you."

"Why would you want to work with me? Because of me, your lab was destroyed, and your elixir research ruined, remember?"

He slotted his fingers together. "I believe you and I would make a formidable team. You're strong, intelligent, and you seem to have no interest in being the most powerful one in the room, which suits me, since that's my role." He flicked his sharp fang.

"And what kind of team are you envisioning? Because my throwing arm is a little rusty for corn hole."

"I'll pretend I know what that is."

A vampire minion entered the room, carrying a tray with a flute of prosecco and a small cheeseboard.

My eyes widened as I spotted my favorite cheese. "Is that Stilton?"

Magnarella dipped his head slightly. "A favorite of yours, no?"

"How did you know that?"

Ignoring the question, he handed the flute to me. I promptly sniffed the contents.

"You have nothing to fear. If I wanted to drug you or poison you, I would've done so when you were bound."

I examined the bubbling liquid before taking a sip. "Nice."

"I'm glad you approve." He motioned to the minion, who leaned forward with the tray of cheese.

I was ravenous thanks to my missed dinner at Otto's. I swiped the Stilton with the dull, rounded cheese knife and smoothed it onto a cracker. It wasn't the moon that was made of cheese, it was heaven; I was certain of it.

"Dr. Edmonds has been working to recreate the god elixir."

"Edmonds is still plugging away? Good for him."

"He is remarkably resilient."

"If you lost your business partners, why continue the program?"

"This would be for my own purposes. I'll be seeking silent investors going forward, which is the point of the gala."

A god elixir in the hands of a vampire like Magnarella seemed even worse than the alternative.

"And what would my role be? I don't have money to invest, and you know silence isn't one of my strengths."

"Knowledge, Miss Clay, and incredible resourcefulness. To that end, I'd like you to meet with Edmonds on Wednesday at ten, so you can see the new lab. It's very impressive."

I laughed. "You trust me to visit your new lab?" That explained the trucks seen going in and out of the compound's grounds.

"There are new safeguards in place to prevent a repeat occurrence."

No doubt. "I'm not a scientist."

"No, but your knowledge of deities is remarkable. I know

people with PhDs in mythology who don't possess your level of information. I'd like to make good use of it."

"You mean exploit it."

"You say exploit. I say when opportunity knocks, you'd be a fool not to answer."

"In other words, you're making me an offer I can't refuse."

"You can refuse, but you may not like the consequences."

"You and I have different definitions of the word 'truce.'" I swiped another cheese and cracker combo from the tray. "One for the road." I shoved it into my mouth.

A familiar figure appeared in the doorway behind Magnarella. I washed down the cheese and cracker with a swill of prosecco.

"Oh, good. My Uber is here."

Magnarella craned his neck. "Sullivan."

"Magnarella. I believe you're entertaining my lady friend."

Lady friend managed to sound worse than girlfriend.

The vampire gestured to me. "Miss Clay and I were simply having a chat about a potential partnership. Business, of course."

"Of course." Kane showed his teeth and Magnarella responded in kind. It was the supernatural equivalent of a Wild West showdown.

"I'm hopeful Miss Clay will see what an incredible opportunity this is."

"It's incredible all right," I said.

Kane stifled a laugh.

"I expect to hear from you by noon tomorrow," Magnarella said.

"What will happen if I decline your generous offer?"

"Let's start with the gala and go from there, shall we?"

"I'll be sure to give you my answer loud and clear."

Kane escorted me from the compound with one arm wrapped around my waist. Although I'd grown accustomed to taking care of myself ever since Pops died, I had to admit, it was nice to feel supported.

We walked in silence until we reached his car in the driveway.

"What was that all about?" Kane asked.

I got into the car. The interior smelled like Kane—pine, sandalwood, and musk, but with an extra hint of mint. "His previous partners cut ties with him, and he wants a new playmate. How did you know to find me here?"

The demon set my thankfully undamaged phone in the cupholder between us. "Otto called. His housekeeper found your phone in the driveway and noticed your truck was still there."

"Heidi?"

"If that's her name."

My chest expanded. Maybe she liked me, after all.

Not that it mattered.

"Did Magnarella threaten you?" Kane asked, as the car passed through the compound gates and joined the road.

"Does a werewolf howl at the moon? Naturally. He can't help himself."

"Why you?"

"He recognizes I have power, although he doesn't know the extent or the nature of it. He thinks having me as his business partner is better than having me as his enemy."

And he would be right.

Kane's hands tightened on the steering wheel. "What will he do if you say no?"

"You heard him. He wasn't specific, but I imagine it involves entrails and eye sockets."

Kane heaved a sigh. "He's an idiot. He had a chance to walk away from all this. He should've taken it."

"I agree. I can't believe Edmonds is still there. I thought for sure he'd be long gone."

"Perhaps the vampire also made him an offer he couldn't refuse."

"There's always a choice," I said. Pops taught me that. Whether it involved suppressing my strength and speed or entreating with ghosts, my grandfather frequently reminded me that just because I could didn't mean I should. I was the Jurassic Park of reborn goddesses.

"I agree," Kane said, "but Edmonds is human, remember."

I cast him a sidelong glance. "Are you telling me to check my goddess privilege?"

"I've seen their struggles firsthand…"

"And I've lived them," I snapped. "I wasn't born with a deified spoon in my mouth. My childhood wasn't filled with nectar and jousts."

Kane cocked an eyebrow. "Jousts?"

"Midnight balls then. I don't know," I huffed.

"Magnarella mentioned a gala."

"He's hosting a flashy event to attract potential investors."

"To fund the avatar program?"

"Yep. He isn't giving up."

"I can't decide which is worse— The Corporation in control of a host of deities or Magnarella."

"I had the same thought. They're both problematic but for different reasons."

"You should attend."

I made a hacking noise. "No thanks."

He cut me a sideways look. "You don't think it's important to see what the new lab is capable of and get a look at those investors? The wrong set of deep pockets could pose a greater threat than The Corporation. It will also buy you time if Magnarella thinks you're considering his offer."

Why did Kane have to be so sensible? "Fine, I'll accept his offer, if only for the purpose of subterfuge. I'm allowed to bring a plus one. Would you like to go? For research purposes, of course."

He gave me a long look. "Only for research purposes?"

I shrugged. "You look pretty good in a tux. That's a bonus." Which meant I'd need a formal dress. That was a problem for Future Lorelei, although I didn't see more money in her bank account than Present Lorelei's. If anything, it would be less.

"You'll need a dress," Kane said, as though reading my thoughts.

"I'll figure something out."

"If you need money…"

I stopped him with a hard look. "I am not accepting handouts." I didn't want Kane to view me as weak or needy or incompetent. If he knew the state of my finances, he might offer to help, and then I'd feel so mortified, I'd have to move again and change my phone number. A perfectly reasonable response to an offer of assistance.

"I wasn't going to offer one," he said. "I was, however, willing to offer you employment."

"At the nightclub?"

"What's wrong with that?"

"The Devil's Playground is not my idea of gainful employment."

He recoiled. "Lorelei Clay, I never realized you were such a snob."

"I'm not a snob. I just don't want to work every day in an environment that caters to supernatural creatures."

"And yet you moved to Fairhaven."

"I wouldn't have, had I known about the crossroads."

"I, for one, am glad you did." Kane pulled outside the gate to the Castle. "Want company?"

"I'm sure you have work to do. Won't the club be opening soon?"

"Josie can manage."

"So can I." I opened the passenger door. "I'm not a helpless kitten, Kane. I can take care of myself."

"Except when you've been kidnapped by a deranged vampire and done something to your leg that requires a bandage."

"I had a plan. I would've escaped in my own time." Right after I'd inhaled the remainder of the cheeseboard.

The demon smiled. "You can just say thank you, you know."

"Thank you," I said and shut the door. He looked far too smug. I began to wish Otto had called someone else.

I strode through the gate and across the bridge, fully conscious of Kane's eyes on me the entire route to the front door. He waited until I entered the house to drive away.

Nana Pratt greeted me in the foyer. "Was that Kane who dropped you off? Did you two have a lovers quarrel?"

"Nana, rules!"

"I'm sorry. You were gone a long time. Ray and I were concerned."

My shoulders relaxed. "You don't need to worry about me."

"I looked out earlier and saw your truck, but then you didn't come in."

"Someone else drove my truck as a favor." And I hoped it was Heidi because Otto had no business driving at all.

"Are you hungry? I roasted the chicken you had in the fridge. I figured you could have it tomorrow."

I scented the air. "You used rosemary?"

"And thyme. I hope you don't mind."

Part of me wanted to chastise her for breaking the rules, but the hungry and tired part of me opted to let it go.

"Thank you. That was very kind."

"Ray and I are grateful to you. If it weren't for you, we'd be in the afterlife without access to our families." Her hands fidgeted. "Speaking of which…"

I sighed. "You want me to check on Steven and Ashley."

"When you have time, of course. Maybe after a nice meal, if you're still hungry?" she asked in a hopeful tone.

"I'll text them." A phone call was a bridge too far at the moment, but I could handle a simple text message.

Nana Pratt looked ready to dissolve into tears. "Thank you, Lorelei. It means the world to me."

CHAPTER 7

I slept ten hours straight. If it weren't for the ward startling me awake, I would've slept even longer.

I sat up and rubbed my arm. The sensation wasn't painful, more like gentle pins and needles.

I looked down at my sweatpants and Eagles T-shirt. This was as presentable as I was willing to get right now.

I hurried downstairs to intercept my visitor. Sian had stopped on the bridge to admire the moat.

I opened the door and waved.

The fairy broke into a broad grin and met me on the porch. "I like your moat, but its presence confuses me. Is it meant to be threatening or inviting?"

"Not sure. The moat was here when I bought the house." I neglected to mention that it was also devoid of water until I made a deal with a mover and shaker in town known as Big Boss.

"I thought moats in the human world were no longer necessary in the modern age."

"The original owner didn't seem to feel that way."

"If you intend it to keep others out, I suggest removing the bridge. It contributes to the mixed messaging."

"But then I wouldn't be able to leave."

He turned to contemplate the bridge. "Perhaps a sign that warns people to beware of the hellhound."

"I don't have a hellhound."

"I can recommend a rescue center."

"I'll take it under advisement."

Sian noticed the cemetery to his left. "Isn't it bad luck to live next door to the dead?"

"Depends on the dead."

"I heard that," Ray said, from somewhere in the vicinity.

Sian seemed uncertain whether I was joking.

"How can I help you?" I asked.

"Would you be kind enough to host me for the remainder of my visit?"

I couldn't imagine Sage booting him out. She was much too polite. "What did Gran do?"

He grimaced. "She seems intent on harassing me to the point where I no longer feel comfortable sharing their quarters."

"Oh, she wants to set you up with Sage?" It was understandable. Two attractive fae under one roof. The possibilities were endless.

"If only," he replied. "While I was in the bath, she decided I required a sponge."

An unsettling image entered my mind, and I quickly dismissed it. "I am so sorry."

"Thankfully, she cannot move very fast. I was able to deal with the situation with minimal embarrassment." He paused. "For both of us."

"Look at that sweet face," Nana Pratt said, alerting me to her presence. "You have to let him stay."

"You might prefer one of the bed and breakfasts in town," I told him. "I hear they're very nice."

He lowered his head. "That would require human currency."

I understood his predicament.

"I apologize for the inconvenience. I was told you lived in a castle and assumed you had ample space." He drew back to admire the facade. "It does seem more than adequate for one person."

"Oh, let him stay, Lorelei," Nana Pratt urged.

"Ask if he can cook," Ray added. "No freeloaders."

"How do you feel about ghosts?" I asked. "Because there are two that haunt this house." I glowered at them.

Sian followed my gaze. "You can communicate with them?"

"Yes."

"Are they friendly?"

"Most of the time. The worst you get from them is a case of the grumps."

"Hey!" Ray objected.

Sian drew an inhalation of courage. "Then I am prepared to endure their presence."

"Endure?" Nana Pratt echoed. "That makes us sound horrid."

I motioned for Sian to enter. "I have plenty of space but not a lot of furniture. It's a work in progress."

He crossed the threshold and immediately took in the sparse surroundings. "I may not have currency, but I do have a woodworking apprenticeship under my belt. I would be happy to pay for my lodging with an item of your choice."

Ray rubbed his hands together. "Now we're talking."

"Ooh, a rocking chair for the front porch," Nana Pratt said.

I glared at them until they got the hint and disappeared.

"I could use another bed," I admitted. It seemed I was hosting overnight guests more than I ever anticipated. Of course, I'd also need a mattress, which was one item I refused to pull out of a dumpster. One step at a time.

"Ah, I see. You only have the one bed."

"I have a sleeping bag you can use."

He bowed slightly. "That would be more than adequate. I am humbled by your generosity."

"Would you like a drink or something to eat? I have leftover chicken. Or there's pizza." Never mind how many days old it was. He'd be fine.

"I am unfamiliar with pizza."

"You'd like it. Only monsters and people without tastebuds find it dissatisfying."

"Then I shall sample your fare."

I ushered him into the kitchen and removed the pizza box from the top shelf of the fridge.

"I just need to zap your slice in the microwave. Cold pizza is good, too, but warm is better."

I hit the button on the microwave and took a plate out of the cupboard.

"Have you made any progress in your search?" he asked.

I spun to face him. "I have a book. That's as far as I've gotten, I'm afraid." I hesitated. "There were unforeseen obstacles."

His face contorted. "Someone is blocking you from finding my sister?"

"No, no. Sorry. Just … other complications in my life."

"I see. I apologize for burdening you with family's problem." His eyelids lowered like a fawn who'd been scolded by a big, bad buck.

Good grief. I'd have to ask Kane for a detailed map because if I died soon, I was going straight to hell.

"It isn't your fault, Sian. I'm sorry I don't have anything to report yet. I know you're anxious to find her."

The microwave beeped, and I set the plate on the table in front of Sian. "One of the few things I missed when I lived in London was real pizza."

He examined the triangle. "An interesting combination."

I sat across from him. "Tell me about your realm."

"Fairie is a place full of wonders. The colors are so vivid compared to here." He seemed to realize the insult. "But it has its downsides, of course. No place is perfect."

"Like what?"

"There are many rules to follow and court squabbles. I'd love to travel more, but Mother prefers I stay with her." He took a generous bite of the pizza, and I watched his eyes roll back in his head. Another convert.

"I'm sure she worries about you. That's what mothers do."

A ping sound startled me. At first I thought it was my phone, until I saw Sian withdraw one from his pocket. "Will you excuse me for a moment?" He left the kitchen to answer the call.

I strained to listen from the kitchen.

"I am perfectly fine, Mother. There is no need to worry." He paused. "It matters not where I am. You rest, and I shall be with you again soon." He heaved a sigh. "Please do not call anyone. I am not with the Unseelie court. You know I have not spoken to her in years. I swore an oath."

I busied myself with a glass of water when Sian returned to the kitchen.

"I apologize for my rudeness."

"Sounds like your mother is worried about you."

He smiled. "She would worry about me even if I were wrapped in cotton wool and stowed away in a tall tower that adjoined her house."

"Must be nice, though, to have a parent who cares that much." I had no idea what kind of parents mine would've been. They never had the chance to find out either.

"Mother can be a bit overprotective. I am an adult now. I make my own decisions."

"Sounds like you had a relationship she didn't approve of."

"There was a particular fairy princess…" He glanced away. "It is all in the past."

"Because she's Unseelie?"

"I would say yes, except Mother has not been keen on any of my potential mates."

"Some mothers are like that with their sons. No woman is good enough for her perfect boy." I shrugged. "Usually those guys are the worst, but you don't seem so bad. You mentioned an uncle. Do you come from a large family?"

"A large extended family. I have more aunts and uncles I care to count, and it seems all they do is bicker." He glanced airily around the kitchen. "It is so quiet and peaceful here in comparison."

I smirked. "Depends on the day."

"Did you inherit this house?"

"No, I bought it online last year."

He nearly spat out his pizza.

"You're actually the first person who hasn't commented on the sorry state of the place."

"Sorry state? This house is remarkable. I can absolutely see the potential."

"Thank you, Sian. You're my new favorite person … or fairy."

"I consider that the highest compliment."

A pleasant sensation rippled through me. What on earth? I checked my phone to see whether it had vibrated. Nope.

I squinted at Sian. "Did you do something to me?"

He looked at me blankly as he swallowed the last of his pizza. "I beg your pardon?"

Now I was suspicious of the innocent fawn. Yep, straight to hell, do not pass Go. Do not take a handbasket.

The doorbell rang.

Well, that explained it. I excused myself and walked to the front door. I glimpsed Kane through the glass. That pleasant shiver was Kane activating the ward? I needed a word with Phaedra about the particulars of the upgrade.

I opened the door and smiled. "Hi."

"Hi yourself."

"What brings you here this early?"

He gazed at me with a sultry look that made my knees buckle. "Do I need a reason to see you?"

"At this hour? Probably."

"I wanted to check on your injury."

"You could've called."

"But then I couldn't see it and confirm it had improved."

I stuck out my leg. "All healed."

He bent to the side. "I could see it better if you weren't wearing pants."

"Should I retreat upstairs?" Sian's head popped into the foyer from the kitchen.

Kane's brow furrowed. "Seems I'm not the first early morning visit, or perhaps his visit began last night?"

Oh, boy. The dismayed look on the demon's face was priceless. Almost worth the price of admission to hell.

I waved Sian forward. "This is my new friend, Sian." I turned to the fae. "Sian, this is Kane Sullivan."

The hardness of Kane's gaze could've ground a statue into dust. "And your new friend Sian is sleeping here?"

"For a few nights." I knew Kane was misunderstanding the situation, but I was enjoying his reaction too much to set the record straight.

Sian offered a bright smile. "I have offered my services in exchange for room and board."

Kane's jaw clenched. "And what kind of services might those be?"

Sian held up his hands. "My skills are renowned where I come from."

"Is that so?" The prince of hell looked ready to cut off Sian's hands with his flaming sword. I had to intervene before the fawn got hurt.

"Down, demon. Sian is a woodworker. He's going to craft a second bed in exchange for room and board."

"And where is he sleeping in the meantime?"

"A sleeping bag in the spare bedroom."

Kane finally shifted his intense stare to me. "You could've told me about this arrangement."

"It only just happened. I'm sorry I didn't have a chance to type out the memo, not that it's any of your business." I waved a hand at the door. "Are you coming in? You're letting in the cold air. My radiators aren't functional enough to be working overtime."

Kane took an exaggerated step across the threshold.

"Don't even think about marking your territory," I whispered. "I don't want the house to smell like pee. Nana Pratt will lose her mind."

"I'm searching for my lost sibling," Sian announced. "And Lorelei has kindly offered to assist me."

"Has she now?" Kane looked at me. "She tends to overextend herself in matters that don't concern her."

"I could say the same thing about you." I smiled at the fae. "Sian, would you mind giving us a minute alone?"

"I would be happy to boil water for tea, Lorelei."

Kane scoffed. "Lorelei is perfectly capable of making tea in her own home."

"I am, but isn't it nice to have someone else willing to do it for me?" I looked at Sian. "That would be great, thank you. Make enough for three. I get the sense Mr. Sullivan will be joining us."

Sian bowed slightly before dipping into the kitchen.

Kane stared at me with an inscrutable expression.

"What?" I asked.

"Is he at least paying you for your detective work?"

"You said yourself I'm the liminal deity for the crossroads, remember? How could I request payment to help him find a changeling?"

Kane stuffed his hands in his trouser pockets. "I'm beginning to regret telling you that."

I tried a different approach. "The sooner we find the changeling, the sooner Mr. Pretty Boy skips back to Faerie."

"You think he's pretty, do you?"

Ooh, a direct hit. Somebody's fourth deadly sin was showing. "Come on, Kane. There isn't a creature alive that would describe Sian any other way. He's like a walking Renaissance painting."

The demon's gaze flicked to where Sian had been standing. "I suppose you're right."

"Hold on." I tugged my phone from my back pocket and opened the calendar app.

Kane leaned over. "What are you doing?"

"Marking this day down for posterity. I don't know if I'll ever hear you utter that sentence again."

Kane's nostrils flared. "What information do we have to help us find the changeling?"

"A nineteen-year-old girl named Rhiannon adopted as an infant by a Fairhaven woman."

"And do we have the name of the woman?"

"Only a first name. Sarah."

Lines rippled across Kane's brow. "Why doesn't he know her last name? Surely the fae recall the full name of the woman with whom they entrusted their child?"

"Not according to Sian."

Kane's frown lines deepened. "Something doesn't add up."

"You're overreacting."

"I am biologically incapable of overreacting."

I barked a laugh. "Because you're a man?"

"Because I'm a demon."

"I didn't realize demons and computers had so much in common."

The frown devolved into a scowl. "Fairhaven is a small town. How many women named Sarah can there be?"

"That's my hope."

"How far have you gotten?"

"I borrowed a book on fae from the library."

He regarded me. "That's it?"

I gesticulated wildly at my leg. "Busy day yesterday, remember?"

"What's your plan?"

"I thought I might call Officer Leo and see if he can help us find her quickly."

"And what do you intend to tell him? That you're searching for a teenager from the fae realm, a world that he knows nothing about?"

"I wasn't planning to be honest. He trusts me."

"There's a less risky option."

I folded my arms. "Let's hear it." Kane was clearly invested in wrapping this up ASAP to get rid of Sian, so his idea *was* likely better than mine.

"I have a friend in town that trades in information."

"Are you talking about yourself in third person?" When I first met Kane at the Devil's Playground, he'd referred to himself as a collector of secrets and assured me he'd one day claim mine—which he did.

"Not at all," he said. "Birdie is a fount of information. I go to her whenever I want to hire someone new at the club. Thanks to her, I've avoided many unpleasant situations."

"Now I'm picturing a giant warehouse of wooden crates on her property like the final scene in *Raiders of the Lost Ark*."

Kane knocked on my head. "I know you're a Luddite, but surely you've heard of computer databases."

"Okay, so you have the geek squad on speed dial. What will you need to give her in return?"

"Leave that to me. How did you injure your leg?"

"I went looking for the werewolves that attacked Anna," I admitted.

"And did you find them?"

"No, they're gone."

He lifted an eyebrow. "Gone?"

"Left town, according to Anna. She found their campsite and scared them off."

"Good to know. I had Josephine patrol the woods around the club, but she saw no sign of them. Did Anna finally tell you the real story?"

"No, she doesn't trust me."

Sian waved from the kitchen doorway. "Tea is ready."

Kane turned his scowl to the visitor.

"He's harmless," I whispered. It was as close as I could get to telling Kane he had nothing to worry about. Anything more would be admitting too much. I said glacial, and I meant it, no matter what my hormones demanded.

Tea was an awkward affair. Kane seemed poised to leap over the table at any moment and throttle the fae. Sian appeared oblivious to the tension, which was for the best. He asked questions about Fairhaven, and I showed him the book from the library.

He paged through it as we finished our tea. "The author thinks we are an extinct race that integrated with humans." He closed the book. "I would not rely on an unreliable source to find my sister."

"I have someone I think can help," Kane said.

Sian's face sparked with hope. "Shall I call upon them?"

"You're better off staying here," Kane advised.

I straightened in my chair. "Really?" The prince of hell seemed to have changed his tune.

"Less chance of him getting hurt or drawing attention to himself."

"True," I said. "Those cheekbones are hard to miss."

Sian touched his face. "I do have very fine features."

"If you need to find anything while I'm out, ask Ray and Nana Pratt. You won't hear them, but they'll hear you."

"I would like to make a start on my woodworking."

"I'll ask Ray to leave the tools at the bottom of the stairs."

Sian's cup stopped halfway to his mouth. "Your ghosts can move physical objects?"

"They're learning. Ray is ahead of Nana Pratt, but she's improving every day."

Sian took a careful sip of tea and placed the cup back on the table. "Do you have wood for the frame?"

"No, but Kane and I can stop at the hardware store on our way back here and bring you whatever you need."

"One that is dense and durable. Oak, maple, walnut, mahogany. I shall make a start on measurements."

I glanced at Kane. "You won't be able to fit the wood in your car. We'll have to take Gary."

Kane shifted uncomfortably. "I'm sure we can manage with the car."

I laughed. "You really hate my truck, don't you?"

"You named it Gary. Seems to me you don't like it very much either."

I sucked in a breath. "Bite your tongue, Kane Sullivan. Gary is reliable and…" I struggled to dig up any more compliments. "Clean," I finished.

"I've seen cleaner trucks at the scrapyard." He stood and walked his empty cup to the sink. "We should go now if we expect to fit in a trip to Hewitt's afterward."

I bit the inside of my cheek to refrain from laughing. Kane and I sounded like an old married couple making plans on a lazy Sunday. Sadly, I didn't envision that life for either of us. We were both trying to build our lives with broken pieces of ourselves. Like my third-grade ceramics class, it seemed the only possible outcome was an ugly mess.

CHAPTER 8

"Your fount of knowledge lives here?"

Birdie's house looked like an abandoned wooden mill from another century. The structure leaned slightly to the left, as though the wind had been pushing it over slowly but surely for decades.

"It's how she keeps a low profile. Not everyone can live in a castle, you know."

"According to everyone in town, I live in a heaping pile of stones. I don't think they're too envious."

"They're not envious of the costs involved in renovating and maintaining a house of that size, that's for sure."

"Look on the bright side," I said, exiting the car. "I'm getting a free bed this week."

As I started toward the front door, Kane redirected me. "We don't need to go to the front door. She's around back."

"How do you know?"

He pointed to the sky. I looked upward to see about a dozen crows circling overhead.

"Feathered friends of yours?"

"No, but they flock to Birdie, pun very much intended. If they're up there, it means she's on the back patio."

I realized he was still holding my hand. He seemed to notice at the same moment because he let go. An awkward moment of silence ensued.

"Do you trust her?" I asked, desperate for the moment to pass.

Kane's response was unequivocal. "Yes."

I nodded. It took a lot for Kane to trust someone. We had that in common.

Together, we rounded the corner of the house to the backyard. A woman sat beneath a plaid blanket that covered her lap, its frayed ends skimming the ground around her. Her stark white hair and a face like a graticule suggested she was at least eighty years old. A pair of glasses hung on a chain around her neck, the silver metal gleaming against the backdrop of her dark green sweater. A set of bright orange and black Tigger slippers poked out from beneath the bottom of the blanket. It was an eclectic look.

Her whole face brightened when she laid eyes on Kane, giving her a youthful glow. "Well, my day just got a lot better."

"Lorelei Clay, I'd like you to meet Kristabel Danvers."

"No need to be formal. You can call me Birdie like everybody else. Everybody I like, anyway." She winked at Kane. "Not to worry. Any friend of Kane's is a friend of mine."

"Need a hand?" Kane motioned to the large bag nestled against her chair.

"No, thanks. They'll get annoyed if you do it. They're spoiled now."

Birdie reached into the bag and produced a cup of food. She scattered the contents across the patio with a flourish. Within seconds, the crows appeared. Dozens of them landed on the lawn and patio, pecking to their hearts' content.

"What do you feed them?" I asked.

"I like to mix it up, so I surprise them now and again.

They appreciate a variety. Today I've got seeds, pistachios, pecans, and corn." She patted the bag. "A homemade blend."

A crow flew closer to Birdie's chair and left a shiny object at her feet.

"I think he dropped something," I said.

"Oh, he definitely did." Birdie leaned forward to collect the object.

"Does he bring you trash?"

"Trash?" Slapping her knee, she howled with laughter. "My dear, this is a crow, not a raccoon. Crows bring gifts."

I shrugged. "One raccoon's trash is another crow's treasure."

She held up the shiny object. "Does this look like trash to you?"

It was a silver dollar. "I think I need to invest in food for crows."

She laughed. "You treat them well and they'll remember. Treat them poorly and they'll remember that too." Her gaze skated to Kane. "I wish I'd known you were coming. I would've made your favorite."

"It was unexpected. I need a favor."

"For you? Anything."

"We're looking for a changeling brought here from Faerie about eighteen years ago. We need to find the adoptive mother, an adult female in Fairhaven named Sarah."

She waited a beat. "That's it?"

"That's it."

"Okay, a first name should be enough to get you a list, but I've got to warn you, Sarah is a popular name around here."

"Whatever you can compile for us would be appreciated," I said.

She tilted her head toward the crows. "If we want their help, I'm going to need a better offering. Kane, would you do the honors?"

He gestured to the back door, and she nodded.

"You're a special one, aren't you?" Birdie said, once he disappeared inside the house.

My guard immediately went up. "What makes you say that?"

"I've known Kane for years, and this is the first time he's brought anybody to see me."

I relaxed slightly. Birdie wasn't a goddess detector, only a Kane fan.

"He thinks you can help me find the right Sarah without going through traditional channels."

Her eyes gleamed with mischief. "Yes, I'm sure that's it."

A moment later, Kane emerged from the house holding an egg. He handed it to Birdie, who proceeded to tap the egg on the side of her chair until the shell cracked.

"Hard boiled eggs are a delicacy for my crow friends," Birdie explained. She broke the egg into pieces and tossed them across the patio. "This will help us get the information."

I leaned over to Kane and whispered, "I thought you said she used a computer database."

"She will, but isn't this far more interesting?" He observed the crows as they went wild for the egg.

"I save the eggs for special occasions," Birdie said. "It makes them sit up and pay attention."

On cue, the largest crow ambled over to Birdie and stopped in front of her chair.

"He's awaiting instructions," Birdie told me.

I stepped forward. "Do you want me…?"

"Oh, he won't listen to you, sweetie, only the hand that feeds him." She shared my request with the crow.

"I don't need any Sarah under the age of thirty," I added quickly.

"Thirty?" Kane queried. "Shouldn't that age be a little higher?"

"I'd rather be conservative than miss someone. What if she lies about her age now? Or what if she was a teen mom? I don't want to skip her because I assumed more than I should have."

Birdie regarded me with shining eyes. "I like her," she said to Kane, before turning back to the crow. "You heard the woman. Now, off you go." She flicked her fingers, ushering him away.

The crow took off into the air while the remaining crows continued to feast.

I wasn't sure what the next step was. "So, I guess you'll call Kane and let him know what the crow delivers?"

Birdie snorted. "Oh, we're not done yet, honey. Would you like lunch while you're here? I may not have Kane's goulash, but I have enough to feed a host."

"Aren't you the host?" I asked.

"A military host, hon."

Kane opened the back door, and I heard a mild buzzing sound as Birdie rolled herself inside. Thanks to the oversized blanket across her lap, I hadn't even noticed the wheels on the chair until now.

I entered the house behind our hostess. The rustic kitchen had a natural, cozy feel, with a flagstone floor, warm wooden cabinets, and vintage dining furniture.

Birdie motioned to the heart of pine table. "You two sit while I get lunch ready."

Kane remained standing. "You know I won't eat if I can't help."

"Oh, you're a stubborn one, aren't you? Fine. You get the bowls and cutlery."

She moved around the kitchen with ease. I hadn't noticed until now that the space was designed with her in mind. The counters and cabinets were lower and the controls for appliances were mounted in the front for easier access.

"You can talk to me while I work, you know. I won't get distracted and slice off a finger." She picked up a knife and cut a loaf of bread into thick slices.

"Have you always had an affinity for crows?" I asked.

"They found me first. My mother once told me they'd circle overhead whenever she walked outside with me in my pram. She assumed they'd targeted me as prey. Poor woman didn't understand their nature. Now they're my regular companions."

Kane nudged me. "You should consider some animal companions. You've got plenty of space for them."

"I think I'm all set." Two ghosts were more than enough.

Birdie observed me. "A dog is often a good fit for a woman living on her own, though I get the sense you're able to take care of yourself."

"Dogs don't like me," I said. Many animals didn't like me; they were afraid, but they didn't know why. Death and darkness had that effect on creatures.

"Why not? My crows didn't seem to mind you." She set a platter of bread on the table, along with a plate of olive oil dip.

"Crows are different." Crows symbolized death and were related to the underworld in many cultures. Naturally, they didn't mind me.

The old woman's eyes narrowed as she joined us at the table. "Ah, yes. I thought as much. You're like my friend Kane."

"I'm not from hell," I said.

"But not entirely human either."

I wondered the same about Birdie.

She motioned to the bread. "Eat."

I didn't need to be told twice. I dutifully dragged a slice of bread through the olive oil dip and tried not to drip it everywhere.

"I associate crows with Apollo and the Morrigan," I said. And there was no chance Birdie was either one of those deities in disguise. I would've sensed that level of power, plus neither god would condescend to live a small life in Fairhaven and consort with the likes of Kane Sullivan.

Birdie's smile revealed a set of slightly crooked and tea-stained teeth. No dentures for her. "A student of myths and legends. What else do you know about Apollo?"

"That's a broad question. He's the god of music." That one was easy, given that music had a heavy presence throughout my childhood. "Also healing."

"That's right. Anything else?" Birdie tore off a piece of bread and stuffed it into her mouth.

I tugged at the memories of my lessons with Pops. "The god of prophecy."

Her eyes glinted with a secret. "Very good, Lorelei."

"You're a prophet."

"Some say prophet. Some say seer. Others say psychic." Birdie shrugged. "I'm not stuck on labels."

It only took a second to work out the connection. "You use the gifts the crows bring you to tell the future about the items' owners." I turned to Kane. "That's why she's your fount of information."

Looking at Birdie, Kane splayed his hands. "I warned you she was clever."

Birdie chuckled and she mopped up the remaining oil with another piece of bread. "I never doubted you, dearest."

"Are you human?" I asked. I didn't sense anything otherworldly about her, which was unusual. I'd developed decent supernatural radar as a survival coping mechanism. If I encountered the wrong nonhuman unawares, I could've ended up in a regrettable situation.

She pinched the pruned skin of her arm. "I'm as human as they come. My parents didn't know what to do with me once they discovered my ability."

I understood that all too well.

"Were you born and raised in Fairhaven?"

"Indeed, I was. My parents were farmers, but that land's

been bought and sold several times over since then. I remember running through the fields as a child and delighting in the line of crows that followed me. I thought I was the pied piper for birds."

"Do you know Jessie Talbot?" Jessie was one of the oldest humans in town. Rumor had it she might have some fae blood in her line, but she tended to stay on the human side of events in town.

"Of course. I used to play pinochle with her. I don't get out much anymore, though."

"What about the Bridgers? You must've known them."

A scowl passed over her face. "Witches aren't my cup of tea, and some of those Bridgers were trouble with a capital T. I steered clear whenever I encountered one of them."

I smiled. "I knew I liked you."

"Finish your bread," she ordered. "Next course is up." She left the table, and the rich aroma of chili reached my nostrils before I saw the cast iron pot. I felt a pang of guilt for leaving Sian to fend for himself in my bare kitchen while I was feasting on homemade bread and chili.

"What do you know about Bone Lake?" I asked.

Her face clouded over. "Nothing good. Why do you ask?"

"Because I encountered a creature there. I got the impression it's killed a lot of people." I didn't feel comfortable saying more than that.

"The creature has been here a long time. It used to leave the lake and hunt animals in the woods." She used a ladle to serve the chili. "I sometimes wonder if something happened to the creature like what happened to me. Not paralysis, of course, but something to prevent it from leaving the lake."

It made sense. I'd only escaped its clutches because I'd fled the lake. And the fire didn't streak far enough to reach the trees, although it should have.

Magic was the most obvious answer.

The taste of tomatoes and spices exploded in my mouth. "Birdie, this is incredible."

"Why, thank you. It's one of my specialties, but I save it for the season. Gets me through the long winter months." She patted her stomach. "Kane is partial to my goulash, though. The two of you should come back for dinner one night. I'll make it for you."

I caught Kane's eye across the table, and he held my gaze. A warm sensation spread from my stomach to my extremities. I credited the chili, but I knew it was more than that.

"If you can see the future, maybe you can skip Sarah and tell us where the changeling is?" I proposed.

Birdie dabbed the corners of her mouth with a napkin. "You know that's not how these things work. There's no crystal ball to show me the child."

"Scrying glass," I corrected her.

"Nor that." She smiled. "I'm too accustomed to catering to the ignorant."

"It's how I've lived my life," I said with a shrug.

She scraped her bowl clean. "If we're finished with lunch, we can get down to business."

I was tempted to ask for a second helping, but I knew it was best to carry on. We still had to stop at Hewitt's, and I had no idea how Sian was getting on with the ghosts.

Kane and I insisted on cleaning up from lunch. Once we finished, Birdie directed us to her office.

The room was nothing like the rest of the house. Metal and small flashing lights surrounded us. In the far corner, a large fan swiveled back and forth.

"It gets hot in here when all the systems are firing," Birdie explained, noticing my gaze.

"What is all this?" I asked. "What about the crows?"

"The crows are only part of the equation." She glided to the closest computer. "They bring me intel, and I use that to uncover more information, which I then enter in my database."

Birdie would've come in handy when I needed to update my ancient computer. To be fair, Steven Pratt did the best he could with what he was given.

"What kind of intel?"

"Oh, it varies. As I'm sure you're aware, Fairhaven borders Wild Acres and a multirealm crossroads. It's important to keep tabs on all the residents and activity."

My palms started to sweat. "Do you have information about me?"

"A small entry." She tapped the keyboard and my name appeared on the computer screen. "There isn't much. Your date of arrival and address. Your truck and the motorcycle you store in an outbuilding. Other than that, you're somewhat of a mystery, Miss Clay."

Kane and I exchanged looks behind her. I was relieved to know he hadn't shared my secret.

"Why do you keep tabs?" I asked.

"Somebody should, or this town could end up a disaster zone."

I thought of my recent experience chasing down gods trapped as animals. "Did you know about the roaming animals?"

"You mean the lion, the wolf, and that whole menagerie?" She cringed. "Oh, yes. The crows told me all about them."

I was uncertain how much information the birds could've possibly conveyed about what really happened. How did you say "imprisoned avatar" in crow?

"What about the werewolves at Monk's the other night? Not Arrowheads. Know anything about them?"

"If there were werewolves here that don't belong to the local pack, they drove because they didn't get here through the crossroads."

That was my theory, too; otherwise, the guards on duty that night would've scented them at the very least.

"I should clarify," Birdie said. "My information tends to center on the locals rather than outside activity coming in. That's why you're in here. If you'd only stopped in a B & B for a weekend, I wouldn't have bothered. But you went and bought Bluebeard's Castle and a coveted spot on my database." She twisted to smile at me. "Now, let's see how many Sarahs over the age of thirty we can find in Fairhaven and hope the one you want still lives in town."

"If we don't have luck with any of these," Kane said, "we'll go back further to Sarahs who moved out of town, but it makes sense to start with the ones still local."

"Agreed," I said.

Birdie centered herself in front of the computer and wiggled her fingers as though about to play piano. Her hands moved rapidly across the keyboard, showing no signs of arthritis or any other ailments. She and Otto could have a keyboard standoff. The speed and dexterity of her fingers suggested they'd be evenly matched.

A long list of names appeared on the screen. Birdie put on her glasses to read them. "So many Sarahs. Why couldn't you be searching for an Armelle or an Addilyn?"

"They're names?" I queried.

She turned to regard me with an air of satisfaction. "You just illustrated my point."

Kane leaned over her shoulder. "Can you narrow down by age now?"

"Do I look like an amateur to you?" Birdie tapped the keyboard and half the names disappeared.

"Twelve residents named Sarah over thirty," Kane said. "Could be worse."

"Would it be possible to print off the names and addresses?" I asked.

The rising whirr of a printer indicated Birdie was one step ahead of me.

"Thank you," I said. "This is incredibly helpful."

"Like I said, any friend of Kane's is a friend of mine."

"What do you do with the information you learn?"

"Depends. Sometimes I'll trade it for goods and services. That's how I met Kane." She winked at him. "Other times I'll pass information to the police or an interested party indirectly. Less often, I'll send an anonymous warning to someone if I learn they'll be in mortal danger in the near future. I can't control the information I'm given, so I can't guarantee answers to specific questions."

"I'll be curious to see what the crow brings back," I said.

"Me too," Birdie said. "That's the fun part."

Kane and I left with the printed sheet in hand and a container of chili. I didn't ask, but Birdie insisted. Psychic, indeed.

"How did she end up in a wheelchair?" I asked, once we were in the car.

He drove along the dirt road toward town. "No idea. I haven't asked."

"Some collector of secrets you are."

"I have no need of Birdie's secret. If she wanted to tell me, she would. I suspect she doesn't wish to be known as the woman in the wheelchair any more than your friend Otto wishes to be known as the blind vampire, so she doesn't discuss it."

"Otto's far happier being known as the curmudgeonly vampire."

Kane grunted a laugh.

"For what it's worth, I think the Crow Lady has a nice ring to it," I continued.

"She's formed an incredible connection with those birds. I'm in awe of her."

"Same." I started to feel guilty about Buddy, the scarecrow I'd placed in my yard in autumn. Live and learn.

"It's amazing how much information the crows can not only absorb but share with her. I have my own methods of gathering intel, of course, but Birdie's is, by far, my favorite."

"What will you give her in return for the favor?" I asked.

Kane kept his gaze straight ahead. "We fly."

"Like in one of those small airplanes?" I seemed to recall meeting a pilot in his nightclub.

"No, when I'm a blackbird. I'll take her with me."

I couldn't picture it no matter how hard I tried. "How do you defy the laws of gravity?"

He spared me a glance. "I can shapeshift into a blackbird and a monstrous beast, but you're concerned about scientific principles?"

"So what you're telling me is that you're a very strong blackbird." I mulled it over. "Do you carry her in your beak? That doesn't seem comfortable for her. And how do you keep her from being spotted by humans? People would freak out if they saw a woman dangling from the beak of a bird fifty feet in the air."

Kane reached over to rub the back of my neck. "I'm amazed what goes through that deified head of yours sometimes."

"I wish she had more control over her gifts. She'd be a hell of an asset for this town."

He glanced at me. "I could say the same about you."

I stiffened. "My gifts are different. In my case, the risks far outweigh the benefits."

"Only because that's what you've been telling yourself your whole life."

Not just me. Pops. Matilda, the Night Mallt.

I shifted in the seat to face him. "Melinoe is darkness. Nightmares. The dead. Tell me, how would unleashing all that on Fairhaven be an asset?"

"Children used to leave little statues of you next to their beds to protect them from nightmares. *You* aren't the nightmare, Lorelei. Not if you don't wish to be."

I didn't wish to be. I didn't wish for any of this, but I was stuck with my goddess powers, for better or worse—and I desperately wanted to keep those scales tipped in favor of better. If that meant denying parts of myself, then so be it.

CHAPTER 9

Sian was thrilled with the list of Sarahs, as well as the quality of timber and leftover chili. "An excellent bounty. Shall we make a start on the list?"

I didn't think it was wise to leave sweet Sian to his own devices. He was a little too wet behind the pointy fae ears to deal directly with the humans of Fairhaven. Fairies with generational experience like Sage and her grandmother blended in far more easily, whereas Sian would be more like Socrates wandering around the San Dimas mall.

"Why don't I heat up the chili for you and then we'll talk?"

"I am excited to try it."

My phone trilled in my hand, and I snapped it to my ear. "Hello?"

"Lorelei, it's Anna."

"Can't West make his own calls?"

"I'm not calling from his phone."

The tone of her voice set my teeth on edge. I left Sian in the kitchen and walked into the foyer to speak in private.

"What's up?"

"Thought you should know I told West what you did to

me at Monk's that first night we met." There was a slight tremble in her voice as she said the words.

"Why would you do that?"

"I told you before, my alpha is my priority. Once you became a threat, he deserved to know."

"Why did I become a threat? I'm trying to help you."

"No one asked you to get involved. Your meddling is going to make things worse."

So her response was to drive a wedge between us by playing on West's fears about me. Anna had to be more afraid of the threat those wolves presented than she was of me. That was the only reason she'd break her silence.

"West didn't seem to mind my meddling when it benefited the pack."

"He won't want it anymore. You can be sure of that."

"I'll bear that in mind the next time one of you shows up on my doorstep begging for assistance."

"I would rather die first."

"Careful, Anna. That's still a possibility." It wasn't my finest moment, threatening a frightened werewolf, but she'd taken me off guard and emotions were running a little high. Just because Kane accepted my identity didn't mean West would. A goddess of nightmares and ghosts wouldn't be welcome here and the pack was more than capable of running me out of town. Anna didn't know anything beyond my brief foray into her mind, but West was smart, and she'd likely given him ample information to figure it out. It was my fault, really. I shouldn't have used my powers on her. I knew better, yet I'd felt compelled to subjugate her. That had been the goddess in me, demanding subordination. A minor loss of control that was now biting me in the ass.

"Why are you calling to tell me this?"

"Do I seem stupid enough to tell you in person?"

I pinched the bridge of my nose. "No, I mean why are you telling me at all?"

"So that you'll keep your nose out of things that aren't your business. West won't want you anywhere near the pack now."

She hung up.

I stared at the phone blankly for a moment, trying to collect my thoughts.

"Lorelei?"

I turned to look at Sian. "How's the chili?"

"Spicy. Is something wrong? You look pale."

My arm started to burn. The sensation was milder than the last time, as though my skin wasn't sure how it wanted to respond.

West was here.

"Sian, do me a favor and go upstairs. Don't come down until I tell you."

"Is anything wrong? I am skilled with a blade."

"Nothing I can't handle. Please, do as I ask." I didn't want the innocent fae to get caught up in supernatural politics. He only wanted to find his sister.

The knock on the door tightened the growing knot in my stomach. I squared my shoulders and prepared to face the consequences of my actions.

West stood on the porch ensconced in a well-worn brown leather jacket and tight jeans. One look at his face told me everything I needed to know about his reaction.

Not. Happy.

I flung open the door and waited. The cold air nipped at my nose. "Want to come in?"

"I'll stay on the porch. What I have to say won't take very long."

"Okay." I stepped outside and closed the door behind me.

"I knew you were bad for Fairhaven. I told you that. If I had my druthers, you'd be gone by sundown."

"Nobody says druthers anymore. Nobody even knows what druthers are."

"That's why you make a good Scrabble opponent."

"Anna only told you about me to get me out of the way. Something about those werewolves has her terrified. Did she tell you how she stole their sketches from the police? Why would she do that?"

"Never mind that. I'm here to talk about you."

Sighing, I sank against the doorjamb. "Fine. What exactly did Anna tell you?"

"That you manipulated her mind. Showed her a nightmare and then threatened her not to tell anybody."

"This isn't the way I wanted you to find out."

"Because you hoped I never would."

"It was a mistake, West. I shouldn't have done it."

He folded his bulging arms across his chest. "I know you're a ghost whisperer. What else can you do?"

"You haven't figured it out?"

"Didn't bother to try. I came straight here as soon as Anna told me. I'd much rather hear the truth from you than a book or computer."

"You won't find much about me anyway. It's mostly speculation."

That got his attention. "Who are you?"

I closed my eyes. There was only one way to get West to trust me. Of course, it meant I also had to trust him. A double-edged sword of truth.

"You're right about me," I blurted. "I'm a danger to Fairhaven. To anyone who tries to get close to me."

"Are you some kind of weapon?"

"In the wrong hands, yes. I'm Melinoe reborn, goddess of nightmares and ghosts."

"Nightmares," he repeated. "You give people nightmares?"

"Among other things."

He nodded, as though I'd just told him I preferred flour tortillas to corn. "Does Sullivan know?"

"Yes."

"Who else?"

"The ghosts at the Castle."

He angled his head to regard me. "What happened to the rest of the ghosts from the cemetery?"

"I helped them cross over. Ray and Nana Pratt asked to stay, and against my better judgment, I let them."

"When you say you helped them cross over, does that mean you pointed them in the right direction?"

I knew what West was really asking. I debated how much honesty I wanted to share.

He must've sensed my apprehension because he said, "You might as well spit it out now."

I exhaled. "I can control spirits if I choose to."

"The ghosts at your place…?"

"They're autonomous. Once in a blue moon, I've shown them how to do something by taking over their movements, but they don't realize I've done it."

"Why not tell them what you're capable of?"

"I don't know," I answered honestly. "I've kept my identity secret my whole life. It feels uncomfortable to share pieces of it, even now."

"Your parents?"

"Human. After they died, my grandparents were left to raise their godly granddaughter. They did the best they could with the information they had."

"Why hide? Why not just live as Melinoe?"

"Because I wouldn't know how to do that. And Pops knew I'd have a target on my back the minute anybody found out my identity. He taught me almost everything I know."

"Even the sword fighting?"

"All of it. He was retired Navy and an avid hunter. He warned me from an early age that organizations would either want to use me or kill me, so I've tried to keep a low profile my whole life." And I'd succeeded, until I moved to Fairhaven.

"Nobody wants power like yours running around unchecked."

If he was this worried about ghost puppets, now didn't seem to be the right time to admit I could bend nightmares to my will and drag them straight through the fabric that separated them from reality.

"That kind of power can only mean trouble for us," he continued. "I'd rather not have it around my pack."

"Then I guess you should stop coming to me whenever you need a ghost whisperer." He couldn't have it both ways; that wasn't fair to me.

His gaze dropped to the slats of the porch. "I guess I should."

The werewolf continued to stand awkwardly for a moment, as though debating whether to say more.

"What's the answer, West? I should live on a mountaintop away from civilization? I'd love to hear it."

"The answer is you shouldn't exist."

His response was like a punch in the gut. "Wow. Tell me how you really feel."

His body remained so rigid that I worried he was about to explode into a giant ball of fur right on my porch.

"You chose your confidantes wisely; I'll give you that."

"What's that supposed to mean?"

"Your spirits are as silent as the grave, and you confided in a prince of hell, a demon without scruples."

I leveled him with a look. "Just because he's a demon doesn't mean he's without principles."

West's cheeks puffed with rage. "He oversees a guild of assassins, for crying out loud. What kind of principles do you think he has? Of course you trusted him to keep your dirty little secret. He's a collector of them, from what I hear. You probably made a deal with the devil to protect yourself."

I'd never felt actual anger toward West before, but I sure did now. Every muscle in my body grew tense. "Kane Sullivan has been nothing but a complete gentleman in every way. Not only has he guarded my secret, but he's offered assistance when he had no reason to do so. He asks for nothing in return."

West was silent for a moment. "I suspected as much, but now I'm sure," he said quietly.

"Sure of what?"

"You're in love with him."

I strangled a laugh. "I can recognize someone's admirable qualities without needing to be in love with them. I recognize yours, even when you're being an unreasonable jackass."

His nostrils flared. "There's nothing unreasonable about protecting my home. Fairhaven is a safe space for humans and supernaturals to grow and thrive together. I want that for everyone who lives here."

"Except me." I pulled myself together. "Whatever you may think, I'm on your side. You may not like that I kept my identity a secret. You may not like that I'm a goddess, but believe me when I say we want the same thing."

He relaxed his arms. "And what about when we don't? So far, our interests have been aligned. What happens when they're at odds? Will you use your goddess powers to make my nightmares come true until I submit to your will?"

I didn't have an answer for him. "Why don't we cross that bridge when we come to it?"

"That's the thing, Lorelei. I can't trust you now if I can't trust you later. It doesn't work like that, at least not for me."

Damn West and his moral high ground. He was going to die on that hill if he wasn't careful. What good is morality when you're dead?

"Listen, West. Something is happening. I don't know what it is, but those wolves are trouble. Anna said she scared them off, but I think there's more to it."

"It's not your concern, Clay. I'm not about to lose the life I've worked so hard to build here, not because of you or anybody else."

"Last chance," I said. "I'm offering whatever help you need."

"The pack can protect itself. We don't need you. We never did." With those words, he turned and walked away.

Unbelievable. I wished I could dump his ass in the lake to be a late-night snack for the three-headed demon. Sort of.

I returned to the foyer and closed the door behind me, resisting the impulse to slam it. I felt something wet on my cheek and realized I was crying. I wiped away the tears with a trembling hand. The confrontation with West upset me more than I expected.

Ray materialized in front of me. "Problem?"

"West is a dick. That's the problem."

"It's the rejection," Ray said softly. "It'll sting for a bit, but it won't last."

"How much did you hear?"

"Not everything because I follow the rules, but enough to feel disappointed in him."

I couldn't resist a smile. "Since when do you follow the rules?"

"He's wrong, Lorelei. You know that, right?"

"Doesn't matter who's right or wrong when the outcome is the same." I retreated into the house and shut the door. I wasn't surprised to see that Ray followed me inside.

"Right now you're feeling every rejection you've ever felt from childhood. That's why you're crying."

I entered the kitchen and tore off half a paper towel to blow my nose. "It isn't because of West?"

"West is the trigger, but the strong reaction, that's the past combining with the present."

I cast a sidelong glance at the ghost. "More psychology books?"

"Not entirely. I told you about that rough patch I went through with my wife."

I nodded, remembering Ray and his daughter Renee's recollection of his near affair.

"I went to see a therapist after that, to figure out what was going on with me."

"That was very open-minded of you." I didn't know many adult men who'd voluntarily put themselves in the hot seat. Then again, I didn't know many adult men until I moved to Fairhaven. "Did it help?"

"Sure did. I learned enough about myself and the reasons for my behavior that I was able to do better going forward." He paused. "Not just do better, *be* better."

"And you think being rejected in childhood because of my abilities is the reason I feel so upset about West's reaction?"

"Makes sense, doesn't it? Every time you showed a sign of power, your grandfather hauled you off to another school."

"He did that to keep me safe."

"Oh, I know his intentions were honorable, but he reinforced the negative associations with your identity. The other people around you reacted negatively, and your grandfather compounded the issue by spiriting you away to another school where nobody knew about your abilities. Must've made it feel shameful just to be yourself."

I stared at Ray, completely unnerved by his observation. "Wow, Ray. That's incredibly insightful."

"The psychology books helped, too. I like reading them in my spare time."

I smiled. "All your time is spare."

"And I like to make good use of it. The human brain is fascinating, but I guess you know that already. People's nightmares must reveal a lot about them."

"They do."

"I bet some of yours involve rejection and abandonment."

A hard lump formed in my throat. "So you think I shouldn't be upset about West?"

"I'm not passing judgment on your response. You feel how you feel, and that's okay, but I thought it might be helpful to understand that you're not crying over Weston Davies. You're crying over every kid who cowered from you. Every time your grandfather yanked you from school and made you start over again somewhere else. It's hard enough to make friends the first time around, but you had to do it so often with the same miserable results, you finally gave up."

More tears welled in my eyes. "Thanks, Ray. As hard as it was to hear that, I feel better."

"Good. Glad I could help. I wish I could've done more of this in my lifetime. Been a more compassionate man for my family."

"Oh, Ray. I have no doubt you were. Look at Alicia. She's a testament to your positive influence."

He chuckled. "The girl who tried to summon a demon to improve her dance moves? Yeah, I can see why you'd say that."

I laughed at the memory of Alicia accidentally summoning Lamashtu, bringer of fever, nightmares, and death. It was only funny now because she lived to tell the tale. It could've ended in disaster if not for Kane and me.

"She's a stubborn kid with a strong personality. It's the reason I like her so much," I admitted.

"Because she reminds you of yourself?"

I looked at him askance. "Are you calling me stubborn?"

He bit back a smile. "In our family, it's a compliment."

"What if West decides to force me out?"

"Do you want to leave town?"

I answered without hesitation. "No."

"Then he won't force you, will he? You're a goddess, Lorelei. He can't make you do anything you don't want to do. That's what scares him so much."

Ray was right about my past melding with my present. West's rejection stung because it reminded me of every rejection I'd ever felt. Every person I helped who then turned on me because I was weird or different. I made it mean something about me instead of letting it be their issue. And now West's issue.

Then it hit me. He was an alpha afraid of power. He'd seen it torn from his father's grasp. He'd been hounded for it. No wonder the werewolf objected so vehemently to anyone with what he viewed as excessive power. It explained his opinion of Kane, too. The problem wasn't that the prince of hell was a demon, it was that he was powerful.

"That isn't all that scares him," I said. West was terrified of losing the life he'd created, of watching everyone around him suffer.

And I understood that fear more than he knew.

CHAPTER 10

With Sian hard at work on the bed upstairs, I summoned Ray and Nana Pratt to the kitchen to review the list of names from Birdie. They'd both lived in town long enough to recognize a couple last names, even if they didn't know the Sarah associated with them.

"I knew Miles and Michelle Stewart," Nana Pratt said. "We went to the same church."

"Any Sarahs in the family?"

"Possibly. They had two daughters and a son." She squeezed her eyes shut, as though trying to force their names to the surface of her mind. "The girls were called Polly and Caitlin. They weren't the happiest bunch. They always arrived at church looking like they'd lost their dog."

I couldn't rule them out. Sarah could've married the son and taken Stewart as her name.

Ray pointed to the next name on the list. "I knew Ines and Frank Ludwig. They had two sons and a daughter. Can't remember their names, though."

"Any other names seem familiar?"

"No," they said in unison.

"Okay, thanks. I'm going to head out and see how many

Sarahs I can get through today. Keep an eye on Sian, will you?"

"Will do," Ray said. "He seems like a nice young man … er, fairy."

"Maybe give him a hand upstairs." I looked at Nana Pratt. "And make sure he eats. I don't want to send him home any skinnier than he already is."

I grabbed my coat off the rack in the foyer and shrugged it on. The list was secure in my purse. The sun was bright today, and the temperature was meant to climb to a balmy fifty degrees. I contemplated dusting off my motorcycle, until my gaze snagged on a familiar silhouette outside the gate.

I stepped outside and motioned for Kane to wait there.

"Have you forgotten how to use a phone?" I asked.

"I prefer face-to-face conversations. Are you on the way out?"

"As a matter of fact, I'm beginning my Sarah hunt."

"Mind if I join you?"

"I wouldn't mind the company." After my argument with West, it was nice to feel like somebody was in favor of my existence, despite his own reservations about me.

He gestured behind him. "My car is already warm."

I smiled. "Anything to avoid Gary. I hope he doesn't hold it against you. One day you might need him."

"Doubtful."

I slid into the passenger seat of the sleek sports car. Kane was right—the seat was nice and warm. It took the truck ages to heat up, if it bothered to at all.

Kane started the car. "Where to?"

I gave him the address for Sarah Stewart.

"How's your houseguest?"

"Building a bed as we speak. The ghosts are keeping him company." I paused. "West knows about me."

Kane cut me a quick glance before returning his eyes to the road. "What prompted you to confide in Davies?"

"He knew enough that it seemed wise to just give him the complete story. Better than letting him fill in the blanks for himself."

"Was it?" he asked. "Better, I mean."

"No," I admitted. "He trusts me less now than he did before."

"He's always been stubborn."

"He has his reasons."

Kane scoffed. "You're defending him?"

"Not exactly, but I understand why he feels the way he does." I snuck a peak at him. "You have concerns about me, too. It isn't like you're so different."

"My concerns are vastly different."

"How so?"

Kane's mouth tightened, along with his hands on the wheel. "Looks like we're here."

He parked in the driveway, and I double-checked the house number.

"This is the neighbor's house," I said.

"I know, but the driveway is empty." He looked at me. "What? Do you think I'd park a car like this on the street?"

"You park on the street outside my house."

"Because you live on a hill away from the rest of town. Nobody will nick my sideview mirror there."

I didn't argue. He locked the car, and we walked across the adjacent patch of lawn to reach the walkway to the Stewart house.

A rusty basketball hoop lorded over the top of the driveway. The garage door was open, offering a full view of bicycles, sleds, and other household equipment.

"Well, there's definitely at least one child in this home," I remarked.

"The changeling is nineteen at this point. Hardly a child by human standards."

"As long as their age ends in 'teen,' they're a kid as far as I'm concerned."

Kane shot me a quizzical look but said nothing.

"What?" I prompted, as we arrived at the front door.

"You want to protect children the way you weren't protected."

"I was protected." Up to a point. Once Pops died, I had no choice but to enter the foster care system.

"You were taught to hide. It isn't the same."

"Now you sound like Ray."

I rang the doorbell. A woman answered, clutching a phone in one hand and a coffee cup in the other.

"Are you Sarah Stewart?" I asked.

The woman immediately moved to shut the door with her hip.

"A woman after my own heart," I murmured.

Kane managed to wedge his Gucci loafer between the door and the jamb before she could fully close it. "This will only take a moment of your time, madam, I assure you."

The woman's head jerked up at the sound of the demon's silky-smooth voice. "What do you want?" she asked, although her tone was softer than the question demanded.

"We're searching for an adopted child who would now be approximately nineteen years of age," he said. "A girl."

"No adopted kids in this house. I gave birth to all four of those whiny brats, and I've got the stretch marks to prove it."

Well, this Sarah was an absolute delight. I was relieved Sian was at the Castle.

"Thank you for your time," Kane said with a slight bow.

The woman used her foot to slam the door in our faces.

"Someone is questioning her life choices," I muttered.

"At least you can cross her off the list."

"Did you hypnotize her?" I asked, as we returned to the car.

"You underestimate me if you think I needed demon magic to appeal to her."

"I'm glad you didn't tack on 'good nature' at the end of that sentence."

He laughed. "She did seem harried, didn't she?" He started the car. "On to the next."

Sarah Ludwig was childless. Sarah Papadopoulos was the mother of twenty-year-old twins.

My stomach gurgled, drawing Kane's attention. "One more house, and then I'm driving you to a restaurant."

"I'd rather eat at home."

"My treat."

I flinched. "I'd still rather eat at home. I have some of Birdie's chili left."

"Suit yourself."

Sarah Berg was our last stop. She had three stepchildren who were all in college. She'd been left to care for their hyper cavapoo, Oliver, while her husband worked. Sarah Berg didn't strike me as a dog person, as evidenced by her exhalations of despair as the dog jumped repeatedly at Kane, ignoring me completely, which was a relief albeit unusual. To his credit, the prince of hell remained calm. Only when Sarah glanced away for a moment did I stare the dog into submission. Whining, Oliver ran away with his tail between his legs.

Sarah's head swiveled to the dog and then to us. "How did you do that?"

I blinked innocently. "Do what?"

Sarah stared after the dog. "I've never seen him do that."

"You should walk him more," I said. "A dog like Oliver has a lot of energy."

"I prefer to walk on my treadmill this time of year," she objected. "It's too miserably cold to walk outside."

I felt a pang of sympathy for Oliver. He'd probably lived his best life with active children around, and now he was stuck indoors, feeling like a caged animal.

"Have you considered a dog walker?" I ventured. "I bet there are more than a few kids in town who would be willing to walk him around the neighborhood for a few extra bucks."

She drummed her fingers on the door. "That's actually a good idea."

"If you need a recommendation, I know a very responsible young lady named Alicia who would take excellent care of Oliver." Ray's granddaughter was always up for a side hustle.

"Tell her to give me a call," Sarah said. "I'd be very interested."

"That was a good deed," Kane commented on the drive home.

"For Oliver."

"It's a good deed for Sarah Berg and Alicia, too."

"It's no big deal. I felt sorry for the dog, that's all."

Kane patted my back. "There's no shame in being one who aspires to ease the burden of others."

"I don't aspire to anything except a quiet day at home."

Kane smirked. "And how's that working out for you?"

I shrugged. "Could be better."

Back at the Castle, the sweet scent of chocolate chip cookies lured me into the kitchen, where Ray was hunched over the computer.

Sian's expression was painfully hopeful, despite the half a cookie dangling from his mouth. I shook my head.

"Cookie," he said, barely intelligible.

"Nana Pratt baked cookies for you?"

"I don't know. They were here when I came downstairs."

I contemplated the freshly baked goods on the cooling rack. I really ought to have a healthy meal first.

Sian finished the other half of the cookie. "I licked the dough from the spoon and scraped the bowl. I hope that is acceptable."

I stared at Sian. The audacity. "Yes, it's fine," I said.

His smile evaporated. "Uh oh. It does not seem fine. Have I overstayed my welcome? If it improves your mood, the bed will be finished tomorrow. Ray was a great help."

It did not improve my mood. He ate my cookie dough, depriving me of one of the greatest joys in life.

I swiped a cookie from the rack and stuffed it into my mouth. There. Pain eased.

"How many Sarahs were you able to rule out?"

I showed him the updated list.

He beamed. "We have both made excellent progress today."

"Me, too," Ray interjected. "I've been researching your lake monster. I found a few references in the books you brought home from the library that warranted closer scrutiny."

"Scrutinize to your heart's content. I need to eat something substantial."

"Oh, I finished the chili," Sian said. "I hope that is acceptable."

I took another cookie from the rack and ate it. I stopped chewing and listened.

"Did you hear that?" I asked, swallowing the lump of cookie.

Ray glanced up from the computer screen. "Hear what?"

"That light tapping sound."

The ghost looked at me with concern. "You know I'm typing on the keyboard, right?"

Sian listened. "I hear it as well."

"It isn't you, Ray." I listened intently. "It might be a squirrel on the roof."

"The roof is too far." Ray drifted over to me. "I doubt that's what you're hearing. Maybe if you were in your bedroom."

"There it is again!" I leaned across the sink to peer through the windowpane and my heart skipped a beat.

"Is that a hand?" Ray asked.

My stomach lurched. "Seems to be."

The hand was too busy trying to open the window from the outside to notice us.

"It's like Thing from *The Addams Family*." Ray leaned forward. "Except slightly greener and… Are those freckles?"

"Decomposition marks." I knocked on the glass. The hand froze.

"Too cold outside for you?" I asked.

The hand scrambled down the side of the wall and disappeared from view.

I looked at Ray. "That was a first."

"For me, too. Then again, there've been lots of firsts since I met you."

"I'll take that as a compliment."

Sian joined us at the window. "Is it truly a hand?"

"Yes, indeedy."

Ray looked at me with a deadpan expression. "You seem awfully chipper about this development."

"Hands are cool."

Sian scanned the backyard. "I can't see it."

Ray pushed his head through the wall for a better look outside.

"I frightened it," I said.

Ray returned his head to the kitchen. "Why didn't it set off the ward? Because it's small?"

"Because it's dead."

"Really? Moved pretty fast for a dead thing."

I gave him a pointed look. "Says the ghost who goes from zero to sixty at the sight of a mouse."

"I don't mind snakes or spiders, but rodents give me the creeps."

I exited the kitchen to retrieve my coat from the rack in the foyer.

"What are you doing?" Ray asked.

"Going to find that hand."

"Why don't you stay inside and let Ingrid and I search for it?"

"Because you won't be able to do anything if you find it."

"And what will you do?"

"I haven't decided yet."

"There's a rake in the shed."

"It's a hand, not a leaf."

"Thought you might want it as a weapon."

"If I want to use a weapon, I have plenty to choose from."

Sian's eyes widened.

Nana Pratt appeared in the foyer. "Bring the laundry basket."

"Why would I do that?"

"You can flip it upside down and trap the hand underneath."

"It's a hand," I replied. "It'll just push off the basket."

Frowning, she dropped her gaze to the floor. "I didn't think of that."

"Shall I accompany you?" Sian asked.

"Stay here," I barked.

I stepped outside and surveyed the yard.

I found the hand resting on one of the headstones like a sunbathing turtle. It saw me and scampered down the side of the stone.

"Wait. I'm not here to hurt you. I only want to talk." I held up my hands as I approached it.

The hand stopped. Slowly, it returned to its perch.

"My name is Lorelei. What's your name?"

The hand used sign language to spell out its name.

"Nice to meet you, Claude."

"What is it?"

I swiveled to see Nana Pratt's lip curled in disgust.

"I told you to wait inside."

"You told Sian to wait inside," Ray corrected me, materializing next to his partner in crime.

I returned my gaze to the hand. "Claude is a revenant."

"I don't know what that is," she said.

"A zombie?" Ray interrupted.

"A relative, but a revenant is older, wiser, and less prone to decay."

"Thank God for that," Nana Pratt said.

Claude gave her the middle finger.

The elderly ghost gasped and clutched her nonexistent pearls.

"It can hear us," Ray said in awe.

"And it's terribly rude," Nana Pratt added.

"Because you're all undead," I explained.

"I am *not* a zombie." Nana Pratt sounded offended by the comparison.

"No, but you fall in the same category."

She didn't seem excited by this knowledge.

"What about vampires? Can they hear us?" Ray asked.

"Real vampires aren't technically undead. That's an old wives' tale." But they still felt my power. The smart ones did, anyway.

"If this thing is like a zombie, then where's the rest of it?" Ray asked.

"Somewhere close by. The parts can't stray too far from the whole. The farther it goes, the weaker it gets." I wasn't sure what the extent of the radius was, but odds were good that the rest of Claude was somewhere in Fairhaven.

"When you say parts," Nana Pratt began slowly, "which ones do you mean, exactly?"

"The obvious ones."

Nana Pratt stared at the hand. "Nothing about this is obvious to me."

"I think what Ingrid would like to know is whether we should be concerned about any dangly bits making a surprise appearance," Ray offered.

I choked back laughter. "I don't know. Why don't you ask Claude?"

Ray glowered at me. "Never mind." He hunched over like he was addressing a toddler. "Where's your body, Claude?"

"Never mind that," Nana Pratt interjected. "Why is it here? What does it want?"

Claude closed his fingers to form a fist.

"He's grey rocking," Ray informed us.

"What's grey rocking?" Nana Pratt asked.

"It's a tactic to minimize conflict," Ray explained. "Make yourself as dull as a grey rock so the other party loses interest."

I looked down at Claude. "We're not trying to manipulate you, buddy. We're only trying to get answers."

"Which is perfectly reasonable, given you've broken into our home," Nana Pratt added.

Ray made a noise at the back of his throat.

"Sorry," Nana Pratt said. "I meant to say Lorelei's home."

The fingers sprang into action and bolted across the ground.

"Wow, it's fast. You'd better run, or you won't catch it," Nana Pratt advised.

"I don't need to chase him." Not when I had an advantage Claude didn't seem to know about.

Nana Pratt shuddered. "Well, do something, please. I can't stay here knowing that thing might be sneaking around."

"You don't have much choice," Ray reminded her.

"I'll see what I can do." I followed Claude to the front yard and heard the bushes rustle as the hand dove in.

"Come on out, Claude. I promise I won't hurt you."

No response.

I sat on the step and slung my arms casually over my

thighs. "I'm going to assume someone sent you here for a purpose. Maybe to steal. Maybe to kill me. Here's the skinny, though, Claude. You can't do either."

The bush rustled. Good. He was listening.

"My guess is you use your hand to scout and then reconnect to your body to finish whatever job you were given." Although revenants had free will, except under certain circumstances, they were unlikely to act of their own accord. Claude wasn't a puppet, though. More of a minion.

"You're a revenant, Claude, which gives me certain leverage over you. Don't make me use it."

Silence ensued.

I waited.

The hand burst from the bushes and scrambled along the pavement to the bridge. I debated whether to seize control, but in the end, I let him go. At this point, I was more curious than worried.

"Did you find it?" Nana Pratt's anxious voice cut through my thoughts.

"He left," I said. "I saw him crawl through the gate."

"Can your witch friend modify the ward to include stray hands?" Nana Pratt asked.

"Phaedra isn't my friend. She's someone I do business with."

"You seem to like her," Ray said. "Why not make a friend?"

"One that isn't an assassin or a demon," Nana Pratt whispered, as though one of them might overhear her.

"Witches and I mix like pineapple on pizza. Not a good idea."

Ray hoisted an imaginary belt. "I'm a big fan of pineapple on pizza."

"Anyway," I dragged out, "Phaedra won't modify the ward again without additional payment." And we all knew I was short on cash.

"Seems like it would be difficult to do," Ray said. "If ghosts fall in the same category as revenants, then we'd activate the ward every time we moved around the property."

I twisted to regard him. "You're a fast learner, Ray."

Nana Pratt looked mildly put out.

"A compliment for him isn't a criticism of you," I told her. "Don't make it mean something it doesn't."

Her shoulders relaxed. "This is still all so new. I'm trying my best to keep up."

I softened. "And you're doing a phenomenal job, really."

"Thank you. That's very nice to hear. I can't say I was very impressive during my human life, so it feels good to tick that box now."

Ray tried to nudge her gently, but his shoulder passed straight through hers. "Ingrid, how can you say that? You were a very impressive woman. Look at your grandbabies. They're a real testament to you."

Nana Pratt scoffed. "I wouldn't describe Ashley as thriving just because she wasn't sacrificed by witches."

I sighed. "Is there some interference you'd like me to run with Ashley?" When I last checked in with Steven and Ashley, I was informed that Ashley had been fired from her job. I should've known Nana Pratt had been stewing over it ever since I shared the news.

"Well, since you asked—maybe you could help her find a new job."

Ray gave her a heavy dose of side-eye. "Are you seriously trying to be a helicopter grandma from beyond the grave?"

"Says the man whose granddaughter regularly visits for advice."

I made a placating gesture with my hands. "Let's just agree that neither one of you is winning any individuation awards today." The fact that they'd chosen to stay tethered to Fairhaven after their deaths to keep a close watch on their families was the flashing neon clue.

"Renee and Alicia need me," Ray said.

"And Steven and Ashley need me," Nana Pratt chimed in. "They already lost their parents. I'm all that's left."

I felt that familiar tug on my heartstrings, the one that had prompted me to agree to let them stay on that fateful day. I'd also lost my family too soon. I understood their anguish and their desire to keep their family ties intact.

I climbed to my feet. "I'll see what I can do for Ashley. I'll also talk to Phaedra about the ward and see if there's anything she can add that affects revenants but not ghosts." Although I wasn't sure how I'd explain my reasons to the witch without revealing more than I intended to. I'd come up with something, though.

I always did.

CHAPTER 11

By the time Wednesday rolled around, I'd nearly forgotten about my required meet and greet at Magnarella's new and improved lab. I wasn't thrilled to revisit the compound premises. None of my experiences there had been positive, and today's visit would be no exception. It was for the greater good, though. Just because West considered me a liability didn't make me one. Thwarting Magnarella's plans would prove I was an asset, possibly a dead one—but an asset, nonetheless.

The temperature managed to reach fifty-one degrees by midmorning, so I opted to ride Betsy, my motorcycle, and enjoy the springlike temperature. It felt good to have the wind rushing past me again.

The gates to the compound were closed, and I had to wait for security to admit me.

"Cool bike," the guard said with a note of admiration. "Looks vintage."

"Thanks, she is." I'd left her in a storage unit with my other belongings when I moved to England. A little love and care upon my return and she was as good as the day I bought her.

"You can leave it here."

"Excuse me?"

"Park it here by the booth. Mr. Magnarella told me to escort you personally to the new lab." He pointed to a golf cart parked on the lawn. "I'll drive you in that."

"Seems like a slower option, but fine."

I joined him in the front seat of the golf cart, and he started to drive.

"How far is the lab?"

"Not too far. It's a separate building now."

I guessed Magnarella didn't want anyone breaking out of the lab and interrupting one of his dinner parties with the supernatural creature they'd slain. Fair enough.

We passed the old entrance to the lab and turned left at the end of the compound, where a shiny new building awaited us.

"Spared no expense, I see." No wonder he needed a gala to entice investors.

"Mr. Magnarella takes his businesses very seriously."

He took the amassing of power very seriously. The businesses were merely the means to an end.

The guard pressed his hand to the keypad and the door slid open. "Have fun. I'll be here when you're ready to leave."

I was ready to leave now, but I knew I had to take the opportunity to see what monstrous activities the vampire had planned.

A second set of doors slid open, and I crossed the threshold of a spacious room. A man in a white lab coat stood at a counter, typing on a computer.

"Hey, Edmonds."

The scientist glanced up at me, and his gaze darted to his pristine lab in alarm.

"Didn't your boss warn you I was coming today?"

Dr. Edmonds smoothed the front of his coat. "He did. I tried to persuade him it was a bad idea, but he insisted."

I surveyed the sterile silver and white environment. "I can't believe you got another lab up and running so fast."

He sighed with pleasure. "It's amazing what money can do, isn't it?"

"That's why you stuck with Magnarella?"

"I'm a scientist, Miss Clay. You have no idea what a difference financial backing can make to an experiment."

"Oh, I think I've experienced it firsthand." I ran a finger along a metal worktop, just so he'd have to wipe away my germs later. "Why this nonsense? Wouldn't you rather cure cancer?"

"Cancer is the old world. The elixir is the new one. With a successful elixir, cancer is only one of many diseases that will cease to be a problem to solve."

"Deities in human bodies are immune to disease?" That was news to me, not that there was much publicly available information on the subject. I healed quickly, yes, but that didn't mean I was invulnerable to disease.

His eyes sparkled with excitement. "Their healing abilities are beyond our wildest dreams. Broken bones. Diseases. Human maladies will be no obstacle to the next version of humanity."

"Next version? Humans 2.0?"

He grinned. "Something like that."

"You've read the old myths, haven't you? Do the gods strike you as entities that serve humanity? They fought like children and used their powers for their own betterment."

"Which is why this version of humanity will be such an improvement. We'll be combining the humility and compassion of everyday people with the power of the gods."

"Humility and compassion, huh? Your social circles must be different from mine."

He smirked. "They are, in that mine include actual humans."

"In my defense, I didn't know I'd be living among so

many supernaturals when I moved here." And by then, it was too late. The Castle was mine, and my bank account was nearly empty.

"If this elixir is done right this time, without the restrictions imposed by our previous partners," he began, "then we have a real chance to change the world as we know it."

"And you'd win the Nobel Prize and whatever other accolades scientists get these days. Maybe a scientific law named in your honor. Kids around the world will be bored to tears by the Edmonds Principle."

He seemed underwhelmed by the possibility. "My interest is in the science, Miss Clay, not the fame and fortune."

"For someone so interested in humanity, you sure seem willing to destroy it." As he moved closer to me, I noticed how gaunt his face looked. "You're sick."

He didn't bother to deny it.

"How long?"

"Months, if I'm lucky."

"That explains the hurry." And the willingness to stick with Magnarella.

"I have an alternate plan if this one fails to pan out by the end."

I knew instinctively what his Plan B was. "Would you really want that life for yourself?"

He shrugged. "It doesn't seem so bad. Immortality in exchange for sharper teeth and a thirst for human blood. The alternative seems much worse."

"Are you that afraid of death?" I didn't share his fear, mainly because of my connection to the dead. I knew there was an afterlife and spirits that lived on in their own way. Edmonds wouldn't be curing disease in the next life, but he had nothing to fear.

"I'm afraid of not fulfilling my potential," he said simply. "I was born into a brilliant family, Miss Clay. Do you have any idea what it's like to be a superior human being, yet still feel inadequate around your parents and siblings?"

"I imagine that's how Hermes felt on Mount Olympus."

Edmonds skipped right over the joke. He might enjoy life more if he had a sense of humor.

"Let me guess, they've all managed great accomplishments in their lifetimes, and you're still struggling to catch up."

"I have yet to complete my scientific purpose, and now I have a deadly illness hanging over me. The universe has been unkind to me."

"The universe is neither kind nor unkind. It simply is. As a scientist, I'm surprised you'd see it any other way."

He angled his head in acknowledgement. "A sensible point. I knew you were more intelligent than Mr. Magnarella gave you credit for."

"He underestimates most people, I find." Because he overestimated himself. Typical man-pire.

"Be that as it may, Mr. Magnarella is willing to continue to raise the funding for this experiment, and for that, I'm grateful to him."

"I guess he's the one promising you an immortal life if you can't create a successful god elixir in time."

Edmonds allowed himself a small smile. "It's in my contract."

So Edmonds used Magnarella and his legally binding agreements to his advantage. Nicely done.

"How do you intend to wipe people's minds without the baku?" I'd killed the rare creature myself, so I knew it was no longer an option for the lab.

"We're developing an alternative method, one that doesn't require a supernatural creature."

"Brain transplant?"

"Something far less intrusive."

He was playing coy. That was fine. I didn't need to know

the particulars because I had no intention of letting his experiment progress that far.

"You must have a team in place. Where are they now?"

"Working remotely today. Mr. Magnarella thought it best to keep our meeting private." He spread his arms wide. "What would you like to know first? I have a wonderful array of potions that I purchased from a shaman in Nevada."

Right now, I was more interested in the boy than his toys. I wanted to understand his relationship to the supernatural world in the hopes of figuring out how to appeal to his better nature, assuming one existed.

"When did you first discover the existence of gods and otherworldly creatures?"

Edmonds seemed taken aback by the question. "Why do you ask?"

"Just curious. I feel like most people in the know have a story about where they were and what they were doing when their worlds got rocked."

Edmonds gazed at the blank wall. "It was my great-grandfather who introduced my family to the hidden world. He was a deminer during World War I."

I wasn't sure where this story was going, but he had my attention.

"He was considered expendable and was sent to clear areas of explosives."

"That sounds terrifying."

"I'm sure it was, but that wasn't the focus of his story. He was far more interested in what he discovered."

"Obviously not explosives or he wouldn't have lived to tell the tale."

"Oh, but he did, you see, which is how he came to learn of the existence of elves. He was left to die alone on that Belgian hill. It was a moss maiden that saved him and nursed him back to health. He should've died, but the elves altered the course of his life. He returned home completely healed. It's the reason my grandmother became interested in science at a young age, and then my father—to see whether humans could replicate some of the elven qualities."

"Sounds like you were destined to study science."

"Oh, yes. Science and bioengineering form the backbone of my family."

"Must have been a fascinating home to grow up in."

The edges of his mouth tightened. "If you were an experiment, yes. If you were one of their children, there were certain expectations."

"You're the youngest?"

"Worse. The middle."

"I'm sorry," I said.

"I watched my older and younger siblings outperform me in school and then university. My parents offered the carrot and not the stick, but even so, their love and validation were tied to performance."

"Which meant less parental attention for you."

He puffed out his chest. "To their credit, it made me a better scientist."

"But an unhappy man," I said.

His shoulders slumped slightly. "Not unhappy. Unfulfilled. There's a difference."

"If you say so."

I strolled along the perimeter of the lab, taking stock of every piece of equipment. I didn't want this visit to be in vain. If there was something in this room I could identify that would thwart the new set of experiments, I hoped to lay eyes on it before I left.

"You intrigue us, Miss Clay."

"You sure about that? Seems more like I scare the crap out of you."

"You were unlike any other subject I had the pleasure of testing."

I shuddered at his use of the word pleasure. There was a

certain abhorrent perversity to it, like a kid who enjoyed torturing animals.

"You only say that because I ruined your science fair project."

"Mr. Magnarella is serious about a partnership. He sees potential in you. Your knowledge alone is worth the price of setting his ego aside."

"There isn't enough room on planet earth to set that ego aside."

He smirked. "Will I see you at the gala?"

"We'll see," I said, which I intended to sound noncommittal, but instead came out sounding ominous and threatening.

My gaze landed on the far counter, where a glass jar held what appeared to be a monstrous foot. My blood ran cold.

"Dr. Edmonds…"

He rubbed his hands together. "Yes, happy to answer any questions."

"Did you, by any chance, experiment on a ghoul recently?"

His hesitation answered for him.

I motioned to the jar. "Only one?"

"In a show of good faith, I'll tell you that we captured two, but one escaped."

"And what happened to the one you kept?"

"We dissected it for research purposes."

Only a psychopath would feel the need to add "for research purposes" to that statement. My animal torturing theory didn't seem too far off the mark.

"Did you find the one that ran away?"

"No, but we didn't look very hard. As you know, we don't yet have quite the level of funding we had, so we need to choose wisely where to spend our time and resources."

The ghoul that died on my walkway hadn't been high or drunk; it had been drugged and experimented on by Edmonds.

"What were you hoping to learn from them?" I highly doubted any gods were eager to slip into a ghoul's body.

"Ghouls are considered lesser beings, and therefore, have warranted fewer studies. Mr. Magnarella caught them creeping around his premises and decided to make use of them." Edmonds smiled. "Waste not, want not."

My stomach churned. "I think I've seen enough for today."

"Are you sure? I could show you the refrigerated items."

My radar pinged. "You don't happen to have any revenants, do you?"

His eyes glinted with curiosity. "I thought those were extinct. Why do you ask?"

"That's what I thought. Thanks for confirming." I wasn't about to throw Claude under the bus; he was in enough pieces as it was.

Dr. Edmonds reached into the pocket of his lab coat. "Before you leave, a parting gift." He removed a pen with the logo of a rising sun. "We ordered a bit of merch to give to our potential investors."

I clicked the pen. "Money well spent, I'm sure."

I left the lab, feeling more strongly than ever that I had to put an end to Magnarella's grand plans once and for all.

CHAPTER 12

The Bridgers were one of the oldest families in Fairhaven. Phaedra still lived on their property, the only surviving Bridger witch on one of the only surviving farms in town. The rest of the properties had been sold off and divided years ago. Given the witches' long history in Fairhaven, I thought Phaedra might be able to help me with my current predicaments.

There was no answer at the door. I rounded the corner of the house to find Phaedra feeding the chickens. The birds squawked and clucked as they jockeyed for position.

I caught Phaedra's eye, and she smiled in greeting. "Hungry?" she joked, holding out a handful of corn.

The chickens nearly lost their minds when their food source turned away from them. Their heads bobbed at a rapid clip as they scurried to stand between us. One hen started to peck the others.

"There's no way birds are descended from dinosaurs," I said.

Phaedra laughed. "Then you've never seen a cassowary."

"Imagine being a T-Rex and seeing your descendants. You'd be so embarrassed."

"I imagine that's how a lot of our ancestors feel," Phaedra said.

The chickens scattered as she tossed more food on the ground.

"On that note, I have a question for you."

The witch closed the bag of chicken feed. "If we're going to talk about my family, let's go inside."

I glanced around the farmyard. "You're worried someone might overhear us outside?"

"No, I'm worried I'll need a drink, and the liquor cabinet is inside."

Fair enough. If my family's legacy involved murder and mayhem, I'd probably feel the same.

The side door squeaked as she opened it, and we entered directly into the kitchen.

Phaedra wasted no time raiding the liquor cabinet. "On a scale of hot toddy to tequila shots, how serious is this conversation going to be?"

"Depends on your answers."

Her face drained of color. "Tequila it is then." She pulled a bottle from the lower shelf. "Two glasses or one?"

"No shots for me, thanks."

She contemplated the bottle. "What if I add cinnamon-ginger tea to it? Reposado tequila enhances the flavor. My mother used to call it her winter brew."

"Sounds intriguing. Anything I can do to help?"

"No. You sit and ask your questions. This will give me something else to focus on."

I took a seat at the farmhouse table as Phaedra gathered the ingredients.

"How are you getting on with the farm? It seems like a lot of work."

She groaned. "You have no idea. There aren't enough spells in the world to help me tackle the never-ending to-do list."

A thought occurred to me. "Would you consider hiring help?"

She poured tequila into a measuring glass. "I'd think you have enough manual labor waiting for you at the Castle. Would you be happy working on a farm?"

"Oh, not me. I'm thinking of Ashley Pratt."

Phaedra started to choke. "You're suggesting that the girl who almost died at the farm at the hands of my family now come to work here? Are you trying to torture her?"

"It might be cathartic for her. She's had a hard time ever since her parents died. Maybe working outside, and alongside someone like you who has her shit together, would be a good experience for her."

Phaedra dumped the contents of the measuring glass into the pot. "I probably owe it to her to give it a try, and I could really use the help."

"You don't owe her anything, Phaedra. You weren't responsible for what happened to her. That being said, it might be a mutually beneficial arrangement."

The witch nodded. "Okay. I'll reach out to her. See what she says."

"Thanks. I appreciate it. Now I have a question about my ward."

She stirred the contents of the winter brew. "Why? Is it malfunctioning?"

"I'm not sure. I have different reactions, depending on the visitor."

Relief rippled across her features. "Right. That's normal. I used one of your hairs to infuse the ward with some of your essence. It helps with detecting threat levels. Say your cousin Jerry shows up unexpected and you can't stand Jerry. Your body will let you know this is an unwelcome arrival."

I thought of the warm, pleasant sensation I'd experienced when Kane activated the ward. Damn. I did not want to feel that good when the demon visited.

"What if I adore Jerry, so the response is initially nice, but then the relationship goes south? Will the ward know when to change its alert system?"

"Automatically. It's designed to be in alignment with you."

"What if I don't know whether the visitor is a threat?"

"Then your response will reflect the uncertainty."

I mulled over her answers. "This is more sophisticated than I realized. I don't think you charged me enough."

She smiled. "I know I didn't."

"One more ward-related question." I drew a deep breath and took the plunge. "I had an unexpected visitor recently. Well, a piece of one. He only sent his hand, so the ward didn't register his presence."

She stopped stirring. "His hand," she repeated.

"Yes, Claude is a revenant."

"An actual revenant." She blinked. "I thought revenants died out centuries ago."

"They're ancient but not extinct."

She grimaced. "Good to know. Maybe I should update my own ward to include them."

"My question is—is there a way to include revenants but exclude ghosts?"

She squinted at me. "Why would you want that?"

"I bought a house adjacent to a cemetery. I don't need the ward activating twenty-four-seven." Okay, it was a minor fib given I'd helped all the spirits cross over as soon as I moved in—well, all the spirits minus two.

"I see," Phaedra said, and resumed stirring. "I understand the dilemma. Revenants and ghosts fall under the same undead umbrella. I'd have to try to parse them, which could prove tricky."

"Does tricky mean expensive?" I queried.

Phaedra snorted. "It very well could. I don't typically

charge by the hour, but I might have to in a situation like this."

"In that case, forget I asked."

"Do you think it came through the crossroads?"

"Possibly." The werewolf guards on duty might've missed the revenant if he sent himself through the crossroads one piece at a time. I didn't want to think too hard about that one.

I set my hands on the table. "Now, my next order of business involves the name Sarah. Ever hear your family mention a Fairhaven woman by that name?"

"Just Sarah? No last name?"

"I'm sure she has one, but I don't know it."

"How long ago would this conversation have taken place? You seem to forget that I basically ran away from home," Phaedra said.

"I didn't forget, but I assume your family gossiped about the people in town when you were younger, and you might remember hearing the name."

Phaedra fell silent for a moment. "There were so many names mentioned over the years. I don't specifically remember any references to Sarah."

"How about a human making a bargain with a fairy? Or a reference to a changeling?"

Phaedra perked up as she delivered our drinks to the table, complete with a cinnamon stick and orange peel.

"This looks amazing." I blew off the steam and drew a small taste to my lips. It managed to be both soothing and spicy, an ideal combination.

"A changeling in Fairhaven?"

"Is that so unusual? The town sits on the border of a multirealm crossroads."

"If my family got wind of a changeling, they would've taken action."

"They didn't seem interested in protecting the town from

other supernatural species. Why would a changeling present a problem for them?"

"Because fairies have magic. They would've viewed the presence of a changeling as encroachment on their turf."

And here I thought werewolves were territorial.

"Would they have kept any notes? Maybe a journal?"

"If they interfered in a bargain between a human and a fairy, they wouldn't have left a written record of it. The fae can be vengeful. They also would've complained until they were blue in the face, so if this happened within my lifetime, I'd remember."

"It was eighteen years ago."

"Then I doubt they knew about it because I never heard it mentioned." Her brow furrowed. "Is there anything I need to know about this changeling?"

"I don't think they're a threat. I'm trying to track them down for a remorseful family member. I'm basically tracking a lost heir, like I used to do in London."

"More like tracking an adoptee on behalf of their biological family." Her lips grew thin.

"You disapprove?"

"You don't know how the changeling will react, do you? Maybe they think they're human. Maybe they're happy and you're about to rip their peaceful world apart."

I considered my own upbringing. What if Pops hadn't known I was a goddess or hadn't told me and someone from The Corporation tracked me down and spilled the beans? How would I have felt?

"I'm only searching for Sarah at the moment. The woman who struck the bargain."

"Don't be naive, Lorelei. What do you think will happen when your fairy friend learns of Sarah's whereabouts?"

"Sian seems like a reasonable guy. I don't think he's here to wreck anybody's life."

"Then tell him to go back to Faerie and leave the

changeling in peace. A bargain was made, and now they must honor it, regardless of any remorse or regret."

"I'll pass along your message." I could see Phaedra felt strongly about this issue, so I decided to switch topics. I took a generous sip of the winter brew. "Wow. This one's a winner."

"Thank you. It definitely hits the spot." She tipped back her cup and drank.

"While I'm here, can you think of any reason your mother or aunts would've checked out a library book about fifty years ago?"

Phaedra laughed, nearly spitting out the brew in the process. "Fifty years ago? I have no idea. We didn't use the library very often, since we have our own in the other room."

"Except presumably your books focus on witchcraft and magic."

She raised an eyebrow. "Are you inquiring whether my mother ever read *To Kill A Mockingbird*? I can practically guarantee she didn't."

"Not literature. This is a book on Albanian mythology."

Her eyebrows drew together as the information sank in. "Albanian," she repeated, as though the word had, in fact, jogged her memory.

"Yes. Does that sound familiar?"

"I remember my grandmother telling a story about a demon. I can't recall the name, but it wreaked havoc on the farm. Eating animals. Causing storms that flooded the crops. The demon was Albanian." Phaedra's gaze seemed to grow more distant as she spoke. "This was all before I was born, so I only remember brief comments made in the years that followed. There was one particularly brutal autumn when my grandmother was convinced the demon had returned because a storm wiped out one of the fields."

"Did they use a spell to cast out the demon?"

Phaedra chewed her lip. "I'm sure they did. Magic would've been their go-to. Do you think it's back?"

"I'm not sure exactly what we're dealing with yet. It may have never left."

"I hope not because if that demon was powerful enough to piss off the entire Bridger coven, I wouldn't want to cross paths with it now. You'd better watch your house. The Castle is an appealing target. All that land and a working moat."

"Do you recall the type of demon?"

Phaedra lapsed into contemplative silence. "No, I'm sorry. I don't."

"Is there any chance your family would've relocated the demon to Bone Lake?"

Phaedra blinked in surprise. "Isn't that place haunted? What makes you ask that?"

"The demon I came across there—there's a chance it's the same one that plagued your farm years ago."

Phaedra laughed. "I highly doubt it. That demon was as relentless as it was monstrous. We'd have heard all sorts of stories in town over the years, or it would've left the area to seek out more victims."

I gave her a pointed look. "But what if the demon couldn't leave?"

Phaedra's eyes sparked with understanding. "You think my family cursed it?"

"It makes sense. They wanted the demon gone."

"They wanted the demon out of Fairhaven, though. Bone Lake isn't too far."

"Yes, but what if they tried and their efforts only resulted in the demon getting trapped in Bone Lake? That would explain why so many hikers have disappeared there over the years."

Phaedra stared into her cup. "Okay, say you're right. Say my coven cursed the demon and trapped it in Bone Lake. Now what?"

"Now I want to release her."

"Her?"

"I think the demon is female."

Phaedra gave an adamant shake of her head. "No, absolutely not. How can you even consider showing that monster mercy? Think of all the damage she's done."

"She's still doing it, only on a more limited scale."

Phaedra looked at me out of the corner of her eye. "Is this because of Kane?"

"What does this have to do with Kane?"

"You think because your prince of hell is reformed, that every demon is capable of change."

"First, he isn't *my* prince of hell. Second, that isn't the reason." At least I didn't think it was. I wasn't that naive, was I?

"I don't remember every detail about the demon, but what I do remember is terrifying. That creature brought pain and suffering to my family. They were at their wit's end."

"These are the same witches who were more than willing to sacrifice innocent people to boost their bank account. Do you really think they would've cared about cursing a deadly demon to remain trapped in a local lake where humans camped?"

Phaedra clapped her pink cheeks. "Oh, gods. You're so right. Tell me what I can do to help."

Relief swelled inside me, but I pushed it aside. There'd be time for feelings later. Right now I needed to focus on the task at hand.

"If it's your family's curse that keeps her locked in the lake, then you can probably undo it."

Phaedra closed her eyes momentarily. "I am so tired of cleaning up their messes."

"I get it. I do. And I wouldn't ask if it weren't important. This isn't about sparing a demon. It's about saving future innocent lives." And about releasing the spirits trapped there with her, although I couldn't explain that part to Phaedra. Although she was becoming a reliable presence, she wasn't quite in the inner circle. That level of trust took time, at least for me.

"I don't understand," Phaedra said. "If we release the demon, don't we risk putting more lives at risk? If you plan to kill her, then you don't need to undo the curse. Just kill her right there in the lake."

"If it were that easy, don't you think your family would've done it?" I knew from experience the Bridger witches weren't opposed to murder to get what they wanted.

She returned to the kitchen to refill her cup with the warm winter tipple.

"The brew is phenomenal. If this witch business doesn't work out for you, you should consider bartending at the Devil's Playground."

"Thankfully, I've built up a reasonable clientele. I wasn't sure it would be possible after the incident."

The 'incident' involved the attempted domestication of a deadly supernatural creature called a culebrón that would've resulted in the sacrifice of Ashley Pratt.

"The few of us who know the details know you weren't involved." I took another sip. The taste was heavenly.

"I still have access to the coven library." She nodded in the direction of an adjacent room. "If they used a curse from one of those books, I can find it."

"I can't pay you, but we can barter." I had no idea what I had to offer, but I'd figure something out.

Phaedra stared at me. "Why on earth would you pay me? This demon in the lake isn't your responsibility."

"It isn't yours either."

"It is if my family is to blame for it, and even if they didn't curse the demon, I'm a resident of Fairhaven just like you. I want this to be a safe place."

I swallowed the last of the delicious spiked tea with regret, resisting the urge to request a second glass. Never mind. My stomach was warm and full, plus I had a potential solution to the Bone Lake problem. Things were looking up.

"Let me know if you find anything worth sharing," I said.

"I will, but no promises."

"I know. It's only a working theory." A working theory I felt confident Phaedra would soon prove correct.

She shook her head ruefully. "It's always something in this town. Stay safe, Lorelei."

"You, too." Staying safe was the story of my life. No need to tell me twice.

CHAPTER 13

I stood in the spare bedroom, admiring Sian's handiwork. "I can't believe you did this in such a short time."

"I told you my skills are renowned."

"I'm sorry I haven't held up my end of the bargain yet."

"The bargain was affording me sanctuary and that you have fulfilled."

The back of my neck began to feel tight, and I rubbed the muscles.

Sian observed me. "Are you hurt?"

"No, I'm fine. It's more of a nuisance pain." And suddenly I realized what had triggered it. "I'll be right back to continue complimenting you."

I hurried downstairs to see which visitor had caused the mildly painful sensation.

Anna Dupree graced my doorstep. She wore her usual snarl, but at least her injuries had healed.

"Hello, Anna."

She glanced furtively over her shoulder. "Can I come in?"

Despite her tough-girl posture, fear emanated from her. When the emotions were as palpable as hers, I didn't even need to access her nightmares to sense them.

"Are you sure you want to?"

Her fingers twitched. "Look, I know you're pissed off, and I'm the last person you want to see right now."

"Not the last person, but definitely not in the top half."

Her gaze darted to the road again. "If you don't want to talk to me, just say so and I'll go."

Curious to learn the reason for her visit, I decided to end her suffering and invited her in.

"Can I take your coat?"

The werewolf looked at her sleeves as though she'd forgotten she was wearing one. "I guess." She shrugged off the coat and held it up awkwardly, despite the fact that the coat rack stood beside her.

I took the coat and hung it on an empty branch.

"Thanks," Anna mumbled. "I usually just toss mine on the sofa."

"If I had a sofa, I'd do the same."

She actually smiled in response to that.

"Can I interest you in a drink? I have about twenty types of herbal tea."

"Got anything stronger?"

"Coffee?"

"I mean booze."

Since she didn't seem the type to apologize, Anna's willingness to appear on my doorstep was the equivalent of flashing neon letters that spelled out 'trouble.'

"Sure. Follow me." I walked to the kitchen and opened the cupboard where I stashed a few bottles of alcohol. "Gin and tonic okay?" I drew the line at offering her the good stuff Kane had procured for me. Puck's Pleasure was for special occasions, and Anna's unexpected visit didn't qualify.

She took the liberty of opening the fridge to inspect the contents. "Got any beer?"

"Help yourself," I said, because it seemed she intended to do exactly that.

Anna pulled a bottle from the shelf and yanked the cap off with her teeth. I waited patiently as she took a long swig.

"West is in trouble," she finally said. "I don't know who else to tell."

"Is this trouble related to the wolves that attacked you?"

She nodded as she swallowed another generous mouthful. "The wolves that attacked me, they aren't from Fairhaven."

"I gathered that from when you chased them back from whence they came, but they attacked *you*. Why is West in trouble?"

Anna glugged more beer before answering. "They're from West's hometown in Minnesota."

A chill ran through me as I recalled West's history. His dad had been the alpha of their local pack when his family was killed by a challenger. Only West managed to escape.

"You think they're here for West? It could be a coincidence."

"They started asking me questions about him at Monk's. I told them I'd never heard the name before. That's how the fight broke out. They didn't believe me. They followed me outside and kicked the shit out of me, trying to get me to tell them the truth."

"Why didn't you fight back?"

"Because I didn't want to draw attention to the incident by beating them to bloody pulps. I thought they'd take out their frustration on me, realize they were mistaken, and disappear."

I folded my arms. "When have you ever met a wolf that gave up that easily?"

"It was wishful thinking; I see that now. I was only trying to protect West."

"Is that why you didn't tell West the truth?"

Her expression grew pained. "I knew it was a mistake not to warn him. They were scouts. They tracked him here for their alpha."

"And you're worried they reported back to him already?"

She nodded. "I tracked them to Bone Lake to kill them so they couldn't share West's location." She drained the bottle dry. "Obviously, you know I failed."

"Why not tell West now? Why come to me?"

"Because West's original pack was much bigger than ours. If they come back to finish the job their alpha started, they won't stop until it's done."

"You're asking for my help?" The request was so unlike Anna that I didn't know how to respond.

"West would skin me alive if he knew I'd run to anyone outside the pack to save us, especially you."

"I'm flattered, but you need to tell West. You've endangered your whole pack by keeping it a secret this long."

Her face hardened. "You don't need to tell me. I wrestled with what to do, believe me. It isn't easy to be here right now, asking for an outsider to help us."

I understood. Asking for help had always been challenging for me, too. I was raised to be independent to a fault, but people weren't designed to live in isolation from each other.

"Why did you tell West about me?" It seemed ironic that she'd betrayed me only to want to resuscitate me now.

"Because I thought I could handle things on my own." She rubbed her forehead. "Obviously, I was an idiot to think so." Her gaze met mine. "I need you to understand something, though. You and me—this isn't a budding friendship. I will steamroll over you or anybody else who gets in the way of the pack."

"A reluctant partnership. Got it."

She squinted at me. "Shouldn't you be offended or something?"

I shrugged. "What you're offering is my comfort zone."

Her face contorted as she processed my reply. "You're a strange lady, Clay. S'pose that's because you're not really a lady at all." Her gaze swept the interior of the Castle. "Well, maybe, of the manor."

At least she didn't call my house the Ruins like the rest of the pack. I considered it progress.

"Tell me what I can do to help," I said.

"Unknown wolves were spotted by perimeter guards about thirty minutes ago."

"And you think they're on the way to kill West?"

"I doubt they'd kill him here. The alpha would want to make a display of it. Show the old pack that the Davies line is officially wiped out."

My palm started to sweat. "Where's West now?"

"At home."

"And you haven't warned him yet?"

Anna waved a hand at the empty beer bottle. "Why do you think I needed a drink? I've mishandled the whole damn thing, and I know that. There's a reason I'm not alpha material."

Panic began to crawl from the pit of my stomach. "Hold that thought. I need weapons."

I raced upstairs to my bedroom and threw open the trunk.

"Is there a problem?" Sian asked, poking his head in.

I continued my weapons selection. "Nothing for you to worry about. Stay here. I'll be back shortly."

"Are you certain? I can assist you." He held up his hands with their baby smooth skin. "These are capable of more than woodworking."

I strapped throwing knives to my thighs. "I appreciate the offer, but your mother is already down one child and a husband. I need to return you in the state I found you."

Sian lowered his hands. "You do not know my mother. Why show concern for her?"

I sheathed my sword. "Because stranger or not, I don't want to be responsible for that kind of pain." I knew what it felt like, and I didn't wish it on anybody, even though I knew it was inevitable. Life and pain were inextricably linked; that didn't mean I had to be a willing participant.

I started toward the door. "And don't even think about following me."

Anna was waiting for me by the front door. I stopped at the coat rack and fished the keys to my truck out of my coat pocket.

"Why do you think it took so long for them to find West?" I asked as we left the house.

"America's a big country. I guess it's like searching for a hop in a vat of beer."

I wasn't sure that was the best analogy, but I let it slide. Now didn't seem the right time to quibble.

Anna's phone trilled. Her face paled as she looked at the screen. "I need to go." She bolted across the bridge.

"Anna, wait!"

"Can't," she yelled over her shoulder. "The trailer park is on fire and your truck isn't fast enough to race a snail." She released the wolf inside her and charged through the gate.

I dashed across the bridge and through the gate to where my truck was parked. "Gary is so much faster than a snail," I muttered. I removed the sheath and tossed it on the passenger seat. I didn't need a sword poking me in the back as I drove.

Naturally, because this was an emergency, the engine refused to turn over.

I stroked the dashboard. "Please don't make a liar out of me, Gary."

The engine sprang to life, and I hit the gas. The back of the truck fishtailed, spraying dirt and gravel in all directions as I sped toward the woods.

In the distance, smoke billowed across the treetops like a filthy grey parachute.

Anna was long gone.

Through the thick haze, I spotted a huddled mass of werewolves by the entrance to the trailer park. Anna was among them, back in human form and gesticulating wildly as other werewolves attempted to put out the blaze.

I grabbed my sword and hurried to join the crowd, scanning the faces for West. My gaze landed on another cluster of werewolves about twenty yards to my left. I counted five. I didn't recognize any of them, and the sight of them set my teeth on edge.

I sprinted to Anna's group. "What's going on?"

She skipped right over the sarcastic reply. "They're trying to smoke out West."

I glanced at the second group of wolves. "Those five are from his original pack."

She nodded. "West is in his trailer. He refused to come out, so they set fire to it."

My chest tightened as I observed the flames. "And he's still inside?"

She grabbed my arm before I could rush forward. "He has a plan, Lorelei. He's not an idiot."

He wasn't a coward either.

"Why isn't anyone fighting them?" Wolves fought each other over much less than setting fire to the alpha's home.

"Alpha's direct orders," Bert interjected. His face was smudged with black. "He said they're only here for him. We can act in self-defense, but that's it."

"Wouldn't it be considered self-defense to keep them from burning down your entire trailer park?"

"They're not trying to burn down the whole park," Bert said. "They made sure to contain the fire."

And members of the Arrowhead Pack were now drenched in smoke and sweat in their attempt to extinguish it.

"Are your two friends from Monk's in that crowd?" I asked Anna.

She shook her head. "I told you; they were the scouts. These five are the extraction team."

"I don't know why West won't let us kill them," Bert growled. "This is an act of war."

Anna shoved him. "Because he doesn't want any of us to die protecting him, numb nut."

"He's the alpha. Of course that's what we're supposed to do."

"Not to West," Anna said. "In his mind, it's the other way around."

Bert dragged his sleeve across his blackened face. "I'm going back over to help. If that wind shifts, all the trailers will go up in flames."

I observed the crumbling trailer. "I hope West realizes that smoke inhalation can kill him even if the flames don't."

Anna typed furiously on her phone. "I told you he has a plan."

My phone lit up with a text from Sage. *He's with me.*

I stared at the screen, initially thinking she meant Sian.

West? I typed back.

Sage sent a thumbs up emoji.

I cut a glance at Anna. "You know where he is."

She nodded without looking at me. "I'm staying here to keep an eye on our visitors."

I snuck away from the crowd and headed back to my truck. I was curious to learn how West managed to escape a burning trailer and make his way to Sage's cabin without anyone noticing.

I drove the short distance to Sage's house. The front door swung open as I approached. Sage ushered me inside and quickly shut the door behind me.

West sat on the sofa, hunched over with his head buried in his hands. He looked nothing like the tough alpha I'd come to know.

Sage brought him a glass of water, which he accepted without looking up.

"How did you know I was there?" I asked.

"Anna," Sage replied. She ran her fingers through his hair in an affectionate gesture before joining him on the sofa.

"How did you escape?"

West stared at the water in his glass. "There's a trapdoor in my trailer that leads to an underground tunnel. Took me years to build, but it was worth it."

"You've been waiting for this day," I said, somewhat surprised.

"More or less. I didn't know they'd set my house on fire, but I figured the day would come when I'd need a secret escape route." He lifted his head. "Is anybody hurt?"

"Not that I could see. Your pack was putting out the fire. The other wolves…"

A howling sound filled the cabin, causing every bone in my body to shudder in unison.

"Are almost here," West said, finishing my sentence. His jaw set. "They must've picked up my scent."

"What do they want?" Gran's voice shouted from the bedroom.

"To kill me," he said simply.

"They're from his old pack," Sage explained.

"Lorelei knows," West said. "Who told you they were here? Was it Anna?"

"Doesn't matter." Regardless of whether I liked Anna, I wasn't about to get her in trouble when she was only looking out for her alpha's best interest.

West's mouth was set in a grim line. "I recognized a few of their faces. Hell, I played Little League with two of them. Jax and I used to fish in the creek together on weekends."

"I don't get the impression they're here to go fishing with you," I said.

"No, they want him to go swimming with the fishes," Gran called from the bedroom.

"No need for a narrator," Sage yelled.

"I'm sorry this is happening," I said.

"I knew they'd find me eventually," West said. "I tried to convince myself otherwise, but I always knew Orson considered me unfinished business." His gaze met mine. "You should leave, Clay. This isn't your fight."

"It isn't Sage's fight either, but now you've brought it to her doorstep." My response was sharper than I'd intended.

West squeezed the fae's hand. "Clay's right. I'm sorry, Sage. I shouldn't have come here."

Another howl. The sound made my blood run cold.

"Let her help, West."

"She has no reason to help me," West said. "I'm the one who accused her of being trouble for the town, and here I am bringing danger to our doorstep, just like she said."

It hadn't occurred to me that he'd feel guilty about his own hypocrisy.

"I don't hold it against you," I said. "You care about Fairhaven, I get that."

"We all do," Sage added. "And you're the pack leader. A threat to you is a threat to Fairhaven."

West rose to his feet. "Everybody stays inside."

Sage jumped up to stand in front of him. "You can't go out there."

"What would you have me do? Hide behind you so they have to break inside and kill three women to get to me?"

"I've lived too long to die for you," Gran yelled.

Sage clenched her hands into fists. "Nobody's asking you to sacrifice yourself, Gran."

"Good, because I won't do it. I was just about to watch the first season of *Good Omens*."

Glass splintered and cracked as a rock burst through the living room window. Sage kept her hands pressed against West's broad chest in an effort to hold him in place.

"Weston Davies," a gruff voice said in a loud voice. "Come out, come out, wherever you are."

West winced. "That's Jax."

"I'd like to meet your old friend Jax." I strode to the front door and stepped outside. The same five wolves from the trailer park now formed a semi-circle outside the cabin.

"Welcome to Fairhaven, fellas," I said. "You seem to be in the wrong location. The tour for Wild Acres starts at the Falls."

The werewolf I assumed was Jax spat on the ground. "Not here for a tour, little miss. We're here for that yellow belly you've got stowed inside."

Jax looked like he hadn't sat in a barber's chair in a decade. His brown hair was tied back in a thick braid. His facial hair culminated in a long beard that likely housed a small family of insects.

"What do you want with West?" I asked. "Did he do something wrong?" Men like Jax expected women to be stupid, so I'd happily play the part to my advantage.

"He stayed alive," Jax replied. "That's what he did wrong. Our alpha would like to correct that mistake."

I took another step toward them, watching to see if any of them cowered in my presence. It happened on occasion to the weaker members of a pack.

The extraction team was apparently made of sterner stuff.

"West has built a life here and shown no interest in going back to whatever hole you crawled out of. Why not leave him be?"

"Not for me to decide," Jax said. "The alpha wants him brought to justice."

"Justice?" I was enraged on West's behalf. "For what? The experience of watching someone slaughter his family?"

"His father was weak," a second wolf shouted. "His whole line is weak, which he's proving right now. We're doing this pack a favor."

I heard the sound of the front door open, and Sage emerged from inside, clutching an axe.

"Why don't you do us all a favor and drop dead?" Sage demanded.

Jax smirked. "West has made some pretty friends here. Maybe we ought to have a little fun first."

I unsheathed my sword. "Oh, I guarantee it'll be fun—for me."

Jax's smile broadened. "I like our odds. What do you think, boys? It's been a little while since we got to play rough." He eyed me. "Hope you like it doggy style."

Charming.

I showed my teeth. "Hope your ass likes the taste of metal."

Jax's bones cracked as he shifted. His transition wasn't as seamless as that of the Arrowhead wolves. If he had an injury that made shifting difficult, I could use it to my advantage.

Gran's window slid open. "Leave my granddaughter alone." She flung a small bottle at another werewolf's head. The contents splashed his face.

He laughed and wiped it away. "You think throwing perfume is going to save you?" His eyes rolled to the back of his head and his body seized. He keeled over, shaking uncontrollably.

Gran chuckled to herself as she slid the window closed again. The elderly fae could be brutal when she wanted to be. I made a mental note never to get on her bad side.

West appeared beside me.

"West, get back inside!" Sage's voice trembled with fear.

"I'm not letting you fight for me."

I twisted to look at West. "Piss off. I'm doing it anyway." And if I had to send a message to the other wolves, using Jax to do it suited me just fine.

I blew a kiss to Jax. "Come and get me, big fella."

Slobber dripped from the wolf's fangs as Jax lunged at me. I sliced off the tip of his ear, wounding him just enough to stun him. Blood spilled from the tiny blood vessels. I grabbed him by the scruff of his neck and kept my sword pointed outward as a warning to the other wolves. I wasn't strong enough to break his neck, but I didn't need to be.

I only needed to access to his head.

I slipped inside and seized control. A whimper escaped him. Poor bastard must've hated to hear that sound coming from his own mouth.

The wolf's body slumped flat on the ground as he lost consciousness and I lowered myself with him. Jax's mind was angry and chaotic, but not abnormally so. There was no spell at work here. I sensed latent affection for West, and nostalgia for the childhood they'd shared. Jax wasn't simply a grade A douchebag following orders. Interesting.

As far as nightmares went, his were fairly standard. Erectile dysfunction. Falling off a cliff. Drowning.

I skipped over the first option for obvious reasons and chose the nightmare behind door number two.

Jax stood in human form on the outcrop of a snow-capped mountain. The air was thin and cold, and there was a large lake in the distance.

"Hi there," I said with a friendly wave.

He looked around in a panic. "Where did you take me?"

"You tell me. It's your cliff." I peered behind him. "Nice view. Is that Lake Superior?"

"How did you teleport me here? Are you some kind of witch?"

I made a noise of disgust. "Okay, now you've pissed me off."

"Then what are you?"

"Your worst nightmare."

His eyes rounded as he glanced over my shoulder. "No," Jax whispered. "He is."

I turned around. The werewolf behind me stood about six feet tall. Stocky build. Nondescript features. His only noticeable trait was the glint of menace in his eyes that put my nervous system on high alert.

"This must be your vindictive alpha," I said.

Jax didn't seem to hear me. The stocky werewolf advanced toward Jax, oblivious to my presence.

"I told you to shift faster, boy," the alpha snarled. "Haven't you been practicing?"

Jax dropped to his knees. "It hurts. My bones aren't mending like they're s'posed to." His voice belonged to a younger version of Jax, not the tough guy outside the cabin.

The alpha towered over a fearful Jax. "You best hope that's not true, because you know what happens to weak links in my pack, boy."

Jax's head bobbed as he struggled to maintain his composure.

"I told you to shift!"

"Yes, sir." Bones crunched, prompting a sharp cry of pain from Jax.

I couldn't let the nightmare continue, for my sake as well as Jax's.

I brought us both back to reality. Rising to my feet, I wiped his blood off my hands.

"We're done here," I said.

Jax's fur and animal parts receded, leaving a man with a bleeding ear in their place.

The other wolves took notice of his condition and reverted to their human forms. The one dripping in Gran's potion staggered toward Jax as the wolf struggled to his feet. For a moment I worried he'd try to fight on, but his silence emboldened me.

"I let you live so you can go home and tell your alpha that Fairhaven and Weston Davies are off limits to you and your pack," I said.

"Bitch," Jax hissed in a pained whisper.

He was angry that I'd subdued him, but even angrier that

I'd glimpsed the abuse he'd endured. Shame was a powerful weapon, and never more so than when we wielded it against ourselves.

West stepped into a patch of sunlight, putting himself directly in the spotlight. "Tell that murdering bastard that if he wants me, he can come and get me personally, if he dares."

Jax pressed the heel of his hand to his ear. "You're a disgrace, Davies. No wonder your line was nearly wiped out. No self-respecting alpha would leave a woman to defend his sorry ass."

"A woman just kicked your sorry ass," Sage shot back. "And no self-respecting alpha would murder an innocent family and consider it a power move."

Jax whistled, and the other wolves fell into line behind him. They slunk away from the cabin in a single-file line.

Sage massaged the back of his neck. "It's over, West. They're gone."

West didn't look convinced.

"You were brave to stand up to them, Sage," I said.

"Never underestimate a fae with an axe to grind," she joked. "What I'd like to know is how you subdued Jax. All you did was cut off the tip of his ear."

"I guess it's a really sensitive spot."

West pulled her closer and leaned his forehead against hers. "I'm so sorry I put you in danger. I should've gone somewhere else. Once I fled the tunnel, your face was the only one I wanted to see."

"Are you kidding? This was the most fun Gran's had in ages."

On cue, the elderly fae appeared in the doorway wearing only a white dressing gown. "I got to use my experimental tonic on that one wolf, and it worked. That's a win-win."

"Dare I ask what was in it?" West asked.

"Probably best not to tell you."

"I told you not to use deadly force," West said.

Her mouth split in a grin. "I was seventy percent sure it wouldn't kill him, but it was fun to try."

A figure burst through the trees. Anna. She took one look at West and her legs nearly buckled beneath her.

"You're safe."

Sage's face scrunched with rage. "No thanks to you. Why didn't you tell him those two wolves that attacked you were from his old pack? He could've been killed."

West touched her arm, and her rage quieted.

"They know about this cabin now," Anna said. "Sage and her grandmother should probably relocate to the trailer park until the threat has passed."

Sage lifted her chin. "I'm not going anywhere. This is my home."

"They came back with five wolves this time," Anna pointed out. "Next time they'll come back with ten or even twenty. You're a weak link. They'll use you to get to West."

Sage took a step closer to her. "I think we both know who the weak link is."

A snarl erupted from Anna and West jumped between them. "Sage can stay. She can ward the cabin before they have a chance to come back." He pinned his gaze on Anna. "You and I will talk later—in private."

Anna began to crumble. "I'm sorry, West. I never meant…"

He silenced her with a lethal look. "I said later. Go home, Anna."

"Speaking of homes, you're going to need one," Anna said, lowering her head. "They couldn't save yours."

"I'll figure something out."

Anna nodded and fled.

"She regrets how she handled the situation," I told him. "She was only trying to protect you."

"The reason doesn't matter. Her silence endangered the entire pack."

"Just don't be too hard on her," I said.

His brow creased. "She ratted you out. Why are you defending her?"

"Because we don't always make our best choices when our actions stem from fear. But that fear stemmed from losing someone she cares about. I get that, and so should you."

I swiped my sword off the ground and walked to my truck without a backward glance.

CHAPTER 14

I arrived home to find two assassins in my kitchen, chatting with Sian over cups of coffee.

Gunther tipped his head back to look at me. "Welcome home, honey. How was your day?"

Camryn noticed the blood on my clothes and grimaced. "I'm guessing not the best. Want me to burn those for you?"

"I'll try a stain stick first, thanks."

Gunther Saxon and Camryn Sable were cousins from a talented family of mages. They were also members of both La Fortuna, an ancient mage society, as well as the Assassins Guild.

"How did you get in?" I asked.

"Sian was kind enough to extend an invitation," Gun said. "We explained that we're friends of yours."

"And he just took our word for it." Cam stifled a laugh. "Isn't he precious?"

Sian blinked, perplexed. "Are you not friends?"

Sighing, I dropped my sheathed sword to the floor with a clatter and walked to the sink to wash my hands. "We are, but I wouldn't typically allow people in my house if I'm not home."

Sian lowered his gaze to the table. "Yes, that makes sense. I apologize. On the bright side, Nerds are a delicious candy. Have you tried them?" He raised the small box and seemed to realize it was now empty. "Perhaps next time."

I dried my hands and sank into the fourth chair at the table.

Gun observed my present condition. "Dare I ask?"

"There was a situation with werewolves. It's been dealt with." For now.

Cam brightened. "The same werewolves that Vaughn fought? I heard he had that sexy post-brawl glow when he broke out of prison. Did he look hardened? Do you think prison changed him?"

"First of all, we didn't break him out. Everything was above board." I assumed. You never knew for sure with Kane. "Second, it was jail, not prison."

"Was his hair tousled? Ooh, was it sticking up in the front in that boy band way I love?"

"I wouldn't say he resembled the member of a boy band. He looked like someone who'd slept overnight in a jail cell."

Her mouth turned up at the corners. "In other words, his hair was disheveled, like he'd just stumbled out of bed in nothing but his boxer briefs?"

Gunther groaned. "You need to make up your mind. Are you interested in him or not?"

"Sounds to me like she is very interested," Sian said.

Cam wrapped a strand of hair around her finger and played with the ends. "I think we can all agree that he's unnaturally hot. That doesn't make us all interested in a relationship with him. I mean, the statue of David is easy on the eyes, but I'm not waiting for an invitation to Florence."

"That might be difficult for him, given he's made of stone," I said.

Camryn flicked a finger. "Oh, he can be turned back, but

no mage is willing to take responsibility for destroying a beloved piece of art." She put the word 'art' in air quotes.

Gun rolled his eyes. "She's convinced David is Medusa's handiwork and that Michelangelo took all the credit."

"Typical white man privilege," Cam added with a sigh of tedium.

"For what it's worth, I think you and Vaughn would make a great couple," I told her.

"Sometimes I think so, but then I remember how similar we are, and I worry it's a bad idea."

"Because you're both mage assassins?" I asked.

She gave me a look of disdain. "Because we're both Virgos."

"A recipe for disaster," Gun agreed. "Neither one of you will be capable of meeting the other one's standards because you're both highly critical and totally unreasonable."

Cam smiled. "I love that you know me so well."

He shrugged. "That's what cousins are for."

Sian's head bounced back and forth as he attempted to follow the conversation. "You are actual assassins? This was not a jest?"

"Not a jest," I said.

The fairy seemed unsure how to react. "Would you like coffee?" he offered. "It should still be hot."

"I'd get it for you, but I don't want to splash any on my clothes." Camryn ran her hands down the front of her white pantsuit. I wasn't one to pay attention to fashion rules, but even I knew white after Labor Day was a fashion faux pas in America.

"White is a bold choice," I remarked.

"It's winter white," she clarified.

"What's the difference between winter white and plain white?" I asked.

Gun clucked his tongue. "I don't even know where to begin with you."

Sian set a cup of coffee in front of me, along with a sealed envelope. "This arrived while you were gone."

"We were tempted to steam it open," Gun said, "but Sian wouldn't let us. The young lad has something called scruples."

"Who delivered it?" I asked. There was neither postage nor a stamp.

"I saw no one," Sian said. "The envelope was on the porch when I opened the door for your friends."

I slid the card from the envelope. It was some sort of invitation.

Gun gasped and snatched it from my hand. "Eternity Fashion House. How? Why? What?"

"You know them?" I squinted at the card. "Where does it say Eternity Fashion House?"

He flicked the logo with his fingers. "That is an instantly recognizable trademark."

"It's the Greek symbol of life." It was a simple spiral embossed with the Greek key design.

"It's the symbol of three illustrious fashionistas who are inviting you, Lorelei Clay, to their offices for a private dress fitting." He slapped the card on the table. "Explain."

"Can't. I have no idea why they'd send this to me." I pondered the invitation. "It could be Magnarella's doing. He wants me to look my best to impress his potential investors at the gala."

Gun and Cam fixed me with matching incredulous expressions.

"I'm sorry," Cam said. "Can you back up a few days and expand on that statement? I know I've been out of town a couple days, but I've fallen woefully behind."

I told them about Magnarella's offer, my visit to the lab, and the upcoming gala.

"Magnarella must know you can't afford a designer

dress," Gun said. "It's in his best interest for you to look flush with cash if he's trying to attract investors."

Cam gave me a pitying look. "How poor are you, Lorelei?"

"I need a new source of revenue very soon," I admitted.

"Why not work as a private investigator? It would be similar to your work in London, and you seem to be doing it anyway, except without compensation." He shuddered. "You really ought to reconsider that."

"If I accept payment, then I'm…"

Gun watched me, waiting for me to finish. "You're what?" he finally prompted.

"I don't know. It feels wrong."

"Are you a comic book superhero? No. You're Lorelei Clay, owner of a house in dire need of furniture."

"I built her a bed," Sian interjected.

"She has a bed," Gun said.

"For the spare bedroom," Sian clarified.

"How useful." Gun's gaze shifted to me. "You have no obligation to work for free just because that work is of a helpful nature."

"I guess I feel a sense of obligation."

Gun scrutinized me. "Why? I don't get it. I mean, it's an admirable quality, but you can't cash it at the store."

"No, I can't."

He regarded me. "How dire is the financial situation?"

I didn't want to fully admit how bad it was. "I can keep the lights on, but the radiators are set to low."

Cam rubbed her arms. "That explains the chill in the air."

Gun brought his cup to his lips. "Assassins make great money, plus healthcare and an enviable retirement plan."

"It's probably enviable because assassins rarely make it to retirement."

Gun winced. "Ouch. Direct hit."

"I wouldn't make a very good assassin."

He pointed to my face. "You have the scowl for it."

I felt my scowl deepen in response. "I don't begrudge you and Cam your livelihoods, but I'm not a good fit for it."

"You certainly have the chops. I've never seen a layperson wield a weapon with such skill and, dare I say, finesse."

"Finesse? High praise from Gunther Saxon, indeed."

He winked. "Takes one to know one. What about Kane? I'm sure he'd be thrilled to have you work alongside him at the nightclub." He chuckled. "I can picture Josie's face now."

"I don't want to work at the club."

"Why not? Josie wears a permanent scowl, and she gets along there just fine."

"I think it would be unwise for Kane and me to spend that much time together."

"Isn't this the honeymoon phase? You're supposed to want to be joined at the hip until the power struggle phase sets in."

"This is the introductory phase. I like my solitude."

He snorted. "Sure you do."

"How much is your mortgage?" Cam asked.

"I bought the house outright. It's the maintenance that's draining my bank account."

Gun shook his head sadly. "You're learning what the owners of Downton Abbey learned years ago."

"You should consider the guild, Lorelei," Camryn urged. "Kane would loop every hole to get you in."

"I do not think one should kill for money," Sian interrupted.

Gun locked eyes with him. "What? You think we should do it for free?"

"It is immoral and unethical."

Gun straightened his shoulders. "My targets are chosen with care and consideration."

"Except you don't choose them," I said. "You agree to the terms."

"Exactly. I have to agree. I don't blindly accept any work that comes my way. I can afford to be selective. Besides, your boyfriend rules with an iron fist. If I decided to stray from the rules, he'd step in."

My chest tightened. "Kane isn't my boyfriend."

"Should I say your lover?"

"I hate the word lover. I'd rather die alone and have my face eaten by zombie cats than describe a partner with that word."

Gun pretended to type on his phone. "Note to self: don't ask Lorelei to sing Part-Time Lover at karaoke."

Camryn's gaze rested on the top half of my clothing. "Would you mind running upstairs to change? The blood is making me feel nauseated."

Sian frowned. "But you are an assassin."

"Yes, but not a messy one. I always carry antibacterial wipes."

I excused myself and ran upstairs to change. Nana Pratt met me at the top of the stairs.

"Where've you been?" I asked.

"Monitoring the situation from a respectful distance."

I advanced toward the bedroom and became aware of the ghost's presence right behind me.

"What is it, Nana Pratt?"

"If you must know, I agree with Sian. I don't understand how you can be friends with them."

"I told you to leave it alone, Ingrid," Ray's voice cut in.

I turned to look at them. "With Cam and Gun? Because they're assassins?"

"You say it like they work at the bank."

"The banks kill people, just more slowly and with less blood."

Ray chuckled. "Good one, Lorelei."

Nana Pratt gave him a sharp look. "No, it most certainly

isn't. How can you defend them, knowing how they earn a living? Taking a life is wrong."

I tapped my fingers against the doorjamb. "Are you really intent on having a morality argument with the goddess of nightmares?"

"You're desperate for money, yet you don't kill for a living."

"Desperate is a bit of a stretch. Kane's a demon. Why aren't you as hard on him as the others?"

"Because he's not a prince of hell anymore, but they're still murderers."

"What if I told you Kane isn't a prince of hell anymore because he was forced out, not because he abdicated his role?"

"I may be old and dead, but my eyes work just fine," she said, somewhat miffed. "I can see he's a better demon than he once was."

She was right. The reason he was forced to flee his circle of hell was because of a failed coup. He'd tried to overthrow Lucifer in order to improve conditions, but instead he was caught and tortured until a daring rescue attempt by Dantalion and other supporters. Kane's redemption tour began long before he moved to Fairhaven.

"He still feels a lot of guilt and shame for the things he did," I said.

"I imagine he does," Nana Pratt said.

"Gun," I called. "Would you mind coming upstairs for a quick second?" I darted into my bedroom and stripped off my clothes.

"What are you doing?" Nana Pratt hissed.

"Conflict resolution," I said, tugging a Villanova T-shirt over my head.

Gun appeared in my doorway, just as I zipped up my jeans. "If it pertains to your outfit, the answer is no," he said.

"It doesn't. Nana Pratt is here. She has concerns about your livelihood."

"I see." Gun sat on the edge of my bed. "Am I here to defend myself?"

"Not defend. Maybe reach an understanding."

Gun scratched his cheek. "Let me see if I can reframe this in a way you'll understand." He cleared his throat. "Nothing is black and white in the same way no one is truly selfless."

Nana Pratt sniffed. "*I* was selfless."

I relayed her reply.

"Tell me how," Gun insisted.

"I was a doting wife and mother, a loving neighbor, a churchgoer, and a hard-working member of multiple community-minded organizations."

I shared her examples.

"And how did it make you feel to do those things?" Gun asked.

She seemed stumped by the question. "How does he think it made me feel? It feels good to do good. Everybody knows that." She paused. "Everybody with a moral backbone, anyway."

"So you continued to do good deeds because it made you feel good to do them," I said.

"That's right."

"So helping others helped you," Gun added. "Do you see how those selfless acts maybe weren't so selfless after all?"

Her mouth opened and closed in silence.

"I'm not saying you shouldn't have felt good about your actions. What I mean is that behavior isn't as easily labeled as you'd like to believe. You did your good deeds and felt good about them. Cam and I consider what we do to be good deeds, and we feel good about them."

"But only one set of those deeds is legal," she protested.

"Legality and morality aren't necessarily the same thing,"

I countered. "And who better to keep assassins in check than a reformed prince of hell?"

"I do not kill the innocent," Gun insisted. "My targets are not anyone the world would mourn."

"Who decides who's worth mourning?" Nana Pratt asked. "He's playing God."

"She thinks you're playing God," I told Gun.

"I see us as doing the Lord's work," Gun responded with absolute sincerity.

Nana Pratt seemed to mull over my response. "Well, the road to hell is paved with good intentions."

"I'm sure Kane would agree," I said.

Gunther rubbed his hands along his thighs. "So, are we good now? My coffee is probably cold."

"I wouldn't say we're good, but I'm willing to hold my tongue," Nana Pratt replied.

I smiled at Gun. "You're good."

Gun rose to his feet. "That Sian is adorable, by the way. Where did you find him?"

"We sort of found each other."

He snorted. "How romantic. I'd love to be a fly on the wall when Kane finds out you have a pretty overnight guest."

"He knows."

"I missed all the fun. Call me next time." Gun exited the bedroom ahead of me.

We passed Sian in the hallway.

"I would like to bathe if now is convenient."

"Now is fine."

Gunther lingered at the top of the stairs. "If you need assistance, I'm available."

I urged him forward. Sian already had one undesirable bathtub experience. No need for another.

We returned to the kitchen where Cam was busy cleaning the table with an anti-bacterial wipe.

"I have no idea where that fae has been," she said, by way

of explanation. She tossed the wipe into the trashcan.

"He said you're helping him find his missing sister," Gun said.

"I am. If you want to practice the lost art of altruism, I have a list of Sarahs to finish visiting."

Gun shuddered.

"This is why you're poor," Cam said. As she passed by me on her way back to the table, we bumped arms. Instinctively, I jerked away before I accidentally caught a glimpse of her mind.

Gun noticed and laughed. "Does Cam have cooties or something?"

"She travels with shamans that cleanse her hotel rooms. She's the last person on earth who would ever have cooties."

"And they are worth every penny," she said, reclaiming her seat.

Gun folded his arms. "Miss Camryn Sable, please take the hand of Miss Lorelei Clay."

Cam extended a hand, wiggling her fingers. "It's okay. I saw you wash your hands earlier."

I steeled myself for the interaction, allowing Cam's fingers to slide between mine.

Camryn shot her cousin a quizzical look. "Now what?"

Gun eyed me with suspicion. "You can let go now." He pulled a deck of tarot cards from his coat pocket. "Mind if I use a card on you, Lorelei?"

My antenna rose. "For what?"

"I've been practicing a move. I need a live target."

I inched back. "I'm sorry. Are you asking to practice your assassination skills on me?"

He shuffled the cards. "No, this is an interrogation technique I'm trying to perfect."

Cam glanced at him. "Since when?" She shifted her gaze to me. "Gunther emerged from the womb with an innate understanding of the magic of tarot."

Gun separated a card from the deck. "An understanding, yes, but you know as well as I do that isn't how it works for us."

Although born with the ability to master tarot, a La Fortuna mage had to earn the magic of the cards. It was an arduous and dangerous process, and not all mages were able to wield the more potent cards in the Major Arcana. Some only managed a couple cards in the Minor Arcana. Useful, but less impressive. Gun and Cam were descended from a far more powerful line.

"You want to use the High Priestess?" I remembered enough about tarot to know this card symbolized the unknown. Gun's little experiment was designed to extract a secret from me, which wasn't going to happen.

He held up the card. "What's the matter, Lorelei? Something you don't want us to know?"

"Many somethings. I'm a private person. You know that."

"She has a moat, Gun," Cam added. "I think it's clear someone who chooses to live behind a moat doesn't want to be known." She gave the table a light punch. "I fully support that, by the way. If you want to go full hermit, you do you, Lor."

Gun regarded me. "I associate her more with a swamp witch aesthetic."

Despite my reservations about witches, I took it as a compliment. "Thanks, Gun."

He pressed the card to his forehead. "Now, can we play? Just one round, pretty please?"

"I miss Scrabble," I grumbled. "Fine. One round, but that's it."

"Are you sure you want to do this, Lorelei?" Ray's voice interrupted.

My gaze slid to the doorway, where he hovered alone. Nana Pratt probably decided to keep her distance from the assassins following her exchange with Gun.

"You haven't told them yet," Ray continued. "What if this is how they find out?"

I pressed my lips together and hoped Ray got the message to zip it.

"They're your friends," the ghost persisted. "If they find out about your identity without you telling them directly, they're going to be upset, and rightfully so."

Ray didn't understand the complications involved, nor was I in a position to explain right now.

"Go on," I urged Gunther.

He focused on channeling the card. "I compel you to speak the truth."

I held up a hand as though swearing a solemn vow. "Consider me compelled."

Gun cocked his head. "She doesn't seem compelled. Cammie, does she look compelled to you?"

Cam examined the tips of her French manicure. "I don't know. Ask your question and then decide."

"Are you sure you do this for a living?" I asked.

Gun glowered at me. "Taunting the mage is never a smart move." He patted the bulge in his pocket, where he'd placed the remaining cards in the deck. "I have plenty of retaliatory options at my disposal."

A burning sensation traveled up my arm. Saved by the ward. "Hold that thought."

"Ooh, do we have company?" Gun asked.

Cam slid from her seat. "Maybe it's Vaughn."

"Why would it be Vaughn?"

"He's here to thank her for breaking him out of prison." Her eyes narrowed. "He's not too grateful, I hope."

"You don't need to worry, sweetie," Gun assured her. "Our Lorelei only has googly eyes for a certain demon prince of hell."

As I rose from my chair, Nana Pratt burst into the kitchen, her breathing labored.

"How are you out of breath?" I asked. "You're dead."

Nana Pratt placed an apparitional hand against her chest. "Right. Of course. There are two large men headed to the front door. They don't look like they're bringing a delivery."

"Good, because I haven't ordered anything."

"What's going on?" Gun asked.

"I suspect our mutual friend Magnarella has decided to send his goons to collect me for an unscheduled visit."

Gun adjusted his collar with a flourish. "Allow me."

He waltzed through the foyer to the front door and opened it as the two large men reached the unwelcoming mat. Square jaws. Buzzed haircuts. They had all the hallmarks of Magnarella's goons.

"We're here for Lorelei Clay," the taller goon grunted.

I watched from the safety of the kitchen doorway as Gun leaned against the doorjamb with a casual air. "I'm afraid Miss Clay is currently unavailable. Would you like to leave a message at the tone? Beep."

The two men exchanged confused glances. "Are you her robot servant?" the shorter man asked.

Beside me, Camryn snickered. "I can't believe he sent these two buffoons to get you. I've heard of self-sabotage, but this is ridiculous."

"Magnarella thinks we have an agreement," I said, although I was curious to see how the situation with Gun played out. At least I was off the hook for the impromptu interrogation session. Small mercies.

"Then why are you letting Gun…" Cam broke into a smile. "Oh, cool. Yeah, let's stay here and watch."

"Consider me her liege lord," Gun explained to the men.

The taller one scrunched his wide nose, stretching the nostrils even wider. "What's a liege lord?"

Gun tipped back his head and sighed. "This is no fun."

"Where is Lorelei Clay?" the shorter goon demanded.

"Do you have an appointment?"

"No, but the boss says she'll come along willingly."

"I very much doubt that." Gun whipped a card from his pocket. From this angle, I couldn't see which one he'd chosen. At least I knew it wasn't a deadly one. Gun was smart enough to follow the rules of the guild.

The taller goon opened his mouth to speak, and the gibberish of an infant spilled from his lips.

"Goo goo gaga," his companion replied.

They stared at each other in horror.

Cam laughed. "Out of the mouths of babes."

The taller one tried to yell at Gun, but the only sound he made was the wailing cry of a tired infant.

Gun used his foot to close the door. Spinning toward us, he dusted off his hands. "Your meeting has been cancelled, madam."

"Magnarella will be thrilled when his men return to the compound incomprehensible."

Gun shrugged. "It'll wear off in an hour, unless you'd rather I stop it now."

I didn't hesitate. "If you stop it now, I'll toss you into Bone Lake."

Camryn rushed forward to peer out the window. "They're gone." She looked at her cousin. "We should probably go and leave Lorelei to find work. The situation sounds dire."

"On one condition," Gun said.

I worried that he'd resume his High Priestess card trick. Instead, he said, "You let me accompany you to New York City in the morning."

"Since when am I going to the city in the morning?"

"Since you received a mysterious invitation to Eternity." He retrieved his scarf from the coat rack and flung it across his neck. "I'll pick you up promptly at nine. Do yourself a favor and ditch your usual footwear. You can't possibly try on couture in black boots."

I smiled. "Consider the gauntlet thrown."

CHAPTER 15

The morning was clear and bright as Gunther and I drove to the city for my mysterious meeting with Eternity Fashion House. The blue sky and reasonable temperature made the traffic slightly more bearable. Gun's upbeat playlist helped. It was the kind of pop music I enjoyed because I had no associations to draw from.

"Maybe this is part of Magnarella's revenge plan," I said.

"What is?" Gun tapped his fingers on the steering wheel in time to the music.

"He's torturing me by making me sit in traffic during morning rush hour."

Every muscle in my body was tense by the time we found a parking spot.

"You didn't have to accept the invitation, you know," Gun remarked, as we walked along 57th Street toward Madison Avenue.

"Would you have let me decline?"

"No," Gun admitted. "This is a once-in-a-lifetime opportunity." He inhaled deeply. "Ah, how I love the aroma of garbage and weed in the morning. Really wakes up the lungs." He beat his chest.

"I hope the smell doesn't cling to me or they might change their mind about the dress."

"Trust me. Everybody here is used to the stench. They probably don't even notice it anymore."

I decided to voice a thought that had been plaguing me since yesterday. "Do you think it's strange that Magnarella's minions showed up after the invitation arrived? If it was from the vampire, wouldn't they have delivered it? Or wouldn't Magnarella have given it to me in person if he expected to see me?"

Gun glanced at me. "Someone's been marching in the thought parade this morning." He stopped short in the middle of the sidewalk, forcing the sea of suits to part around us. "This is the address."

I double-checked the number on the invitation. Yep. This was it.

"This building is amazing." Gun tilted his head back to admire the tall structure. "How have I never noticed it before?"

"Because it's a New York City skyscraper. It blends in with all the other ones."

"Au contraire. This building is a magnificent work of art. See how it has the attributes of the neo-futuristic style, but also Art Deco and Gothic influences." His voice grew quiet. "I've never seen anything like it."

I urged him forward. "Come on then. Let's see if the inside is as impressive as the outside."

We entered the lobby, which was, to Gun's dismay, far more ordinary than the facade. He performed a slow spin, taking in the interior features, or lack thereof.

"I think they spent all their money on the exterior," he lamented.

"Or maybe they splurged on their offices."

He drew back from me. "Look at you, walking on

sunshine. I always say, give a girl a dress and watch her twirl."

"What if it's a pencil dress?"

Gun broke into a smile. "A relevant fashion term? Someone did her homework last night."

"I like to be prepared."

We approached the security desk that blocked the entrance to the elevators.

"Names?" The security guard barely glanced up from his phone.

"Lorelei Clay. I have an appointment with Eternity." That line sounded far more mysterious and exciting than "I'm here to get measured for a free dress."

His gaze flicked to Gun. "And you?"

"I'm her traveling companion."

The guard's features relaxed. "Like she's the Doctor and you're her Rose Tyler?"

"Gunther Saxon, not Rose Tyler, and she's not a doctor."

"You're a fan of *Dr. Who*, I take it," I said to the security guard. I'd lived in London long enough to recognize the reference.

He beamed. "Great show, right?"

"A legend in its own time ... lord."

He chuckled. "I like your style, Miss Clay."

"I don't," Gun murmured. "Puns like that are beneath you."

"You're headed to the eighth floor." The security guard motioned behind him. "The elevator bank to your far left."

"Thanks."

"Your friend stays here, though. He doesn't have clearance."

"Clearance?" Gun echoed. "I thought this was a fashion house."

"It is, and your name isn't on the schedule, which means

you shall not pass." He shifted his attention to me. "You get that, right?"

"I sure do, Gandalf."

The security guard glanced at his screen. "I need to use the letter 'z' in a word. Any suggestions?"

"Wordle?" I asked.

"Online Scrabble."

Even better. I stood on my tiptoes for a better glimpse of his screen. "Between the letters on the board and your tiles, spell muzjiks. It'll give you the most points."

Gun swatted my arm. "Why are you helping him when he won't let me in?"

"Because it's Scrabble. It's my calling in life."

The security guard squinted at his screen. "You're not allowed to make up words. The computer will know."

"It's a real word. It means Russian peasants."

He shot me a dubious look as he tapped his screen. A slow smile spread across his face. "What do you know? I won! Thanks. That's the first time I've ever beaten Larry. He's the security guard across the street. Went to private school in the city and thinks he's smarter than everybody else." He let loose a wicked cackle. "Suck it, Larry."

"Glad I could help."

The guard's smile faded. "But your friend still stays down here. Rules are rules."

I shrugged at Gun. "Worth a try."

Gun groaned. "Fine. I'll take a stroll and enjoy all the sparkly window displays."

"Sorry," I said.

"I'll survive. Passing the time is basically part of my job description."

The guard grunted. "You and me both. Do you work security, too?"

"In a sense," Gun said.

"Oh, here, Miss Clay. You need this." The guard handed

me a keycard. "You won't be able to operate the elevator without it. Just drop it in the slot over there on your way out. Works like a hotel keycard."

"I'll meet you out front when you're finished," Gun said. "Take a few selfies for me, so I can live vicariously through you."

I wasn't sure that was ever a good idea, but I nodded anyway.

I pocketed the card and headed to the left. Even the elevator doors were fancy, lined with the same Greek key design as the Eternity logo.

The doors parted, and I used the keycard to activate the button for the eighth floor. I instantly recognized the music as an instrumental version of 'Holding Back the Years.' My grandmother had been a fan of the original song by Simply Red.

Before I could stop it, a memory took hold. My grandmother grabbed Pops by the hand as he walked by and pulled him into a slow dance embrace. Neither of my grandparents had been big on expressing emotion, but I still recalled the way they'd looked into each other's eyes in that moment. The love between them had its own pulse. It must have been so difficult for him to lose her. I knew how hard it was for me, and she wasn't the love of my life.

I forced my attention back to the present moment. Living in the past served no purpose except to undo me, and I already had Kane loosening the knots of my carefully constructed persona. I had to stay focused on what I could control.

I fixated on the directory instead. Floors eight through twenty-eight were dedicated to the offices of Eternity. No small operation in a building this size.

The doors to the eighth floor opened, and I shut my eyes, momentarily blinded by brightness. Once my eyes adjusted, I stepped out of the elevator into a gleaming white space.

Marble flooring. Marble columns. Floor-to-ceiling windows that framed the morning light. No receptionist desk. No sign of anyone, in fact.

"Hello?" I said. My voice echoed.

I turned to check the floor number, thinking I might've made a mistake.

"Not to worry," a voice said. "You're in the right place."

A statuesque figure burned a hole in the brightness. It was as though she'd been carved from a beam of sunlight. Everything about her was golden. Hair, dress, spiked heels. Even her eyes seemed to glow with the energy of two small suns.

"Miss Clay, I presume." Her voice was surprisingly youthful. It seemed to conflict with her more mature appearance.

"Please, call me Lorelei."

"Lorelei, I'm Chloe. It's an absolute pleasure to meet you." She extended a pale hand. There was something otherworldly about her, and I didn't want to discover the details the hard way.

I offered a self-deprecating laugh. "Trust me, you don't want to touch this. My hands are filthy from the subway," I lied.

She withdrew her hand, unfazed. "I understand completely. I carry cleanser wherever I go for that very reason. I prefer my hands as pure as a newborn's skin."

I couldn't picture Chloe riding the subway. She struck me as the type of woman who only traveled in a black executive car with tinted windows.

"Is your office under renovations?" I asked.

"Oh, no. This is the private floor where my sisters and I work. We prefer to keep the space clear and bright. Keeps those creative juices flowing. Speaking of juices, may I offer you a refreshment?"

"I'm fine, thank you."

"Let me know if you change your mind. Kindly step into

my office and we can get started. I'm sure you're a busy woman with much better things to do than try on dresses."

I pictured myself at home, fixing the lever in the toilet tank. "It isn't often I get to dress up, so I appreciate the opportunity. My friend Gun persuaded me this would be a good opportunity to wade into the feminine waters."

Chloe's smile was as blinding as the rest of her. "The feminine waters. I like that."

I followed her into an adjacent office. The room was larger than average for a city office with a brass, onyx, and glass design theme that matched the building's eclectic exterior. The Greek key was present here as well, lining the door frame and a glass curio cabinet.

"How long have you worked for Eternity?" I asked, resisting the urge to ask whether it had, in fact, felt like an eternity.

"Since its inception. I own this company, along with my two older sisters, Annie and Laz. You'll meet them in a few minutes."

A family business. Nice.

She motioned for me to sit in the chair opposite her desk. It was made of plush black leather with arms that displayed the Greek tricolor key design.

"Before we get started," Chloe began, "I'd like to run through a few preliminary questions. Standard procedure, of course."

"Of course," I said, sensing there was nothing standard about this place. It radiated supernatural vibes the way Kane radiated sex appeal.

Okay, not the analogy I meant to make. I cleared the demon prince from my thoughts and tried to focus.

Chloe settled behind her desk and consulted the shiny gold laptop in front of her. "Can you confirm that Lorelei Clay is your legal name?"

"Yes."

"Any middle name?"

I hesitated. "Why do you need that?"

"Not to worry, Miss Clay. I have no interest in gaining answers to your security password questions. It's simply that we have no record of you."

"Well, you must have some record of me since you sent me an invitation to your office."

"That's the reason we invited you. We were curious to see if there'd been an administrative error somewhere along the way. It's an extremely rare occurrence, you see."

"Actually, I don't see." At this point, I was thoroughly confused. "Vincenzo Magnarella didn't arrange this meeting?"

"No." She looked at me expectantly. "And your middle name is…?"

"I don't think that will help."

"The computer will be the judge of that."

I sighed. "Bertha. It's a family name," I added quickly.

Her gaze locked on mine. "Bertha? Who would do that to an innocent child?"

"It's in memory of my great-aunt." My grandmother's sister was officially named Bertha, although people only knew her as Honey. According to my grandparents, my parents had been close with Aunt Honey, who died while my mother was pregnant with me. Why they couldn't have given me Honey as a middle name, I'd never know.

"Your great-aunt must've been someone quite special to pass that name down the line. It's grounds for generational trauma, if you ask me."

My generational trauma spanned centuries and was far worse than an old-fashioned middle name, not that Chloe needed to know that.

"Bertha," she repeated, scanning the screen. "You're right. There's definitely no Bertha either."

"That information is confidential," I added. My middle

name was a secret I was prepared to take to the grave, apparently unlike the one that identified me as a goddess. Priorities.

She tapped her fingernails on the desk. "It seems that all your information is confidential. I can't fathom why you're not on the list."

"For the gala?"

She peered at me over the edge of her laptop. "That isn't the list I mean. According to our records, you don't exist."

"Then how did you know my name and where to find me?"

Her mouth quirked. "Crows are sometimes loyal to more than one mistress."

Betrayed by a bird. That had to be a first.

A knock interrupted my next question. Two women entered the room, each one as stunning as the other.

"Lorelei, I'd like you to meet my sisters." One sister was dressed completely in black and the other one in winter white. I'd have to remember to tell Camryn she was on trend.

The woman dressed in black introduced herself as Annie. Her bronzed skin gave her a healthy glow, although I could tell from the threads of silver in her dark hair that she was the eldest of the three sisters.

"And I'm Laz," the woman in the winter white pantsuit said. Her white-blonde hair was swept back in an elegant chignon. I noticed the bangle bracelet on her slender wrist featured the same Greek key design.

Annie pondered me. "Would you mind standing so we can take a closer look at you?"

I felt fairly confident I wasn't standing to be measured for a dress. I debated whether to bolt for the exit, but my survival instincts weren't in overdrive, so I opted to stay. There was something oddly comforting about these women.

Chloe joined her sisters in walking around me in a tight

circle. They stopped to scrutinize my face, like they were teenaged girls searching for an elusive zit.

I touched my forehead. No bumps.

Annie snapped her fingers. "We need the poultice."

I leaned back. "There's nothing on my face."

Laz produced a small square cloth from her pocket and passed it to her sister.

"Hold still," Annie told me, as she placed the cloth on my forehead. It smelled like rain and felt like morning dew against my skin.

"I'll be honest," I said. "I didn't know what to expect this morning, but it definitely wasn't this."

Annie removed the cloth and took a step back, seemingly satisfied. "There. Do you see?"

Chloe gasped. "I do."

"See what?" I asked.

"This explains it," Chloe continued. "She's marked. It's faint, but it's there."

Laz continued to stare at my forehead from an inch away. Her breath smelled like peppermint. "Fascinating."

"Marked?" Was I some sort of prey? Had The Corporation somehow marked me as a target? Or Magnarella?

Chloe's smile bordered on relieved. "We know your name."

"Yes, because I told you."

"Your real name," Laz said with emphasis.

Did the poultice reveal some sort of invisible goddess tattoo? My mind raced with possibilities. "Who are you?"

Annie flicked the cloth into the nearby trashcan. "Haven't you figured it out yet? We're known as the Moirai."

My throat ran dry. I wasn't sure why I was speechless. I'd met my share of otherworldly beings, but these three sisters… They were legendary.

"Clotho, Lachesis, and Antropos? *The* Fates?"

Chloe's laughter sounded like tinkling sleigh bells. "You make us sound like a singing group."

"And we go by more modern names now," Laz added. "It's important to keep up with the times."

"Your parents might've tried that instead of Bertha," Chloe remarked.

"It's a family name," I insisted. I couldn't believe the Fates had summoned me. Now the fashion house's circle of life motif made more sense. The sisters were hiding in plain sight, living their best eternal lives as divas in the city that never sleeps.

"This isn't the first time we've met," Laz said.

"Though it's been many centuries since your last incarnation," Annie chimed in.

I didn't retain those memories in this form. The human brain wouldn't be able to cope. It would be like trying to load a laptop with… Okay, who was I kidding? I didn't have the technical knowledge to complete that kind of analogy.

Annie contemplated me. "But why are you hidden, even from our view?"

"I wish I had an answer for you."

"Melinoe in the flesh," Laz mused. "I was not expecting this."

"And it takes a lot to surprise us, as you might imagine," Chloe added.

"Thank goodness you're not one of those ridiculous avatars." Laz shuddered. "They're abominations."

"Just so I understand the situation," I began, "you lured me here under false pretenses because you have no record of me. Am I here so you can…?" I glanced at Annie. "You're the one who cuts the thread of life. I guess I should ask you."

"The truth is we don't know what to do with you," Annie replied. "That's the reason we brought you here. It isn't normal."

"There's nothing normal about me."

"Oh, I wouldn't go that far," Laz said. "You wouldn't have been able to blend in so well if you weren't somewhat normal."

"You've escaped our notice for…" Chloe surveyed me. "How old are you?"

"Thirty-five."

"A drop in the ocean for us, but still," Laz said. "It's embarrassing to miss someone that should be on our list. We'll have to file a report with our compliance department."

"And if we don't know about you, we can't…" Annie mimed cutting a pair of scissors.

I shifted uncomfortably. "I guess that's a win for me."

Annie's voice dropped to a low level of intensity. "We want to know *why*."

"I wish I could tell you, but I don't know any more than you do."

"Untrue," Chloe said. "Who were your parents?"

"Dana and James Clay."

"Mother's maiden name?" Chloe asked, spinning around the laptop to face her.

"Frost."

Chloe typed on her laptop. "I see them both here, but there's no record of a child."

Pops had been adept at hiding me, but he was only human. He wasn't hide-me-from-the-Fates good. There had to be another explanation.

"My parents died in a car accident when I was very young. Maybe the timing messed up the official records." It sounded lame even to my own ears, but I didn't know what else to say.

Annie peered over her younger sister's shoulder. "It wasn't an accident."

"It was," I insisted. "A car crash."

"Yes, I understand that part," Annie replied smoothly, "but the death itself… The outcome was not accidental."

I blinked, stunned by the revelation. "You're telling me someone murdered my parents?"

The edges of Annie's mouth turned down. "I'm afraid so."

My heart beat faster. "How can you know that?"

"Because we're the Fates and we know things," Annie said.

"The kind of information you can only dream of knowing," Chloe added.

"Congratulations," I said.

Laz jabbed Chloe in the ribs with a bony elbow. "No need to humble brag."

"That's not a humble brag," I pointed out. "That's just straight-up bragging." I folded my arms. "If you're so clever, tell me the type of demon that tried to kill me in Bone Lake the other day."

Chloe elbowed her middle sister. "You can field this one."

"She is called a kulshedra," Laz said.

She. Laz knew the demon was female. "How do you know that? Did you put her there?"

"We are the circle of life," Chloe explained. "Birth, life, and death."

"But only I know death," Annie interjected. "My sisters are clueless in that regard."

"We're like meteorologists," Laz said. "We merely forecast."

"According to my friend Ray, that means you don't know anything," I said.

Chloe tittered her appreciation.

I pivoted toward Annie. "My parents… Did you cut the thread?"

"Whether I operated the scissors or not, I can't tell you who murdered them. It is beyond my ken."

I wondered whether Pops had known, whether it was a secret he'd hidden from me to keep me safe.

My gaze slid to Laz. "You're in charge of measuring the length of thread. Did you choose their fate?"

Laz showed no remorse. "Your parents had to die in order for your destiny to be fulfilled."

My blood burned hot. "A minute ago, you didn't know my parents had a child. Now you're telling me their deaths were necessary for my sake?" I didn't wait for an answer. "You said I was marked. Is that how you identified me as Melinoe?"

The three sisters exchanged glances. A silent conversation seemed to follow.

Chloe answered first. "The mark was made by another."

I resisted the urge to rub my forehead raw. "For what purpose?"

"What does it tell you?"

"That your fate was chosen for you," Chloe said.

"Isn't that what fate is?" I asked. "Your destiny being chosen by another?"

Annie tapped the pads of her fingers together. "Fate can be a fickle beast."

"Are you talking about yourself in the third person? Because people don't tend to like that."

"What my sister means," Chloe began, "is that there is no one path. Certain elements of a life are set in stone, but the choices you make along the way... Those are yours alone."

I still didn't understand the mark. "What does the mark look like?"

Chloe smiled. "No need to worry. Even if one can see it, it doesn't detract from your beauty."

"I live in sweatpants and T-shirts," I shot back. "I'm not worried about my beauty." I wanted a description for research purposes. If there was one thing I knew about the Fates, it was their affinity for vague commentary.

"It's a rose," Laz said.

"A rose, as in the pretty flower?" That seemed like an odd choice.

"Yes."

"You're telling me I have the symbol of a rose on my forehead that's invisible to me and just about everybody else in the world."

Laz nodded. "Correct."

"Why can you see it? Because you're the Fates?"

"Because we had the power to reveal what was hidden," Annie said. "Whoever marked you possesses equal or lesser power to us, but not greater."

"Because if it were greater, then you wouldn't be able to see the mark either?" I asked.

"Exactly," Annie said.

"Can you tell me who marked me?"

"We cannot," Chloe said simply.

"Can't or won't?"

"Cannot," Chloe repeated.

"The rose as a symbol doesn't tip you off?" If the Fates didn't recognize the mark, what chance did I have?

"It's a symbol that belongs to many pantheons," Annie said. "It would be difficult to know with certainty."

Her body stiffened. Her arms jerked outward, and she clutched her sister's arm.

"Is she having a vision?" I asked.

"Muscle cramp," Annie squeaked. "It'll pass in a minute."

"I have a banana in my office," Laz offered.

"She won't eat it. I told her to take the magnesium supplements, too, but nooo," Chloe said. "Big sister always thinks she knows best."

Annie's body relaxed and she exhaled slowly. "There. All better."

"There's something else you should know," Chloe began, but one look from Laz silenced her.

"Too much," Laz whispered.

I looked from sister to sister. "Too much what?"

"It changes nothing," Annie said.

"It changes *everything*," Chloe countered.

An involuntary shiver passed through me.

"Your family," Chloe began.

"Who? My grandparents? The foster families?"

Laz drew a horizontal line in the air, which sealed her sister's mouth closed.

"What my sister means is you must take care, Melinoe," Laz warned.

"Why? What do you see?"

"Your road divides like the stem of a rose," Laz continued. "Many branches and leaves, and many thorns."

I winced. "That sounds painful."

"Life *is* pain," Laz said. "You have lived enough lives to know that much."

"Better to be dead then?"

"That's up to you, although clearly you feel it's worth the price as you insist on returning." Annie sounded mildly put out that she'd have to put those scissors to work on me again someday.

"But for what purpose?" Laz asked. "That is the mystery."

"Because I get bored easily? I have no idea. I don't leave myself notes." Sure would've been helpful if I had.

Annie cupped my chin in her cool hand. "You will play a significant role. I see it written in the stars."

"A role in what? The local production of *Newsies*?"

"You reject the call," Laz said. "Interesting."

Annie unsealed Chloe's lips, prompting a dirty look from her younger sister.

"The call?" I didn't understand. "I'm not rejecting anything."

Laz turned to her sisters. "She isn't ready."

"She isn't ready," they murmured in unison.

Exasperation threatened to spill out of me. "Ready for what?"

"What is to come next," Laz said.

Annie regarded me. "Choose wisely, beloved Melinoe, goddess of ghosts and nightmares, proprietress of our innermost secrets. The sweet fragrance oft distracts from the pain of the thorns, but the damage is done nonetheless."

"I'll be sure to get that tattooed on my arm as a reminder."

"Our time is up," Chloe announced.

I shot a quick glance at Annie. "As long as it isn't my time."

Chloe glanced at her phone. "No, I have hot yoga in twenty minutes, and I need to change."

"What happens now? Do you add me to your list?"

"We can't," Laz said. "You're beyond our power."

I touched my forehead again. "Because of the mark. Doesn't that make me a threat?"

Annie arched an eyebrow. "Why? Do you intend to be a threat to us?"

"Not a threat to you, but a threat to the system. People in power generally take issue with a cog that strays from the wheel."

Chloe closed her laptop with a gentle snap. "We have ways of keeping track of you now."

The crows. Maybe I'd keep Buddy outside the Castle after all. The scarecrow could serve double duty.

"Wait, what about the dress? I really do have an event to attend." And I didn't have the money to afford one.

Chloe tapped her phone. "Kelsey, I'm sending Miss Lorelei Clay to the twenty-eighth floor. Would you be so kind as to assist her with a dress from the winter collection?" She snapped the phone closed. "Done."

"I'm glad we were able to get to the bottom of this, for the most part," Annie said, escorting me to the elevator.

"What did Chloe want to tell me about my family?"

Annie wagged a finger. "All in good time."

I slammed the heel of my hand against the button to summon the elevator. "Would an apology kill you?"

The Fate looked at me blankly. "I have no idea what you mean."

"You snipped the thread. You took my parents away from me. I get that it's your role in the universe, but you can still offer a 'sorry for your loss' or something that makes you seem less like a monster."

Her fingers moved to her throat. "A monster? Miss Clay, my sisters and I each have a duty to fulfill. While there are certainly many monsters in this world, we are not among them."

"I guess it depends on your definition." The elevator doors parted, and I stepped inside.

Annie clasped her hands behind her back. "We'll meet again, Miss Clay."

"Not if I have anything to say about it. Like you said, I'm beyond your control."

I hit the button for the twenty-eighth floor and went to get my damn dress.

CHAPTER 16

The drive home from the city with Gunther consisted of the mage fussing over my dress and me fussing over the Fates' cryptic messages. It was basically two people each having a one-sided conversation, not to mention the added stress of avoiding any mention of Melinoe. That part I kept to myself. As much as I wanted to tell Gun, I wasn't ready.

"Big deal," he said. "You have an invisible rose on your forehead. Better than a tiny clown face."

"Someone marked me, Gun. Someone powerful enough to hide me from the Fates. And what about my parents? And Chloe's comment about my family? Why did Laz silence her?"

"Because it was information you aren't meant to know."

"Or aren't meant to know yet." But now that I knew there was information to learn, I wouldn't be able to rest. Information that "changes everything," according to Chloe. How could I ignore that?

Gun cut me sidelong glance. "You have enough to worry about right now. Try to set aside the vague messages until you're ready to deal with them."

He was right.

"Plus, your dress is stunning."

I groaned. "So you've told me fifty times in the past hour."

"I mean it. Kane is going to go full demon when he sees you. The horns are going to pop out and everything."

I frowned. "He has horns?"

"I don't know. I picture him with horns, don't you?"

"Not really."

"Huh."

Now I was picturing Kane with horns and the image only made him more attractive. I decided to change the subject.

"Ever hear of a demon called a kulshedra?"

"I know they're a rare, female serpent thingamajig."

"Very descriptive."

"And their natural enemy is a drangue."

"Right. A drangue." A winged semi-human with supernatural powers destined to fight and defeat the kulshedra. They were born solely for this purpose—basically Buffy the Kulshedra Slayer.

"Why do you ask?"

"There's a kulshedra in Bone Lake. I'd like to relocate her."

Gun pulled the car outside the gate to the Castle. "I might be able to assist you with that."

I noticed Cam leaning against the gate. "Did you tell Cam to meet us here?"

"Of course. She's dying to see your dress. Since we're not attending the gala, this is our chance to look upon divine inspiration."

I couldn't deprive her of that. I exited the car and carried the dress inside.

"I need to see," Cam said, hurrying after me. "Gun says it's incredible, like it was woven by magical spiders."

I cast a look at Gun over my shoulder. "Magical spiders?"

"It shimmers like a web."

"I'll show you when we're inside," I told Cam. "I don't want to get it dirty."

The mages trailed behind me into the house. I entered the parlor room and unzipped the garment bag.

Cam's mouth dropped open. "Whoa. That is perfection. I wish I were a little taller so I could wear it after you."

"She'll need shoes," Gun said. "Maybe you can help her with that."

"Happy to."

"You said you can help with the kulshedra," I reminded him.

"Yes. I bet we can find you a drangue." He regarded Cam. "Do you think there's one on the international roll?"

Camryn took out her phone. "I'll give Josie a call and ask her to look."

"Don't tell her it's for me," I said quickly. "She won't want to do it."

"You're right. She won't."

I glared at Gun. "You don't have to agree with me so readily."

"Don't take it personally," Cam said. "Josie doesn't like anybody."

"Except Kane," I countered.

Camryn tapped her phone. "She's loyal to Kane. There's a difference. Now shush. I'm putting her on speakerphone."

The phone rang twice before Josie picked up. "What is it, Sable?"

"If it isn't Miss Josephine Banks, my favorite vampire in the whole world," Cam cooed.

Josie's sigh was audible. "Flattery will get you flayed. What do you need?"

"Can you be an absolute doll and check the international guild roll for any drangues?"

"What's a drangue? Never heard of them."

"Winged creature, semi-human, supernatural powers, invulnerable."

"Are you sure you don't mean an angel?"

Camryn narrowed her eyes at the phone. "I think I know the difference between an angel and a drangue."

"What is it?"

Camryn faltered. "What's what?"

"The difference. It will help my research."

"You don't need it to search the roll. Everyone's species is listed. Just type 'drangue' in the search bar and see who comes up."

Josie sat quietly for a beat. "You don't know the difference, do you?"

Cam's grip tightened on the phone. "I certainly do," she snapped, her cheerful disposition slipping in the face of Josie's stoic torment.

"If you say so."

"I do."

"Okay then. Please hold."

Camryn's jaw clenched as she hit the mute button. "She must sense your presence, Lorelei. She's usually not this prickly with me."

Gun laughed. "I love that it's Lorelei's fault that you don't know the difference between an angel and a drangue."

The blood rushed to Camryn's face. "You know what? I'm not treating you to dinner tonight. I've lost my appetite."

"Are you there, Sable?" Josie's voice broke through the sound of Gun's laughter.

Cam clicked off the mute button. "Yes."

"There's only one drangue on the roll, but he's on medical leave until August."

Cam stared at the phone. "One drangue. Wow."

"Should I check for any angels?" Josie offered. "Given they're so similar."

Cam's fingers curled around the phone, and I worried she

was about to crush it against the wall. "No need, but I appreciate the offer."

"Tell me something," Josie said. "Am I still your favorite vampire in the whole world?"

Gun slapped a hand over his mouth to cover his laughter.

"Of course you are," Cam replied with anemic conviction.

Josie grunted. "This was fun. Be sure to call me again the next time you need a favor. It made my day." She hung up just as laughter erupted from Gunther.

"Sorry it didn't work out, Lorelei," Cam said, speaking loud enough to be heard over Gun's convulsions.

"I'll tell you what," Gun said. "She's definitely *my* favorite vampire in the whole world."

Camryn scowled. "I hope you like salad because that's all I saw in your fridge earlier."

"I'm more than capable of taking myself to a restaurant."

"Maybe so, but it isn't nearly as enjoyable without me."

"I've always felt disappointed not to have cousins," I said. "But I'm starting to feel better about it now."

Camryn jabbed a finger in my direction. "See what you've done, Gun? You've made Lorelei happy to have no family."

"Why don't you have cousins?" Gun asked.

I shrugged. "Because not everybody does."

"Our families are large and annoying," Cam said. "Consider yourself lucky."

"Kane's going to consider himself lucky when he sees you in that dress." Gun leaned over to kiss my cheek, and I steeled my mind in the nick of time. "Thanks for the adventure today. I enjoyed it, even if I didn't get to peek behind the curtain."

I waited until they left to call Phaedra.

"I'm glad you called," she said.

"You found something in your family journals?"

"No, but I spoke to Ashley. We agreed to a trial run. She seems eager to help out with the animals in particular."

"That's great news. I hope it works out." I couldn't wait to tell Nana Pratt. "I have information that may narrow down your search. Did you happen to see the word kulshedra in any of the journals?"

"Hang on. That word rings a bell."

While I waited, I walked upstairs in search of Sian and found him napping on the sleeping bag beside the bed he'd built, which was still in need of a mattress and would be for the foreseeable future. I tiptoed out of the room and returned downstairs to the kitchen.

"That's it!" Phaedra declared. "They even tried to hire a drangue to defeat the demon, but they couldn't find one."

"And when the drangue didn't pan out, they probably took matters into their own hands," I suggested.

"Knowing my family, it's very likely. I'll keep reading and see what I can find."

"Thanks, Phaedra. I owe you one. Again."

"You owe me nothing. If my family trapped a demon in Bone Lake that's responsible for killing people, then I have a duty to remove it as a threat."

"There's a black bird on the gate," Ray announced.

I thanked Phaedra again and hung up the phone.

I wasn't expecting Kane, not that it mattered. He had a habit of showing up without warning, as did many other residents of Fairhaven. I was beginning to think the ward, gate, and moat were less effective than I intended.

I opened the front door and scanned the horizon. Not a blackbird. A crow.

"False alarm," I said. As I moved to close the door, the crow swooped toward me, cawing madly. A shiny item around its neck glinted in the sunlight. I left the door ajar and waited.

It was either a message from Birdie or a message from the Fates. I was dying to know which.

The crow landed on the porch, dropped the item on the mat, and flew away.

I stooped to examine the delivery—a clear snack bag. Inside the bag was a tiny scroll tied with a metallic silver band, as well as a pale pink pacifier. Birdie's findings, presumably.

I removed the band and unrolled the paper. Written in chicken scratch was a single name. All those computers and Birdie still wrote by hand? Her inkjet printer must've been out of magenta and refused to print anything at all.

I continued to stand on the porch and study the name. I managed to work out Sarah, but the last name was pure scribble.

"You look like you're trying to solve the world's problems on the world's smallest piece of paper," Ray remarked.

I held up the paper for him. "Can you decipher the last name?"

He squinted. "Lots of loops, that's about all I can see."

"Nana Pratt," I called. "We need you."

The elderly ghost materialized out of thin air. "Did you spill something?"

"No. I can't read Birdie's handwriting." I showed her the paper.

"It says Peele. See there. The loops are the three 'e's."

Now that she'd pointed them out, they were plain to see. "Either of you know the Peele family?"

They shook their heads.

I had a name, and a pacifier that suggested Sarah Peele was the adoptive mother of the fae. That crow was worth its weight in gold. No wonder Birdie fed them.

I retreated into the house, feeling a surge of hope. This was helpful. I'd have to send Birdie a thank you basket.

I stopped short in the foyer as I fully processed my thought. When did I become the sort of person who sent thank you baskets? What had Fairhaven done to me?

Sian appeared at the base of the staircase, stretching his arms over his head. "Good news?"

"How'd you know?"

He pointed to my face. "You're smiling. An uncommon sight."

My face fell. "Is that the fae version of telling a woman to smile more?"

Sian blinked. "I do not understand. Why would I not want you to smile more? You deserve happiness."

Gods, Sian was too sweet and innocent for this world. He needed to scurry back to his realm before we corrupted him.

"As a matter of fact, there is good news. A breakthrough in the case." I dangled the bag in front of him. "I believe this pacifier belonged to your sister, which means I have the name of the adoptive mother."

He removed the bag from my hand and gazed at the pacifier. "Can we see her now?"

"I think it's best if I go alone first." I had no idea what kind of person Sarah Peele was. There were too many variables, and I didn't want to put Sian in harm's way. He was here to mend his mother's heartbreak, not cause it.

"Lorelei!" Nana Pratt burst straight through the wall like her fluffy robe was on fire.

"What's wrong?"

"That thing is back, and it's brought a friend." Her voice trembled.

"Which thing?" Nana Pratt had a long list of dislikes, so the options were many.

"The revenant," she said in a hoarse whisper.

"Where?"

"Front porch."

I hustled to the foyer before the creeper could make an entrance. I threw open the door and screamed. On the porch was Claude's hand cradling his head. His eyes widened at the sight of me looming over him.

"Hi again," he said.

"You can talk."

"Only when my head is with me. Glad you're fluent in sign language. You'd be surprised how many people aren't."

I regained my composure. "What brings you back so soon, Claude?"

"No choice. I needed to act before you strengthened your ward."

"Yes, I'm working on that. You beat me." I hoped the lie sounded believable.

The ghosts now flanked me.

Ray angled his head, studying the return visitor. "Are those supposed to be ears?"

"Hey, you'd be missing earlobes, too, if you'd lived as long as I have."

I examined the grayish-green head. "Actually, you're well preserved for a guy who's centuries old."

Nana Pratt recoiled. "You call that well preserved? It looks like a lizard that was left to rot in the sun."

Claude's gaze slid to the ghost. "Must be like looking in a mirror, toots."

Nana Pratt didn't miss the insult. She whirled toward me with her hands clenched into fists. "I thought you were going to speak to the witch."

"Later," I told her and turned my focus back to Claude. "Care to explain why you insist on trespassing?"

"You've got a nice place here. Very homey."

"That's only because you don't require furniture," Nana Pratt said.

"Lorelei, are you well?" Sian joined me at the door and hiccupped at the sight of Claude. "You have returned with an additional body part."

"He's like a snowman that keeps falling apart and you need to rebuild it." I had good memories of playtime in the snow with Pops. Igloos. Snowmen. Even a Medusa once. Now snow was nothing more than a nuisance.

"What does the revenant want?" Sian asked.

"That's what I'm trying to find out, but he's being tight-lipped." I leaned down to address the trespassing body parts. "You might as well tell me why you're here. Maybe I can help."

Claude stared at me for a long moment, as though actually considering my offer. Then the hand tossed the head like a football clear across the yard. The hand scrambled after it. I watched as the head landed on the bridge and rolled to the other side.

"What an odd creature," Sian remarked.

"You need to fix the ward," Nana Pratt said, visibly shaken.

"I spoke to Phaedra. She isn't sure she can include revenants without including ghosts, too. I can't take the risk."

"He seems harmless," Ray said. "More of a nuisance than anything."

"And very rude," Nana Pratt added with an air of indignation.

"On the plus side, Ashley has a new job. She's going to work at the farm with Phaedra."

Nana Pratt frowned. "My granddaughter is going to work for the witch whose family tried to sacrifice her?"

"She's going to work at the farm. She loves animals. It'll be a great experience for her."

"An honest day's work in the great outdoors is just what that girl needs." Ray nodded his approval. "Well done, Lorelei."

Nana Pratt appeared less convinced, but I'd give her time to process.

I lost sight of the revenant as he passed through the gate. Whatever he wanted, I had a feeling he'd be back to get it very soon.

CHAPTER 17

Sian was less interested in Claude the revenant than the pink pacifier in his hand.

"Will you go now?" he asked.

"According to the latest records, she lives on Bronte Street," Ray said from his place at the computer.

"Are you certain I cannot accompany you?" Sian asked. I didn't miss the pleading note in his voice.

I debated the offer. "I'm sorry. I think it's better if you don't." Two strangers on a doorstep were far more intimidating than one, and I wasn't sure how the family would react. "I'll report back as soon as I can."

I shrugged on my coat and walked to my truck, casting glances from left to right in case Claude decided to lurk in the bushes.

The drive to Sarah Peele's house gave me a quiet moment to reflect on the information I'd been given by the Fates. The revelation that my parents had been murdered was a tough pill to swallow. Every time I tried, I choked.

Had Pops known or had he truly believed it was an accident? I couldn't imagine why he'd shield me from the truth when he'd been open about everything else.

Unless he hadn't.

Someone murdered my parents. Because of me? Because of them? Wrong place, wrong time?

The thoughts curdled my stomach. I was almost relieved when I turned onto Bronte Street. Any excuse to stop the rumination.

The neighborhood was your typical suburban subdivision. One of the many farms that once occupied Fairhaven had been sold off and divided several times over to allow for this neighborhood. Most of the houses were two-story brick in the Colonial style. The lawns were maintained, and the only sign of disrepair was a broken slat in a fence. A dumpster straddled the width of the neighbor's driveway like a hulking metal monster. Somebody was cleaning house.

A cat shot out from behind a bush, nearly tripping me. I caught myself before I faceplanted on the walkway. The cat turned to hiss at me before darting across the yard.

I rang the doorbell and waited. The muffled music of Stevie Nicks played inside. I pressed the bell again and the song ended.

The door opened. A middle-aged woman looked at me in surprise. Her hair was pulled back in a messy ponytail. She wore sweatpants and an MIT T-shirt that looked like it had been washed a hundred times.

Sarah Peele was my people.

"I'm sorry," she said. "Have you been out here long? I like to crank up the music when I'm cleaning, so I didn't hear the bell."

"Not long," I said. "Are you Sarah Peele?"

Her brow creased. "I am. Can I help you with something?"

"I'm looking for a woman who arranged to meet a friend of mine earlier this week, except she didn't show up." I tried to keep the information vague in case the information I had was wrong.

"I'm sorry. I have no idea what you're talking about."

I almost believed her, except for the framed family portrait on the wall behind her. It included Sarah and two children, a boy and a girl. The kids appeared close in age. The brunette boy favored his mother. The girl, however, was fair and blonde and looked remarkably like the fae currently living in my house.

Crows for the win.

I dove straight in. "Why did you agree to meet in the woods with information about your daughter? Why not lie and say they had the wrong family?"

Her mask fell away. "Because the message came from the original account on the changeling forum. There seemed no reason to lie."

"Did you think they wouldn't come looking for you?"

She glanced furtively around the neighborhood. "Come in before the whole neighborhood discovers I have a child from Faerie."

I entered the house and inhaled the lemon fresh scent. At least she hadn't lied about cleaning.

She stopped in front of the family portrait. "I guess this is what gave me away."

"I had other evidence."

She nodded and continued into the kitchen.

"No Mr. Peele?"

"Not anymore. He left not long after I brought my daughter home."

"And your son? He isn't fae."

"No, he's mine." She motioned to the stool at the kitchen counter. "Can I get you anything?"

"I'm good, thanks."

"So who are you?" Sarah asked. "I can tell you're not one of them."

"My name is Lorelei Clay. I'm working on behalf of the family to locate your daughter."

"I see." She poured herself a cup of coffee from the pot. "I guess they were unhappy when I failed to show up."

"More like confused."

"I didn't know what to do. I hardly expected to receive a message like that after eighteen years. I agreed to the meeting and then pretended none of it ever happened."

Avoidance. One of my favorite games.

"What did your husband think when you came home with an infant? Did he know?"

She offered a rueful smile. "It was the beginning of the end of our marriage."

"He didn't want kids?"

"No, he did not. He'd made that clear when we were still dating, and I'd agreed."

"What changed?"

She hesitated. "I did. At the time, I didn't see myself as a mother, so I went along with Tony. We were going to travel all the time. Retire early." She heaved a sigh. "The tradeoff was worth it, though. I don't regret a thing. Not giving up my career. Not losing my husband. None of it. Raising children is the best decision I ever made." She set down her coffee cup. "I'm curious. How did you find me?"

"I have experience tracking lost heirs."

She perked up. "Heirs? Did someone die?"

"Her father."

"Well, I guess it bought him eighteen years. Hope it was worth it."

I looked at her. "What do you mean?"

Sarah seemed too lost in her own thoughts to answer. "Her mother *sold* her to me. Can you imagine? Do you really expect me to give her up to a family willing to sell their own child?"

I held up my hands in acquiescence. "Whoa. Nobody's asking you to give her up. I'm only here to pass along information."

"Information about *my* daughter. I'm her mother, Miss Clay. I'll do whatever it takes to protect her."

"Her brother is the one searching for her. His name is Sian."

"A brother?"

I nodded. "Yes, and he's lovely. Their mother is unwell. Sian was hoping to reconnect them before she passes."

Sarah hesitated. "She's going to die, too?"

"Yes, which is why Sian has been desperate to find you. No one wants to take your child away, Ms. Peele. They couldn't even if they wanted to, right? She's a legal adult now."

She clutched the neckline of her T-shirt. "It's been my greatest fear that someone would come and take her away." Tears streaked her cheeks. "First, my brother. Then the baby's biological mother. I never even considered a sibling coming for her."

"You said your brother. Did you mean your ex-husband?"

"No, Tony knew I was serious about keeping the child. He didn't argue. He just packed up and left town. Three weeks later I was served divorce papers."

"Why did you worry about your brother taking the child from you?"

"He's the reason I ended up with my daughter in the first place. Adopting the child was his idea."

"I'm confused. The baby was intended for him?"

"Yes," she said slowly. "In a way."

Okay, now I had more questions.

"My brother was livid when I lied and told him the deal fell through. He isn't a nice person when he doesn't get his way. That's why I kept my married name even after the divorce. There was no way I wanted to be an Edmonds again."

"Edmonds," I repeated. "As in Dr. Edmonds?" That couldn't be a coincidence.

Her face paled. "You know him?"

"He didn't send me, Sarah."

"Oh, that much was clear. He already knows all the information you were asking."

"He must've been unhappy with you for breaking your agreement."

"He doesn't know I kept her. I faked a pregnancy so that he would think she was mine. We haven't spoken in years, though. We had a rocky relationship at the best of times. He was obsessed with being the best, at the expense of everything else."

"Why did your brother pay you to obtain the child?"

She fidgeted with the hem of her shirt. "Because he knew it would draw less attention for a woman to take a changeling."

"But you knew his intentions weren't good."

She paused. "I didn't know for sure, but I suspected. He was always ambitious to a fault."

"Why not return the child to her mother when you realized you couldn't go through with it?"

"A mother who would sell her own baby? Never. Once I held her in my arms, I knew I couldn't let her go."

I recalled my conversation with Dr. Edmonds. "Your brother mentioned he came from a family of overachievers."

"Oh, yes. I was still an engineer when my brother asked me to collect the changeling. Once I divorced, I gave up my career to look after my children. I took a job as an art teacher for the elementary school. I always enjoyed drawing, but my parents preferred me to focus on math and science."

"Why not move away from Fairhaven? Weren't you concerned your brother would figure it out and steal the child?" Knowing what I knew about dear Dr. Edmonds, I wouldn't put it past him.

"I considered it, but part of me didn't want to take her too far from the crossroads, just in case."

"In case what?"

Her gaze dropped to the counter. "In case I couldn't handle her."

"What would you have done? Send a child through the crossroads and hope for the best?"

"No, of course not, but I might've tried to find some of her kind to ask for guidance. As it turns out, that wasn't necessary." Her gaze flicked to an elementary school photo attached to the fridge with a Fairhaven magnet. "She's thriving now. I couldn't be prouder."

A thought occurred to me. "There was no trade."

"Pardon?"

"Usually, changelings are swapped with a human child, but you didn't have a human child to swap."

"No. I simply paid the woman."

Human money was useless in the fae realm. There was more to this story. "Paid her with what?"

"An elixir that my brother made. That was the deal."

"What did the elixir do?" Eighteen years ago meant it would've predated the god elixir.

"Wendy's biological father had a disease that affected the male line. The elixir would prolong his life."

Now I understood her previous comment. "So the fairy mother sacrificed her child to keep her husband alive, and possibly her son." My chest tightened at the prospect of Sian carrying the disease, too.

"I would've let him die if it meant giving up my child," Sarah said.

I didn't doubt her for a second.

"Where's your daughter now? Based on what you've told me, I'm guessing not away at college."

"No, and believe me, I felt guilty about that, but she didn't want to leave Fairhaven either. She's been happy here, Miss Clay. I promise you that."

"I never doubted it."

Sarah wiped a stray tear from her cheek. "Will you take her back to the other realm to meet her mother?"

"Not personally, no. My job was only to locate her."

"But her brother will," she said, matter-of-factly.

"Only to see their mother and say goodbye. Then she'll be back. I promise."

Sarah burst into tears. "What if she doesn't come back? What if she loves it there so much, she decides to stay?"

I resisted the urge to remind her that if you love someone, set them free. If someone said that to me under the circumstances, I'd probably hit them.

"Where can I find your daughter?" I asked gently.

Tears welled in her eyes. "Please. She doesn't know her real origin. I always said it was a regular adoption. My kids don't know about other realms. I've always warned them to stay away from Wild Acres and the Falls."

"And their uncle," I added.

Her face tightened. "Yes, especially him."

I nodded toward the other photo on the fridge. "What about your other child?"

"Anonymous sperm donor," she said. "Once I had a child, I figured I might as well give her a sibling. I thought it might compensate for the single-parent household."

"Do they get along?"

She smiled. "Yeah, they do. Michael is Wendy's biggest cheerleader."

"Sounds to me like you've created bonds of love that can't be broken," I said. "I wouldn't worry about losing your daughter to the miracles of the fae realm."

She wiped away a tear. "Thank you. Hearing it from someone else helps a lot."

A single word lodged itself in my brain. "Did you say her name is Wendy?"

"Yes."

My gaze returned to the photograph on the fridge. My

pulse sped up as I recalled the sprightly young woman who'd captured the likenesses of Anna's attackers.

"Does she work as a sketch artist for the police?"

Sarah's smile radiated maternal pride. "She does. She's extremely talented."

"Another artist," I said. "The apple doesn't fall far from the tree."

"Right? You'd think creativity would be nature, not nurture."

"The fae are an artistic bunch," I said. "It's possible your family has traces of fae blood, you know. Fairhaven has been integrating supernaturals into its community since its inception. It isn't unreasonable to suggest that one of your great-grandparents was a fairy." That could explain their impressive family pedigree.

Sarah examined her hands. "Wouldn't that be something? Fairy blood in my veins, too." She laughed. "Who knows? Maybe I'll live to be over a hundred."

Her comment triggered another memory that I debated whether to share. In the end, I decided it was best to tell Sarah and let her choose her response.

"You should know that your brother is sick," I said. "He has months to live." Unless he was able to extend his life by other means, of course, but I omitted that part.

She met my gaze. "Sick?"

"Cancer."

"Am I supposed to feel something?"

"No, just thought you'd want to know."

She grunted. "I can only imagine the experiments he's running right now in the hope of outsmarting the inevitable. I'm glad he never got his hands on Wendy. I shudder to think the experiments he would've conducted on an innocent child."

It seemed Sarah knew her brother better than I thought.

"Would you mind if I was the one who broke the news to

Wendy? It seems wrong to hear the truth from strangers, even if one is her brother."

I gave her my phone number. "Call me when you're ready, and I'll drive Sian over. Just to be clear, he won't try to take her against her will. The decision is entirely hers."

"I appreciate you saying that. From everything you've said, he seems like a good guy. I'm sorry he might be ill."

I took a moment to let that reality settle in. "Yeah, me too."

CHAPTER 18

Sian was thrilled to learn about Wendy, although his angular face clouded over when I ended with Sarah's request to run interference first.

"Is my house that bad? Does the sleeping bag smell like mildew?"

"Not at all. I was only hoping to return home to my mother very soon. I dislike leaving her alone this long."

"I understand. Hopefully, Sarah will call later today with good news." And hopefully before I had to leave for the gala.

Sian bit his lip. "You feel confident Sarah Peele will tell my sister the truth?"

"I do."

He nodded, as though making an internal decision. "Then I will be patient."

Patience for Sian meant pacing the length of the foyer. I felt my nerves fray just watching him.

"Why don't you exercise patience outside? There's a scarecrow in the yard that could use a little extra stuffing. His name is Buddy."

Sian lifted an eyebrow. "Your scarecrow has a name?"

I nudged him out the door. "Don't judge me. In my world, if it moves, it gets a name."

I closed the door behind Sian and found myself face to face with Ray.

"Then how do you explain the headstone you named Rocky?" he asked.

"It was an empty grave with a blank headstone. It was basically begging for a name."

A gust of air delivered Nana Pratt to my side. "The handsome werewolf is almost to the gate," she preened. "Quick, run a brush through your hair."

"I do not need to make myself presentable for Weston Davies." If defending him from attackers didn't change his opinion of me, unknotted hair wasn't going to make a difference.

By the time I reached the front door, West had activated the ward. I asked the ghosts for privacy.

"Why can't we stay?" Nana Pratt complained. "He isn't your beau, although I can understand if you're conflicted. He's very good-looking and doesn't have any associations with the bad place."

I looked at her. "You can't say hell?"

Her gaze lowered to the floor. "Just because I'm dead doesn't mean I'll say any old word. You won't hear me cussing either."

"Hell is a place. It's like refusing to say Fairhaven."

"No reason to shame her for it," Ray interjected. "If Ingrid doesn't feel comfortable, what does it really matter?"

Nana Pratt offered him a grateful nod. "Thank you, Ray."

"I'm sorry," I said. "I'll try to be more respectful next time."

Nana Pratt lifted her chin slightly. "I would appreciate that."

I opened the front door. "Now scram."

West approached the porch with cautious steps. "Clay."

"Davies. Something I can do for you?"

He cast a furtive gaze around the yard. "Can we talk inside?"

"Are you sure you want to come in? Could be dangerous. It's my house, after all."

He winced. "Fine. I deserved that."

I stepped aside and gestured for him to enter. "I'm only kidding. You're always welcome, West." Just because he had reservations about me didn't mean I felt the same about him.

"Would you be more comfortable if we played a game of Scrabble while we talked?" I asked, closing the door behind us.

He grunted his amusement. "I don't need the distraction unless you do."

"No. I'm all ears, unlike your friend Jax."

He broke into a smile. "I bet he's still fuming about that. I think that's the ear he pierced when we were twelve."

I steered West to the kitchen. "Well, he can still wear his favorite earring. It's the tip that's missing, not the lobe."

He scented the air. "Has Mrs. Pratt baked any cookies?"

"I'm afraid you missed the most recent batch." Between the cookies and candy, I'd be sending Sian back to Faerie with intense sugar cravings.

"That's too bad," West said. "Her cookies would make this conversation a hell of a lot easier."

"She would've baked more if she'd known you were coming. She's got a sweet spot for you."

"Glad to hear it. She seems like a nice lady."

"She's a better housemate than I expected, that's for sure."

"Must be strange, having them around all the time."

"There are rules." Sort of. Kind of. Not so much anymore.

He glanced around the kitchen. "Are they here right now?"

"No, I asked them to wait outside while we spoke."

"That was considerate."

"I know you're a private guy. I was being respectful."

He exhaled. "Speaking of respect, I owe you an apology, Clay."

"Oh?"

"I'm sorry. I had no right to be so hard on you. I was so busy calling you out for being a potential threat to this town when I was the actual threat. I endangered my pack. Sage and her grandmother. You. I want to make it right."

"Your concern is valid, and I won't hold it against you." And I loved him for it, in a platonic sense. He looked out for his pack the way Pops had looked out for me. There was so much love and compassion wrapped up in that furry hide. No wonder Sage was smitten with him.

"What did you decide to do about Anna?"

"That's internal pack business." He paused. "But you should know I took on board what you said back at the cabin."

I nodded. "Orson is terrible, by the way."

He grunted. "Tell me something I don't know."

"He abused Jax. Broke his bones over and over again, trying to get him to shift faster when he was younger."

West peered at me. "You saw that?"

"One of Jax's worst nightmares. He lives in constant fear. He's probably lived that way for so long, he doesn't recognize the feeling anymore. It's just a natural part of him."

West winced. "Leave it to you to make me feel sorry for the guy."

"I'm not saying he isn't responsible for his choices now, but his perception has been twisted over time and compounded by fear."

"Can't say I'm surprised. Orson believed fear was the only way to rule. I never wanted to be that kind of leader."

I offered him a small smile. "Achievement unlocked."

"You scared the shit out of Jax. I guess you use fear to get what you want, too."

His comment stunned me. "That was different."

He slid into a chair at the table. "Was it?"

"It was self-defense," I protested.

"They weren't attacking you. It was me they wanted."

I lapsed into astonished silence.

"I'm not criticizing you, Clay. I see what your intentions were. Identify the leader of the five and stun him into submission as a de-escalation technique. Congratulations, it worked."

"Do you think they'll be back?"

He studied the grain of the wooden table. "To be honest, I don't know what I think these days. I suspect so. Orson has wanted to rid the world of me for a very long time. I don't see Jax's report putting him off."

I planted myself across from him. "Then let me help."

"I can handle it. I never should've let you get involved in the first place. This is my fight."

"Why are you being so stubborn? I'm not some damsel in distress who's going to get in the way. I'm a valuable asset. Use me."

"I can't."

I resisted the urge to shake him. "Why not?"

"If for no other reason, Sullivan would draw and quarter me if anything happened to you on my behalf."

I laughed. "You greatly overestimate his…"

West held up a hand. "You can stop right there. I've seen the way he looks at you. I wouldn't have thought he was capable of feelings, but I've been wrong before, and I'll be wrong again."

"You're wrong right now—to not let me help you."

West raked his hand through his hair. "Trust has to be earned."

"Why not give it freely unless you have a reason?"

His face hardened. "Because you end up with a dead family, that's why."

And now it made sense. West had trusted the alpha who murdered his family.

"Was Orson a family friend?" I prodded gently.

West averted his gaze. "We're not in kindergarten, Clay, and this isn't a sharing circle."

"I told you my story. Do you have any idea how hard that was for me to share? My grandfather drilled into me, day in and day out, that I had to isolate myself to survive. That too much connection endangered my life and the lives of anyone close to me."

"Sounds like he and I have that concern in common."

I snorted. "You're more of a crusty old man than he ever was."

"He must've loved you a great deal." West paused. "Guess we both lost our parents at a young age."

"I was too young to remember. It must be so much harder for you."

He shook his head. "A great loss is a great loss, Clay. Doesn't matter how or when it happens. Only matters that we have to endure it."

"Sage loves you, you know."

"I know, and I've put her in grave danger. I never should've sought sanctuary in her house. It was selfish of me."

"She's your safe space, West. Of course you wanted to go to her in your time of need. That's only natural."

He turned an absent gaze to the kitchen window. "I need to find a way to end this before anyone loses more than the tip of an ear."

"I agree. What's your plan?"

He shifted his focus back to me. "It's pack business."

"It ceased being pack business the second those yahoos rolled into my town. I'm the liminal deity of the crossroads, West. The safety of Fairhaven is my responsibility."

He wore a vague smile. "When did that happen? Did I miss the official ceremony?"

"VIPs only. You weren't invited."

"Does that mean I no longer need to post guards there?"

"No, I appreciate the extra sets of eyes, but maybe you could include me in the text chain. Any creepy crawlies come through the gate, your guards alert both of us."

West contemplated the request. "They won't like that."

"Doesn't matter. You're the alpha, remember? You give the orders."

"You know I operate more democratically than that."

I regarded him across the table. "West, I get that you want to distance yourself from the kind of alpha Orson is, but that doesn't mean you shouldn't lead your pack at all. You can still be a good, decent alpha and occasionally issue orders that not everybody likes."

West was so afraid to lose another pack that he sometimes went too far the other way to appease them. No fairy girlfriend. No commands. No trust.

He cracked a smile. "Then I guess you can still be a good, decent goddess and occasionally scare the shit out of someone who deserves it."

"Touché, Davies. Touché."

After West left, I continued to sit at the kitchen table, lost in thought. I glanced up to see Sian lingering in the doorway.

"Your friend is gone?"

"Yes."

"Is the matter resolved?"

"As much as it can be."

"Have you heard from Sarah Peele yet?"

"Not yet."

Sian scrutinized me. "You do not seem concerned."

"It's possible she had to wait for an opening in her daughter's schedule. It's also possible Wendy had a negative reaction to the news."

"Who would react negatively to learning they are one of the fae?"

I smiled. "It isn't as simple as that. She's learning her whole life has been a lie. It's pretty heavy stuff. It wouldn't surprise me if it takes a week to hear from her."

Sian's face hardened. "A week is too long."

"I'm sorry, but we have to exercise patience, or we risk chasing her away. That isn't the outcome you want."

"No, it is not." Sian joined me at the table. "When did you discover your life was a lie?"

"Excuse me?"

"You spoke with authority on the subject. I imagine there is deception in your past."

"That's just how she speaks," Nana Pratt interrupted. "It's her tone."

I glared at the ghost over Sian's shoulder. Now seemed like the right time to broach the subject of Sian's health. I didn't feel right breaking the news to him; I only wanted to set him on the path to enlightenment.

"While we're on the subject of deception, I learned something from Sarah that I think you should know."

Sian perked up. "My sister is not musically inclined? I suspected that would be the case. Not all fae are."

"I wish it was as simple as that." I inhaled deeply. "The good news is a human child wasn't sacrificed because there was no swap. Your mother sold your sister in exchange for an elixir, one that would prolong your father's life."

Sian blinked. "My father only recently fell ill. My sister was brought here eighteen years ago."

"No, Sian. Your father was ill for a long time and would've died much sooner without the elixir." I swallowed the lump in my throat. "It's a sickness that only affects the male line."

Sian turned away, digesting the news. "My mother always puts a drop of the same liquid in my morning drink that she gave to my father. She said it was a nutritional supplement." His hand moved to rest on his chest. "Am I ill as well?"

"I think that's a question for your mother."

He gazed at me through pained eyes. "She sacrificed my sister so that my father and I could live. I do not understand. Why could she not purchase the elixir through other means? Why her own child?"

"I suspect the person she bargained with would only accept a fae child as payment."

"Why would Sarah Peele insist on a fae child?"

"It was her brother who made the arrangements. It's a long story. His intentions weren't good, and Sarah decided not to hand over the child. She faked a pregnancy and raised Wendy as her own, so that her brother wouldn't try to take the child later."

My arms began to tingle. The sensation was neither pleasant nor unpleasant. Neutral. I walked to the front door to glimpse my visitor.

A woman charged across the bridge, appearing decidedly unneutral. Her hands were balled into fists, and she looked "fit to be tied" as my grandmother would've said. Blades of grass seemed to wither around her as she marched toward the front porch.

"Who in the hell is that?" I asked.

Sian's face turned a shade paler than the wilted blades of grass. "Oh, no. That is my mother."

"Your dying mother?" His assessment of his mother seemed a little skewed. From where I stood, Sian's mom looked capable of strangling a kraken with her bare hands.

Mama Fae spotted her son through the window. "Sian Rowan Blevins! You come out here this instant."

I looked at Sian. "Do you need backup?"

Shaking his head, Sian stepped onto the porch. "How did you find me?"

"I tracked your phone. It took me a couple days, plus a payment to that pest Mauricio to track your phone beyond Faerie borders, but I managed it." Her expression was nothing short of triumphant. Her gaze skated to me. "And who is this?"

"Lorelei Clay," I said. "This is my home."

She stood back to appraise it. "I guess this is what passes for a home in the human world."

I shot Sian a quizzical look. This was the dying fairy in mourning, crying out in her fitful sleep for her lost daughter?

"Mother, you should not have followed me here. I told you I would return home soon."

"What are you doing here? Of all the places you could go, why would you come to Fairhaven?"

He folded his arms and looked down his nose at her. "Why do you think?"

Her face registered shock. "Great gods above. You came to find Rhiannon. How did you know?"

"You often cry out in the night for her." He glanced at me. "That much is true."

"Which part isn't true?" I frowned at his mother. "Are you dying?"

She barked a hearty laugh. "I am not dying at this particular moment. I am angry and confused, but I intend to live a very long life."

Now I was beginning to feel angry and confused.

"Sian, there are reasons I did not tell you…"

Sian held up a hand. "I know about the elixir, Mother. I do not blame you." He swallowed hard. "Am I like father? Am I ill as well?"

"I certainly hope not. I could not stand to lose you, too."

"Then why add the elixir to my morning drink?"

"As a precautionary measure."

Sian's face flooded with relief. I might've teared up a little too.

Mama Fae gestured to me. "Why would you do this? Why not come to me directly about your sister?"

"I was not sure how my sister would respond to the news. If she reacted poorly, I did not want you to know and cause you more pain."

Mama Fae gave us an expectant look. "And?"

"And we found her," I said, "but Sian is still waiting to meet her."

"Which is why I have remained here longer than I intended."

Mama Fae looked crestfallen.

"It isn't necessarily bad news," I interjected. "Her mother wanted to explain as much as she could first."

"Her name is Wendy," Sian added.

"Wendy," Mama Fae murmured. "A pretty name."

I stood back from the door. "Why don't you come in and I'll make tea?"

"Tea sounds good." Mama Fae swept past me and entered the house.

"The kitchen is straight back and to the right," I called after her.

I blocked Sian's path. "Not so fast." I rubbed the back of my neck. "Your mother is something else."

"She is unhappy with me at the moment."

"Yeah, I might be on board with that sentiment. What's the real reason you want to find your sister?"

"I told you. I have heard my mother's cries in the night. She is mourning my father's passing…"

I tipped my head back and pretended to snore. "Cut the bullshit, Sian. What's the real reason or, so help me, I will call Sarah right now and cancel the whole plan."

Sian heaved a sigh. "Remember the Unseelie fairy I mentioned? The one I said I have not seen."

"Yes," I said slowly.

"It is true we have not seen each other, but we have stayed in contact. We would like permission to marry. I thought if I could bring my mother joy in her darkest hour, she might be willing to give us her blessing."

"You mean you thought if you could manipulate her, she'd change her mind. And you thought you could manipulate me into helping you." Which he did, effortlessly.

"You are angry."

My shoulders sagged. "No, Sian. Just disappointed." I paused. "That's worse in the human world, by the way."

"I truly do desire to make my sister's acquaintance. It is not only for mother's sake, although my mother will also be disappointed when she learns of my treachery."

I sighed. "It isn't treachery. She knows your heart was in the right place."

Sian fixed his gaze on me. "And you?"

"You don't owe me anything. I'm not your mom."

Sian hung his head. "But I was not entirely truthful with you."

"Yeah, I sort of got that when your mother crashed through my gate like the Hulk."

"I am deeply ashamed," Sian said. "Lying is abhorrent to my kind."

"You didn't outright lie. You skirted the truth."

His cheeks grew flushed. "I sincerely apologize. I hope you can find it in your heart to forgive me."

"You're a son with great love for the family he has and the one he wants to create for himself," I said. "There's nothing to forgive."

"Thank you," he whispered.

We joined his mother in the kitchen, and I put the kettle on to boil.

"What in Faerie is that contraption?" his mother asked.

I followed her incredulous gaze. "My computer."

She bellowed with laughter. "And here I thought this realm was supposed to be lightyears ahead with technology."

My phone jolted me from my stupefied state, and I spotted Phaedra's name on the screen. "Excuse me for a moment. I need to take this call."

"Is it Sarah?" Sian asked, and I shook my head in response.

"I'll make the tea," Nana Pratt trilled. "You deal with the phone call."

I ducked into the dining room. "I could really use good news right now."

"I think I found it!" Phaedra's voice was so loud, I had to draw the phone away from my ear.

"The curse?"

"Yes. There's a curse in one of the books that someone annotated. It seems to fit the demon's situation."

"Witches annotate curses?"

"Only the anal ones."

My pulse raced. "How quickly can you meet me at the lake?"

"I need a little time to gather the ingredients to break it, but I should be able to acquire everything."

"A little time as in two days or two hours?"

"Two hours."

"Then I'll see you there in two hours," I said and hung up.

"You have the gala," Nana Pratt interrupted.

I whirled around to face her. "I thought you were making the tea."

"It's brewing. You can't possibly go breaking curses now. What will you do if the demon attacks you?"

I raced upstairs to my bedroom. "What I always do. Defend myself."

"You'll need to rewash and style your hair," the ghost chided as she trailed behind me.

I unlocked my weapons trunk and pondered the best

options to keep the demon at bay. The escrima sticks would be good for blocking and poking, although not impervious to fire. I removed them from the trunk and set them aside.

"Why not the double-sided axe?" Ray asked.

"I'm choosing defensive weapons. I only want to keep the demon from killing me."

"Why not kill her?"

Still in a crouched position, I turned to regard the ghost. "When have you known me to kill for the hell of it?"

"You'd be ridding the world of a dangerous monster responsible for the deaths of dozens of innocent people," Nana Pratt interrupted.

I zeroed in on her. "So you do think it's acceptable to kill sometimes, just like Gun and Cam."

She glanced away.

"To our knowledge, the kulshedra wasn't killing anyone until she was trapped in the lake," I continued. "The problems she caused at Bridger farm involved livestock and crops."

"That justifies the lives the creature has taken since then? That's like saying murder is okay if you're already in prison for grand larceny."

He made a good point. "I'll take throwing knives and a sword, too. How's that?"

"The demon already murdered a lot of people, Lorelei. I don't want you to be one of them."

"Ray's right. You don't want to miss the opportunity to wear that pretty dress."

I hopped to my feet. "Not a person, remember?"

"You said you're a goddess in a human body born to a human family. That makes you as much of a person as Ingrid and me. Just because you have godly gifts doesn't make you indestructible."

"You don't need to worry about me, Ray. Phaedra's a talented witch. She and I can handle this."

"Why don't you call your boyfriend for backup? He's got an arm that turns into a flaming sword, or he can turn into that scary monster. Alicia said he's terrifying."

"Kane is not my boyfriend, and I don't need backup."

"Why not?" Ray asked.

"Because I have managed my own affairs for my entire adult life…"

"Not the backup," Ray interrupted. "Why isn't he your boyfriend?"

I felt the tension creep through my body, tightening muscles that I needed loose for the lake.

My phone rang again. No rest for the insanely busy.

"Hello?"

"Lorelei, this is Sarah Peele."

I closed my eyes and swallowed a groan.

"Wendy would very much like to meet her family."

I glanced at the weapons spread around me. "Now?"

"If that's all right with you. Is Sian with you now? Because I can drive her over."

I released a breath. "Yes, of course it's all right. It's actually good timing because Sian's mother is also here."

Dead silence greeted my statement.

"Sarah?"

"I thought she was on her deathbed."

"It's a bit more complicated than that, but it means Wendy can meet them both right here on Fairhaven soil."

"Yes, I suppose that's a plus. What's your address?"

"Bluebeard's Castle."

"You're joking. You're the crazy lady who bought that money pit?"

"Señorita Loco at your service." In so many ways.

I hung up and called Phaedra with an update. The kulshedra would have to wait.

. . .

Sarah opted to wait in the car outside the gate and sent Wendy alone to the Castle. Sian and his mother decided to meet her in the adjacent cemetery for privacy. I didn't have the heart to tell them there was no such thing with Nana Pratt and Ray around.

I paced the foyer, glancing outside every so often to make sure Sarah didn't come tearing up the walkway on the fumes of fear and regret.

Nana Pratt poked her head through the wall. "It's going well so far."

"No one's upset or angry?"

"No. Wendy is showing them pictures on her phone that she's drawn and they're making the appropriate noises."

My hands fidgeted. "Should I say hello or leave them alone?"

"I think it might be goodbye. Sian is talking about heading back to Faerie with his mother."

I grabbed a sweater and sauntered outside to the cemetery where the three fae were chatting and laughing. Wendy seemed at ease with them. I wondered whether she felt as comfortable in the human world as she would in Faerie. I sometimes wondered how I would feel in Melinoe's natural habitat, but the underworld didn't hold much appeal for me.

Wendy was the first to notice me.

"Sister, this is Lorelei Clay," Sian said. "She is the friend who found you."

The young woman beamed. "Can you believe I'm a fairy? What little girl doesn't dream of meeting one? And to find out I am one? A literal fairy tale."

"I'm glad to see you're all getting along."

"It has been wonderful," Mama Fae said; her eyes were moist with tears. "A dream come true, not only to see her again, but to be forgiven." She fanned herself. "And here I thought my heart had turned to stone."

"And now we must return to Faerie," Sian said. "I have certain matters to attend to." He winked at me.

"Will you visit them?" I asked Wendy.

"Very soon, if my mother agrees." She gave me a shy smile. "This has been the most exciting thing that's ever happened to me. Thank you for finding me, Miss Clay."

Mama Fae smoothed Wendy's hair in an affectionate gesture. "Thank your mother for me, too, for taking such excellent care of you. I could not have wished for a better outcome."

Sian bowed. "Lorelei, your warm hospitality will not be forgotten."

"I think warm is overstating it," I said. "Those radiators are past their best."

"Hey, Cinderella," Ray called. "You'd better get ready for the ball. I don't think any of those fairies seem like godmother material."

I said goodbye to my guests and hurried inside the house to change. As I pulled off my top, I glanced at the phone to see a final message from Sarah that simply read, *thank you*.

CHAPTER 19

The ghosts fussed over me as I prepared for the gala. They'd respectfully left the bedroom when I changed into my dress but returned to critique my hair and makeup. Priorities.

"How does it feel to have reunited a family?" Ray asked.

I took a moment to reflect. "Amazing, actually. I spent years tracking lost heirs for the dead. It was nice to finally track someone for the living, even if it was under false pretenses."

"I still like Sian," Nana Pratt said firmly.

"So do I," I admitted. "As far as bending the truth goes, he wasn't so bad." My own lies were much worse as far as I was concerned.

The ward pulsed through me, sending pleasurable sensations to my extremities. Now that I understood how to interpret Phaedra's magical formula, I knew which visitor had arrived.

I checked my hair and makeup in the bathroom mirror one last time. The smoky eyeliner seemed excessive but given that my body was clad in a divine dress, it seemed only right to make an extra effort with my face.

"You've spent more time looking at your reflection this evening than the entire time I've known you," Ray said. "You remind me of Renee in her teenage years."

I ducked out of the bathroom. "I can't help it. I'm stressed about tonight."

"Because you'll have to admit you have feelings for Kane?"

My head snapped to attention. "Why would I have to do that? No, because of Magnarella and his investors. We have to stop this project from moving forward without leaving a bloodbath in our wake." For all we knew, the investors were simply clueless humans with capital to spare. They might not know the details of the vampire's proposal, only what he chose to share with them.

Nana Pratt floated into the bedroom, fanning herself. "Oh, my. I've never seen your beau look so handsome. You can hardly tell he was once in league with devils."

I dropped a small dagger into my purse and snapped it closed. "Demons," I corrected her.

The doorbell rang, startling me. I dropped my purse on the floor and then promptly stepped on it, twisting my ankle.

Laughter boomed from Ray. "Boy, do I wish I could follow you to the gala. This is going to be a night to remember."

Nana Pratt clapped her wispy hands together. "Ooh, you can command us to go with you, can't you?"

"No," I said firmly. "I can't."

"You can," she insisted. "You controlled my hand when you showed me how to use the putty knife to remove the wallpaper. I bet you can do a lot more than that. Let us come with you. We promise to be good. We can even help you."

Nana Pratt had been paying closer attention than I realized.

"You knew I did that?"

"Of course, dear. You were being helpful. There's no harm in that."

I hesitated. "Help me how?"

"You can't be everywhere at once. We can eavesdrop on all the people you aren't able to talk to."

"Divide and conquer," Ray added with an enthusiastic punch to his palm.

I actually found myself considering the option.

"It would be a nice change of scenery," Nana Pratt said. "Not that I mind the grounds of the Castle. I'd rather be here than…" She jacked a thumb over her shoulder to indicate the afterlife.

"It could be dangerous," I said.

"Not for us," she shot back. "We're already dead."

"Just because you're dead doesn't mean you're beyond certain kinds of torture."

"Like what?" Nana Pratt asked. "I'm immune to bullet wounds and vampire fangs."

"There are others way to hurt someone that don't involve their physical bodies."

Ray's expression turned solemn. "She means our loved ones, Ingrid. The reason we stay tethered to this place. Our living relatives could become collateral damage if we upset the wrong people."

Worry lines formed over Nana Pratt's wrinkled brow. "I see. I'm starting to understand why Lorelei has kept to herself all these years. You don't have to worry about endangering anyone you love if you don't love anyone."

My chest tightened. "I need to open the door for Kane."

"Kane has taken care of that himself." The prince of hell stood framed in the doorway of my bedroom, looking more debonair than I'd ever seen him. Nana Pratt was right. Wowzers.

"Hi," I said, momentarily distracted by his sudden appearance.

"Hi." His gaze traveled slowly from my head to my feet. "I'm sorry I let myself in. I thought perhaps you hadn't heard the bell." He shook his head. "You look like a star that's been plucked out of the sky. Simply breathtaking."

"Are you sure you want to wear such a low-cut dress?" Nana Pratt asked.

"Come on, Ingrid," Ray chided her. "It's the twenty-first century."

"I don't mean because I'm a prude. I mean because of the vampires. Won't all that skin be like waving a red flag in front of a bull?"

I smiled at the elderly ghost. "I can handle myself."

"We have spectators, I presume," Kane said.

"We do."

His gaze flicked to the bed. "It wouldn't be the first time."

I shoved him toward the door. "Not a chance, Romeo. This is a work event, remember?"

"A work event that doesn't involve a paycheck doesn't seem right," Ray said.

"Especially for someone like you who needs money, Lorelei," Nana Pratt chimed in.

Kane couldn't seem to tear his eyes off the dress. "Your trip to the city was worth it, I see."

I didn't tell him about my encounter with the Fates. There was too much to unpack yet.

I spread my arms wide to give him a better view. "You like the dress?"

His eyes sparked with mischief. "It's the body underneath that interests me more."

I urged him downstairs. "Let's go before you forget why we're doing this in the first place."

He snaked an arm along my waist. Luckily, I'd been prepping myself all day in anticipation of his touch. There'd be no accidental trips down his memory lane tonight if I could help it.

"We're going to dance the night away, isn't that it?"

I swatted his hand away. "No. This is purely professional."

"What about us?" Nana Pratt called after me. "Are we coming?"

I stopped at the front door and swiveled to face the ghosts. "I command you both to attend the gala with me this evening."

Kane's eyes widened. "What are you doing?"

"Bringing reinforcements."

"Is that wise?"

"We need more eyes and ears than we have. No one will know they're in the room."

"I thought they were anchored to this property."

"They are, unless I choose to untether them, which I have for tonight."

Kane stared at me. "Now I'm wondering what else you can do that you haven't told me."

I gave him a demure look. "So many things," I whispered.

Kane placed his hand on the small of my back and guided me out the door. "And I can't wait to experience each and every one of them for myself."

"If you're going to flirt like this the whole night, I'm definitely going to eavesdrop on other people," Ray grumbled.

Kane escorted me across the bridge and through the gate to a sleek silver car. The passenger door opened automatically, revealing a glowing blue interior.

"You didn't have to spring for a rental just for this," I said.

"It isn't a rental. It's a concept car."

"I thought those never actually got made."

Kane's mouth split in a self-satisfied grin. "They do for me."

Nana Pratt contemplated the strange car. "How does this work for us? Should we get in, too?"

"Yes, you're basically the barnacles to my whale until we're safely inside the compound."

Kane's eyebrows lifted. "Did you just liken yourself to a whale?"

"It makes sense for the analogy." I motioned for the ghosts to enter the car and followed suit, sliding into the ridiculously comfortable seat. I felt like I was melting into a pad of butter.

"I've never ridden in a car as nice as this," Ray said. "This will be a real treat."

My hands stroked the supple material. "Where have you been hiding this beauty?"

"I have a small fleet of vehicles, depending on my needs."

"You and Otto have that in common, I guess." I gave him a sidelong look. "Any more secrets I should know about, or is this the last one?"

Stony silence greeted my question. Alrighty then. More secrets, it is. For both of us.

He eased the car onto the road. "I didn't notice any telltale lumps. How many weapons are you wearing this evening?"

"Only two, but I'll leave them in the car in case of emergency. I have a small dagger in my purse that will likely be confiscated. Magnarella will have a security checkpoint at the entrance. No sense losing my favorite weapon to some goon that won't appreciate it."

Nana Pratt poked her head between the seats. "I thought this was strictly a recon mission. Why do you need weapons?"

"Like I said, in case of emergency. Where Magnarella goes, trouble follows."

Kane grinned. "And here I thought that was your motto."

I twisted to observe the two ghosts crammed into the back of the two-seater. "It's a good thing you two are incorporeal."

Nana Pratt stuck her head straight through the glass of the window, like a dog enjoying the breeze.

"This is going to be so much fun," she enthused. "I wish I'd worn a nice dress to mark the occasion."

I looked at her robe and slippers. "You still can. I told you before, you can wear whatever you want. You only have to concentrate and think of the outfit you want."

"It's a pale pink dress with a matching cardigan. I wore it to Steven's graduation with a white carnation on the lapel."

Her clothing remained the same. "And how did you feel when you wore that dress?" I prompted. Sometimes a little emotion plus imagery was necessary to complete the change.

Nana Pratt smiled at the memory. "Like the queen attending a family function. Not too showy but very feminine."

"That's how you *looked*. I asked how it made you *feel*."

Her smile faded as she considered the question. "Happy," she answered softly. "Content. Capable."

I nodded. "Look down."

The elderly ghost gasped as she drank in her wardrobe change. "I'm Cinderella at the ball."

"Which makes you the fairy godmother, Lorelei," Ray interjected. "Much better than a whale, don't you think?"

"How about you, Ray?" I asked. "Want to change out of your plaid shirt? Maybe throw on a suit for tonight?"

"I didn't like wearing suits when I was alive. No interest in wearing one now."

Kane kept his gaze fixed on the road ahead. "Fair warning. If Magnarella so much as breathes wrong in your direction, I'm stepping in."

I gave him a hard look. "Is that so?"

He noticed my expression. "Hold on. Allow me to rephrase. I know my help isn't needed because you're more than capable of taking care of yourself, but would you like my assistance nonetheless?"

"If I need your help, you'll know."

"I can't read minds, Lorelei. I'd like to know what you expect of me this evening."

"I don't expect anything."

Ray craned his ghostly neck to observe us from between

the seats. "Look at you two. It's like watching the mating dance of the two most awkward birds on the planet. Is this what it's like for all otherworldly beings? Because it explains a lot."

"I think it's sweet," Nana Pratt chimed in. "I like that he's acknowledging that she's capable of acting independently but is still offering support if she wants it."

"That's called interdependence," Ray announced. "But Lorelei shouldn't expect him to be a mind reader. She needs to communicate clearly and directly."

It seemed Ray and Nana Pratt were both spending time with psychology books. Next time I went to the library, I was bringing home the latest John Grisham to distract them.

"I'll follow your lead then," Kane said, although he didn't seem convinced.

"Sounds like a plan."

"Please go inside," Ray said. "This is painful to watch."

I turned back to glare at him. "You can meet us inside."

Kane bypassed the valet and parked in one of the spots near the entrance marked for VIP guests.

He escorted me to the end of a short line, where we were greeted by security guards and a metal detector. These guards weren't vampires. As we inched closer, I realized they were mages.

"Know any of the guards?" I whispered.

"They're not local."

Smart. Any Fairhaven mages would recognize Kane on sight. They were probably on his payroll, too.

The guards made a show of scanning people and checking bags, but it was clear to me they were told to search for weapons of a more magical variety as well.

The guard pulled the small dagger from my purse and inspected it. "Do you always carry a blade to formal affairs?"

"At the last formal event I attended, the cheese was sliced far too thick. This time I came prepared."

The guard snorted. "I'm almost tempted to let you keep it."

I offered an engaging smile. "What if I promise to only use it on food?"

He pocketed the dagger. "Come see me when you leave and I'll let you have it back, if you're nice."

Kane stepped in line beside me and placed a proprietary hand on the small of my back. "Why don't I come see you when we leave, and I promise not to break your neck if you give it back?"

The guard's swallow was audible. "Yes, sir."

"He doesn't even know who you are," I whispered, as we entered the ballroom.

He squeezed my waist. "It isn't simply my name that's effective."

The ballroom reflected Magnarella's over-the-top style. Servers adorned in peacock feathers that would've looked right at home on the Vegas strip. An orchestra played in the far corner. More food than the local grocery store. And, of course, an ice sculpture of the vampire himself smack in the center of the ballroom.

Ray sucked in an imaginary breath. "Will you look at this room?"

Nana Pratt appeared equally floored. "I've never even been to a wedding as nice as this, and I went to Sharon and Mitchell's wedding at the Marriott in New York City."

"Takes money to make money," Kane said with more disdain than enthusiasm.

"I'm going over to make sure the punch bowl isn't spiked," Nana Pratt said.

"You do that." Alcohol in the punch was the least of my worries.

"I'll go eavesdrop on those folks near the stage," Ray offered.

"Good luck," I said. I caught sight of the host across the

room, chatting with a group of men in tuxedos. "Do you think all these people are potential investors?"

"No, I think some of them are here to influence the decisions of potential investors." Kane inclined his head toward two women in skimpy dresses that barely covered their backsides. "I recognize those succubi from the club."

One of the succubi noticed him and blew him a kiss.

Magnarella spotted me and lifted a glass in greeting. Even from this distance, I could distinguish blood from a Cabernet. If he was drinking openly, then that meant everyone in this ballroom had knowledge of the hidden world. Made sense. It was unlikely a god elixir would be funded by the average human, no matter how deep their pockets. Unless they agreed to be silent investors, any potential investors would want updates on the progress of the project. There was no getting around the supernatural aspect of it.

Magnarella downed his drink and placed the empty glass on a passing tray, never taking his eyes off me.

Kane's grip on my waist tightened. "Let's dance before the night is ruined by our host."

"I think we should circulate. That's the reason we're here, remember?"

His eyes locked on me. "Yes," he said distractedly. "Of course."

"Miss Clay and Mr. Sullivan," Magnarella's voice carried across the ballroom as he advanced toward us. "I am so pleased to have you with us this evening."

There was no avoiding the vampire now.

I flashed a bright smile. "Wouldn't miss it. A promise is a promise."

He snapped his fingers and a server appeared beside us. "My special guests require refreshments."

"After we work up our thirst on the dance floor." Kane spirited me away before the vampire could say another word.

"We should've asked questions while we had his full attention," I hissed over the sound of the music.

Kane kept one hand draped along my waist and slid his other hand into mine. "Do you really believe he would tell us anything valuable? The only information we'll learn here tonight is from unsuspecting guests."

True.

"They play this piece beautifully," I said, casting a glance at the orchestra.

"Chopin?"

"Beethoven. 'Violin Romance no. 2 in F Major.'"

His head tilted as he gazed at me.

"What? Is it my eyeliner? I knew it was too smoky."

"I didn't notice your eyeliner. I was too busy admiring your eyes." He seemed to catch himself and retreated from the compliment. "I heard you're the one who subdued the wolves at Sage's house."

"Only one wolf. The leader." I suddenly became painfully aware of the short distance between his mouth and mine.

"Risky, wasn't it? Using your powers in front of others."

"I only wanted to de-escalate the situation before anyone was killed, which I did. The only ones who know what really happened are West and Jax."

Kane flinched. "West *knows*?"

"It was necessary."

The other guests blurred around us as we continued to dance.

"How did it feel?"

"Telling West the truth?"

"Subduing the werewolf."

"I didn't stop to think how it felt. I needed to act, and I did."

His brow wrinkled. "That doesn't concern you?"

My body stiffened in his arms. "What about it should concern me?"

"That you were so quick to resort to your powers in a time of perceived crisis."

I blinked. "You've uttered multiple wrong words in such a short sentence. Impressive."

"West is more than capable of defending himself. You should've stayed out of it instead of endangering yourself and others."

I balked. "Now you sound like Pops. What's gotten into you?"

The pads of his fingers pressed into my skin. "You, Lorelei Clay. You've gotten into me."

And it terrified him.

"You're the one who dubbed me the liminal deity. Should I have let them kill Sage and Gran and kidnap West?"

"I suggested nothing of the sort, but if you intend to use your powers more frequently in Fairhaven, you should practice."

I scrutinized him. "Why do you care whether I practice?"

His voice grew low and intense. "Why do you think?"

"You think if I can learn to control the darkness within me, that we have a chance."

"You see that, don't you? I've come too far, Lorelei. I can't risk falling back into the depths of that hell. I agreed to move forward at the pace you set, but unless you do the work, time alone is meaningless."

I continued to sway in his arms as I mulled over his words.

He leaned forward, his lips brushing my earlobe, and whispered, "Tell me you don't want it as much as I do, and I'll walk away right now. We never need speak of it again."

I wanted it. I wanted it more than I'd ever wanted anything in my life, and I resented him for it. I'd tried so hard to keep my life simple. Manageable. Fairhaven changed all that.

I found my voice again. "I don't want death and darkness for either of us. You know that."

"But?" Kane prompted. "I hear a 'but' coming."

"I can't make a promise I don't know that I can keep."

"You can promise to try."

"And that would be enough for you? You'd risk your humanity solely on my pledge to try?" I was willing to bet on myself in many scenarios, but the ability to embrace Melinoe without becoming consumed by her... Pops hadn't been convinced it was possible and neither was I.

"I'd risk far more than my humanity," he replied. His intense gaze threatened to burn a hole through the sheer fabric of my dress.

The song ended, and we broke apart, except for my hand, which he continued to hold.

"We should mingle," I said, feeling breathless. "Remember the reason we're here."

"*You* are the reason I'm here, Lorelei Clay. And don't forget it." His hand slipped from mine, and he disappeared into the crowd.

"Thought I saw two familiar faces."

I turned abruptly. "West?"

"What? You're the only ones allowed to collect intel?" The alpha stuffed a bacon-wrapped scallop into his mouth.

"Did you sneak in?" I asked.

"I'll try not to be insulted. A surprise invitation showed up at the trailer park. Figured it was a sign that someone wanted me involved."

Over his shoulder, I spotted Sage as she emerged from the restroom. She looked resplendent in a green dress that cinched at the waist. The skirt billowed like a forest canopy.

"I take it you're the only Arrowhead here," I said. There was no chance he would've brought Sage as his date otherwise.

"I'm keeping this event low-key," he replied. "I didn't want anyone getting worked up for nothing."

"Uh-huh." I smiled. "Hi, Sage. You look pretty tonight."

Sage linked her arm through his. "Lorelei! It's so great to see you. Are you here alone?"

"I'm with Kane. We're conducting a little investigation."

"I didn't think you were here for the drinks." She pulled a face. "Steer clear of the blood bar in the VIP lounge. They're offering body shots. I'll leave the rest to your imagination."

My gaze swept the room. "Have you learned anything useful so far?"

West raised the glass of beer to his lips. "Based on that ice sculpture, I'd say Magnarella thinks very highly of himself."

"I said useful."

West took a swig. "He's desperate for cash."

Sage glanced at him. "What makes you think that? Look at this gala. The food alone probably costs more than Gran and I spend in a year on food."

"Exactly," West said. "He's showing off because he wants to convince the investors he's successful—a sure bet."

"Losing his financial support had to be a huge blow to his bottom line," I added.

West rubbed his thumb along the outside of his glass. "It's brave of you to be here, Clay."

"Should I mark this day down on my calendar for posterity?"

"This has to be like walking into the lion's den for you."

"More like a hyena's, but I take your point."

West looked past me. "I see your buddy Sullivan doing what he does best."

I pivoted to see the demon dancing with the two succubi we'd seen earlier.

"He has his reasons," I said, ignoring the twitch of muscle next to my right eye.

"And I can see four of those reasons from here," Sage

remarked with a sigh. "My boobs do not look that good without the help of a bra."

I tapped West's foot with my own. "This is the part where you're supposed to compliment her."

He waved his hand. "I value my life. I don't weigh in on discussions about body parts."

Sage kissed his cheek. "You're a smart man, Weston Davies."

Kane noticed me in the company of the werewolf and quickly extracted himself from the succubi.

"You two should take the opportunity to dance," I said. "Say what you want about Magnarella, but the music is excellent."

Sage smiled up at West as he twirled her onto the dance floor. I intercepted Kane by the ice sculpture, which I now realized displayed Magnarella, not in a business suit, but in his birthday suit. Delightful.

I quickly averted my gaze. "Did you notice he modeled the ice sculpture after Michelangelo's David?"

Kane kept his attention firmly on me. "I'm trying not to notice any details, no matter how small."

I smiled. "You look like you were enjoying yourself."

"The succubi were very informative."

"Is that so? And what did you have to offer in exchange?"

I didn't hear his response. I was too distracted by the image of Sage barreling toward me. Her hair had fallen loose from its updo, and mascara bled from her eyes.

I practically shoved Kane out of the way to reach her. "Sage, what is it? Where's West?"

She gripped my arms, struggling to catch her breath, and I steeled myself against the chaotic state of her mind.

"They took him. Dragged him off the dance floor. Nobody even tried to stop them."

"Who took him?" I caught sight of Magnarella across the

room, deep in conversation with a small group. Of course, the vampire rarely did his own dirty work.

"Wolves." She sucked in a breath. "Three of them."

Wolves? Since when did vampires work with wolves?

"Which way?" Kane demanded.

Sage released her hold on my arms. "Follow me."

We hurried along the perimeter of the room. I prayed we didn't attract any attention.

"What's the rush?" Ray asked, appearing beside me. "Are we done?"

"West is in trouble. Stay here and keep eavesdropping. I'll meet you at home."

"We can be somewhere outside the Castle grounds without you?"

"Of course you can, as long as I will it. You and Nana Pratt will stay here until guests start to leave, then you'll go home."

"We don't need a car?"

I suppressed a laugh. "The Castle is your anchor. You'll get snapped back there. No transportation required."

"Ooh, I'm interested to see how this goes." His form dissipated.

I hurried to keep up with Kane's long strides and Sage's frantic pace. We rounded a corner to a corridor with a single door marked 'Staff Exit.'

Sage pushed open the door, and we spilled into the night. Now would've been a good time for a La Fortuna mage to turn up. Between Gun and Cam, one of them would be able to identify the guilty vehicle. Unfortunately, we were on our own.

"Miss, wait!"

I whirled around to see a security guard chasing after us. It was only when I spotted the familiar dagger in his hand that I realized which guard it was.

He offered me the handle. "I thought you might need this."

"Thanks."

Sage stared at the parking lot in anguish.

The guard pointed to the open gate. "I saw a white van drive away a minute ago. Thought you'd want to know."

"Did you happen to notice which way it turned?"

"Left."

"Thanks."

He adjusted his collar. "The name's Chaz."

"Thanks, Chaz."

They were headed for the interstate, the highway north of Fairhaven. That road traveled east-west.

"They're taking West back to Minnesota," I said.

Sage's face radiated despair. "Why wouldn't they just kill him? Why kidnap him?"

"Because their alpha plans to strike the final blow in front of the whole pack," I said. "It's a show of strength."

"And dominance," Kane added.

"Please help him," she pleaded. The agony in her voice stoked a fire in the pit of my stomach.

I turned to Kane. "Do the bird thing."

"The bird thing?"

"Shift into a blackbird and track them from the air. They'll never suspect it."

"Then what? Fly all the way to Minnesota?"

I held out my hand. "Key."

The demon slapped a key in the palm of my hand.

"Now go!" I didn't wait to watch him shift. I sprinted to the car with Sage right behind me.

"What are we doing?" she panted.

"Not we, me," I corrected her. "You drive home and stay with Gran. West will kill me if anything happens to you."

The figure of a vampire sliced through the shadows, along with two of his henchmen. The three bodies blocked our path to the car.

"Yes, Miss Clay," the vampire said. "An excellent question. What *are* you doing?"

"This isn't about you. I need to help a friend."

"Do you mean the werewolves from Minnesota?" He was so proud of himself; he could barely contain his glee. "I was aware there was a history between their pack and Mr. Davies, but I had no idea they intended to do him harm."

"Asshole!" Sage advanced toward the vampire. I sidestepped to prevent her from reaching him. Magnarella would snap her delicate neck without a second thought.

"Funny, you don't look like a werewolf." He sniffed the air. "You don't smell like one either."

"I don't need to be a werewolf in order to care about West," Sage shot back.

"Why did you help them?" I asked. "Their beef has nothing to do with you."

"No, but I saw an opportunity for leverage, and I seized it with both hands."

"Leverage," I echoed.

Magnarella held up his phone. "Agree to our partnership, sign the contract, and your friend Mr. Davies will be released. No harm done."

"You can't promise that. His old pack is determined to wipe out his line for their own peace of mind. They'll never release him, no matter what they promised you."

I had to get to the car, or I'd never catch up to the van in time, even if Kane was able to track it.

"I suppose that's a risk you'll have to take." The vampire waved the phone at me. "I need an answer, Miss Clay. My lawyers are waiting inside with the necessary paperwork."

Sage's hand dipped into her dress.

"Your dress has pockets?" Why hadn't the Fates thought of that?

"Run!" Sage shouted, pulling a small vial from the enviable pocket. She released a green liquid in the air.

I ran.

I hit the button on the key and watched the door rise. By the time it was completely open, I was already behind the wheel. I had yet to drive an electric car, but there was a first time for everything.

I sped out of the lot, wheels sliding, and blasted past the confused guard at the gate. I prayed that whatever potion Sage used on Magnarella and his goons, she'd given herself ample time to escape.

CHAPTER 20

I ignored the pompous robo-voice in the car that insisted on telling me how much I was currently exceeding the speed limit. Unless I saw flashing red lights in the rearview mirror en route to saving West's ass, I didn't much care.

Up ahead, I spotted a white van on the side of the road. Two of the doors were wide open.

Shit.

I pulled alongside the van and peered inside. No sign of its occupants.

The silhouette of a large bird drew my attention to the forest. Its wings closed as it sailed to the ground, morphing into the prince of hell as it landed.

"They're gone," I said.

"West broke out of the van and headed into the woods," Kane explained. "The others are tracking him."

West was running for his life, and the other wolves were running to take it. At least West had the home court advantage. He knew Wild Acres better than almost anybody.

"Then I guess we'd better hurry." I ducked back into the car to retrieve my weapons.

"Not that I won't enjoy the show, but how do you expect to run through the woods in that dress?"

He was right. Aside from the obvious challenges, I'd twinkle like the lone star in a sky of darkness. As much as it pained me, I had to ditch the dress.

The heels were the first to go. I was surprised I'd managed to make it this far without blisters. That was adrenaline for you. I shimmied out of the dress, giving Kane quite a shock until he realized I'd worn a nude bodysuit underneath.

"Here, take my jacket. It's too cold for that." He removed his suit jacket and helped me into it.

"Ever the gentleman, even in a crisis," I said.

"Just try not to get blood on it. It's vintage."

"No promises."

I sprinted into the woods, searching for large paw prints. They were easy to spot in the dirt. Their path was even easier to see thanks to the messy trail. There were broken branches and crushed bushes all along the route.

It was only when I glimpsed the shimmering surface through the trees that I realized where we were.

Bone Lake.

"Where did they go?" I asked, as we arrived at the lake's shore. The trail ended here, but there was no sign of West or his kidnappers.

Kane put a finger to his lips and listened.

"Don't get too close to the water," I whispered. "You won't like what you find in there."

A low growl reached my ears. Kane and I shifted position so that we stood back-to-back.

Twigs snapped and leaves rustled as a team of wolves crept toward the lake.

"Those aren't Arrowhead wolves," Kane said.

"Didn't think so."

The wolves stayed low to the ground as they inched toward us, snarling and snapping their jaws.

Kane glanced at me. "Is that supposed to be intimidating?"

"I think so."

"Shall I show them how it's done?"

"I'd be disappointed if you didn't."

Before the demon could shift into his monster form, the trees above us shook and spit out a giant wolf. Brown fur. Muscular haunches. A gaping maw designed to instill fear in the bravest of hearts. He landed between the parties with a grace that belied his size and shook the leaves from his coat.

West.

The wolf faced the approaching pack. A powerful growl-bark tore from his throat. The ground trembled beneath our feet in response. I'd never seen this side of West. This was an alpha hellbent on defending himself and his home.

Even Kane looked impressed. "I like this West. Shall we help or will that be deemed offensive?"

As mighty as West was, he was still outnumbered. I wasn't convinced he could defeat his opponents on his own.

I held up a throwing knife. "Fair warning. I'm an excellent shot and you are all big, fluffy targets."

A black wolf separated from the pack. His eyes glowed amber in the starlight. He was larger than the others, except for West. His muscular frame and excessively sharp teeth suggested he was the strongest and deadliest of the pack.

It seemed the alpha had taken West up on his offer to come for him personally.

West didn't want any casualties the last time they'd attacked him. I wondered whether his stance had changed.

"A little direction would be helpful right now, West," I said.

The Arrowhead alpha was focused solely on his opponent. The black wolf howled, prompting the other wolves to dissolve into the shadows.

This was personal. Got it.

Kane and I gave them space, although I didn't want to stray too far in case West needed us.

Kane squinted. "By the devil, is that Magnarella?"

The vampire stormed through the woods toward the lake. He locked eyes with me, and his lips parted to display his formidable fangs. The left side of his face glowed with a greenish hue and the left-side collar of his shirt had disintegrated. Whatever Sage had released into the air had marred the vampire's smooth complexion.

He didn't look happy about it.

The vampire seemed oblivious to the wolves as he marched toward me with his hands balled into fists. He seemed incapable of seeing anyone except me, the target of his ire.

I brought my hands together, injecting as much mockery into the movement as physically possible.

The vampire stared at me with vague disgust. "Did you seriously just slow clap my entrance?"

I glanced at Kane. "I give it a five out of ten. You?"

"As far as entrances go, I've seen better at the club on karaoke night."

"This could have been a magnificent partnership," Magnarella seethed. "Tell me, Miss Clay, do you ruin everything you touch or is it limited to my business?" He kept his fiery gaze firmly on me as he reached the shoreline of the lake.

Kane started forward, but I grabbed his sleeve to hold him back. "This is mine to resolve."

"I'm not going to stand here and let him lay a finger on you."

"What about fangs?" Magnarella asked. "I only intend to bite you hard enough to snap that troublesome neck of yours. Mr. Sullivan is welcome to do whatever he wants with your corpse after that." He smiled. "I know demons tend to develop certain kinks in hell. I'd hate to deprive him of that distinctive pleasure."

Out of the corner of my eye, I saw Kane's nostrils flare.

"I visited your lab. I attended your gala. And now we're done."

"I warned you there would be consequences should you refuse."

Beyond him, the water rippled. Too subtle for Magnarella to notice, but then again, he probably didn't know about the dangers of Bone Lake. Such concerns were beneath him.

"I said we're done now." I curled my fingers around Kane's hand and encouraged him away from the water's edge.

Mocking laughter rang out as Magnarella pivoted to face us. "Do you think you can simply walk away from me, and I'll allow it?"

"I'd like to see you stop me," I said, as three enormous heads broke the surface. The vampire didn't have time to react. The middle head swooped down and snatched him from the lake's edge in one swift movement. I heard the crack of bones as the kulshedra chewed and swallowed her late-night snack and receded into the water.

Kane's jaw slackened. "Did that actually happen or is this one of your nightmare realities?"

I stared at the spot where the vampire had been standing. "It happened."

Kane's grip on my hand intensified. "Are we in danger?"

"Always."

"Josie mentioned your need for a drangue…"

"A winged hero with supernatural powers."

His mouth twitched. "Who needs a drangue when you have me?" He uncuffed his sleeves and rolled them to his elbows.

I grabbed his arm. "Stop. I don't want you to kill her, Kane."

"Pardon? You don't want me to kill the vicious three-headed demon that wants to kill us?"

"Correct."

His brow furrowed. "You are a wonderfully complex and interesting woman, Lorelei Clay."

"Funny, it sounds like a compliment, but…"

He leaned down and kissed my cheek. "No but. It's a compliment. Enjoy it."

We hurried to the perimeter of the woods, out of the kulshedra's reach. The two alphas were locked in a heated battle, oblivious to the world around them. Multiple sets of eyes glowed in the darkness behind them, a stark reminder of another imminent threat.

"I'm going to circle around and approach them from behind," Kane whispered. "Between us we can make a tasty wolf sandwich."

"Tasty?" I mouthed.

He winked and dissolved into the shadows.

I stayed put and tried to decide whether he was actually planning to eat them. Who knew what that monster form was capable of?

The threat crept into the moonlight, preparing to offer support to their leader. I made a move toward them and hoped my presence would impact any weaker members.

The kulshedra beat me to it. Fire sprayed the shoreline, throwing up a barrier between us. I rushed to the safety of the woods as the scent of scorched hair burned my nostrils. Fur smoked, and painful howls filled the air. The affected werewolves shifted to their human forms simultaneously. They rolled in the dirt until the flames were extinguished.

More wolves burst through the trees. My muscles relaxed when I recognized the markings of Anna and Bert. Someone had alerted the Arrowhead Pack.

The wolves lunged at the members of the opposing pack

while they were still recovering from the kulshedra's attack. I lost sight of the alphas.

"We meet again."

I spun around to see Jax approaching me from behind. "Sorry about the ear. I had to get my message across in the most efficient and effective way possible."

He grunted. "I probably won't kill you efficiently, but I can promise it'll be effective."

I tossed down my throwing knife and held up my hands, palms out. This was as submissive as I was willing to get. "Jax, this isn't who you are. I saw what your alpha put you through. I'm sorry you had to endure that."

His face twisted in anger. "I don't need your pity."

"You and West were friends once upon a time. He doesn't want to see you hurt, even now. Doesn't that speak volumes about the kind of alpha he is?"

Jax spat. "He'd kill me if he had half a chance."

"Not true and you know it. West is someone who puts the welfare of his loved ones above all else. And he's never, ever cruel."

Anna cut through the trees in human form. Blood streaked her hair and face. "You good here, Clay?"

I kept my gaze fixed on Jax. "Undecided."

Jax growled and dashed toward the shore just as the waters parted again. The kulshedra was back for an encore.

Anna whistled and the Arrowhead wolves wisely retreated into the woods. Orson's howls carried across the lake as he ordered his pack to attack the bigger threat.

Panic seized me as his wolves shifted from human form. My heartbeat thundered in my ears, drowning all other sounds.

"No!" I rushed forward as they launched themselves at the three-headed demon. This pack had to be more terrified of their alpha than the kulshedra to obey the command. I couldn't begin to imagine the type of leader he was. Arrowhead lucked out the day Weston Davies showed up on their doorstep.

I waved my arms from the shoreline. "She's trapped in the lake. Retreat and she can't hurt you!"

The kulshedra wasn't acting out of malice, only basic instinct. They misunderstood the situation—there was no need to engage. Werewolves usually operated at a higher level, despite their primal side.

But not tonight.

Working as a team, they bit and broke and crushed the kulshedra's body. The demon's serpentine tail smacked two wolves clear across the shore and into the woods.

Every nerve ending in my body screamed for mercy. I had to stop them from killing her and each other.

Pushing through the panic, I closed my eyes and concentrated, extending my supernatural sensors to the spirits in the lake. I felt each and every one of them. Their pain. Their confusion. Their desire for peace. I fought to keep an emotional separation between us, the way Pops had taught me. I was their goddess, and I was in control, not the spirits.

I summoned them to the surface, to the aid of the very creature that had killed them. The irony wasn't lost on me, but I was more interested in respecting life than retribution. I wasn't a fury devoted to exacting justice, or a fate preparing to cut a thread. I was Melinoe, goddess of ghosts and nightmares. Yes, I had the power to create those nightmares.

But I also had the power to end them.

Collectively, the spirits rose from the depths like a sunken galleon from the bottom of the sea. They didn't appear as human as Ray and Nana Pratt. Some wore layers of wet reeds. Others had lost their human shape, their bodies lacking arms or legs. Years stuck in the lake had twisted their forms and possibly their minds. It was a dangerous gamble to call upon them, but desperate times called for desperate measures.

And there was one surefire way to secure their loyalty.

I seized control of the spirits—all of them. My muscles twitched in response as they resisted. I had no experience with so many at once, especially ones so feral, but I had to try. I kept my focus on the spirits, infusing them with the ability to manipulate the physical world.

Then I willed the ghosts to charge.

The wolves were so focused on the demon, it took a moment for them to register the otherworldly presence. It was only when they were torn from the kulshedra with great force that they realized there was an invisible hand at work. The ghosts dragged the werewolves from the demon's body and flung them into the lake.

It became hard to breathe. I felt pressure on my chest, as though the ghosts were all piled on top of it in their corporeal forms. My strength waned as I tried to redirect the spirits to drag the werewolves to land. It wasn't in the same ballpark as manipulating Nana Pratt's hand. The effort of puppeteering so many at once took its toll. My knees buckled, and I sank to the ground. The tether snapped, and I no longer felt the weight of the spirits.

The relief was short-lived.

Nearby the water rippled and a cold panic seized me. I couldn't move. I'd wrung every ounce of energy from my body. My lips parted to call for help, but my frail voice was drowned out by the sound of the kulshedra's roar.

I stared helplessly at the creature, wanting desperately to tell her that I had a plan to release her from the curse that trapped her in the lake, out of sight and alone for decades. That she deserved her freedom.

If only I hadn't waited.

The demon's eyes observed me with a mixture of hunger and sorrow. I knew which feeling she would choose to honor.

My body felt like it was gliding over gentle waves. Only

when I saw the tree branches overhead did I realize I was moving.

I craned my neck for a glimpse of my rescuer but saw no one. It made no sense. I was definitely moving. In fact, I was now out of the danger zone.

The ground shook as three heads crashed to the earth in unison. I choked back a cry. All my efforts had been in vain.

I focused on my breathing as I worked to regain my strength. A hand scrambled to my side and tugged me to a seated position. I sagged against the trunk of the nearest tree.

"Claude?" My voice was barely a whisper.

The revenant patted my hand.

"Thanks for lending a hand."

Claude smacked my arm before scurrying into the woods. I didn't have the energy to call him back. For whatever reason, the revenant had saved me. I'd analyze it later. For now, I was grateful.

"I don't know what you did to them, but I know it was you!"

Orson staggered toward me, drenched in blood. Each step closer promised vengeance. There was no sign of West or Kane or anybody else.

I scanned the ground for my weapons, but they were too far away.

The alpha threw himself on me, toppling me to the side. I didn't—couldn't resist. Pain seared my abdomen as a rib cracked from his weight. Sharp claws slashed my arms.

He was starting to shift.

I grabbed the hair at the nape of his neck and used my last remaining strength to wrest control of his mind.

An image of West appeared, at least he resembled West. He was a few inches taller and wider, and his nose was more crooked, but he was otherwise Weston Davies. Shadows of wolves lowered themselves to the ground in submission. This nightmare version of West snapped Orson's neck like a popsicle stick and skinned the wolf to wear his black coat as a prize.

The image of West slipped away, replaced only by darkness. I inhaled sharply. It was easier to breathe again, despite the broken ribs.

"Lorelei." A voice cut through my jumbled thoughts.

"Kane," I murmured.

"Talk to me, Lorelei."

West. The voice belonged to West.

"Is he dead?"

"Yes."

I exhaled.

It took a few minutes to regain my bearings.

West crouched beside me. "How bad are you hurt?"

"I'll live."

"Did you see his worst nightmare?"

I nodded.

"Surprised he had one. What was it?"

"You."

West's eyebrows lifted. "You're joking."

I moved to a more comfortable position as my strength returned. "He was afraid of you, West. That's why he hunted you all these years. He knew how strong you'd become. He feared you'd return to reclaim your place in the pack and kill him, and that the other wolves would embrace you as their leader."

"Well, one part of his nightmare came true." West gazed at the lake. "How did you fight those wolves in the lake without touching them?"

"I didn't fight them."

He offered a patient smile. "Okay, let's try a different line of questioning. I know you were responsible for what happened out there. What did you do?"

"The kulshedra killed a lot of people over the years. Their spirits have been trapped here, along with the demon."

The alpha looked at me with an inscrutable expression. "You controlled them."

"Yes."

"All of them?"

"Yes. I'm sorry. I know you didn't want any bloodshed. I didn't mean for the wolves to die."

"If there's one thing I seem to learn over and over, it's that life doesn't always happen the way we want it to. Resistance to that reality only brings pain and suffering. Better to accept what is and keep moving forward."

I groaned, prompting him to check closer for wounds.

"Your arms are bleeding."

"It isn't that. It's your philosophical outlook on life. Does this mean you've accepted my presence in Fairhaven?"

He chuckled. "You had to make it about you, didn't you?"

I glanced at the woods. "Where's your pack?"

"I sent them home."

"Have you seen Kane?"

"No."

My gaze snagged on a familiar figure who'd been observing us from a safe distance. My stomach curdled.

"Gun?" When did he get here?

He raised a hand in greeting as he approached us.

"I'll give you two a little space," West said, and withdrew.

"Was there a beacon in the sky to converge at Bone Lake?" I asked.

"I was with Josie at the club when Kane called. He thought you all might need backup." The mage regarded the carnage. "Looks like he was mistaken."

"Where's Josie?"

"Someone had to stay behind. Dantalion is still out of town, and it's karaoke night. You know how those sirens can be." He clasped his hands in front of him. "So, how was the gala? I see you ditched the dress. I hope it's somewhere safe."

"It is. Where's Kane?"

"Haven't seen His Royal Hellness yet. I got too caught up in the show." He inclined his head toward the lake. "And here I thought violent chaos was my natural habitat."

Right. Gun had seen more than I realized.

"I owe you an explanation."

His hands cupped his hips. "Damn right you do. I'm fairly certain I watched you command a legion of ghosts to attack a pack of wolves."

"How did you know they were ghosts?"

He gave me a deadpan look. "This isn't my first kulshedra rodeo." He paused. "Okay, actually it is, but I know a ghost when I see one—or don't." He grimaced. "You know what I mean."

"Technically, there weren't enough of them to qualify as a legion."

Gun released an exasperated breath. "You're too smart to play dumb, Lorelei. Please stop. It's insulting to both of us."

"I understand that you're angry, but I can't do this right now, Gun. I'm exhausted." Even a goddess needed time to recharge her otherworldly batteries.

"I thought you were just a ghost whisperer. What else don't I know about you?"

"Hold that thought for now. Come over tomorrow and we'll talk, I promise. Bring Camryn."

Gun couldn't let it go. "Can you at least tell me what you are?"

I closed my eyes, on the verge of a record-breaking migraine. "Please, Gun. I said tomorrow."

His voice dropped to a whisper. "Just tell me what you are. I deserve that much. I bought you a coat rack."

I looked at him. "I'm a goddess."

"I don't understand. You're an avatar, like from the elixir?"

I shook my head. "Not an avatar. Natural-born. My original name was Melinoe."

I was an anomaly. An accident. A cruel joke by the universe.

Gunther stared at me for a long moment, as though viewing me through fresh eyes.

"I thought we were friends," he said in a low voice.

His words were like a punch in the gut. "We are."

"Then why did you lie?"

"I didn't. My name is Lorelei Clay. I am everything I told you."

"You are so much more than what you told me."

My head throbbed. "Can we put a pin in this? There's a lot to say, and I can't manage it now."

"Why didn't you trust me enough to tell me the truth? Is this because I'm an assassin?" His eyes blazed with recognition. "It wasn't Nana Pratt expressing misgivings about me, was it? It was you."

"No, I swear it wasn't. I don't judge you or Cam…" I had no right to judge anyone given my own performance tonight.

Gun backed away. "Right. Because the gods are universally known for their kindness and compassion."

"Gun, you know me."

"Apparently, I don't." He turned and stalked off into the woods.

I'd give him time to cool off. Then maybe he'd forgive me. I hoped.

I struggled to my feet in search of Kane. I found West first. The werewolf was crouched beside the body of the fallen alpha. Orson appeared to have died midshift. There were traces of the black wolf sprouting from his face and arms.

"You okay?" I asked.

"He's been my worst nightmare for most of my life, and now he's gone."

"Not to worry. If there's one thing I've learned, there are more than enough nightmares to go around."

"That isn't comforting."

"Wasn't meant to be."

The snap of a twig jolted me. I half expected to see Kane. Instead, Anna stood poised between two oak trees.

"I told you all to go home," West said.

Anna took hesitant steps toward her alpha. "Sage and her grandmother are safe at home. Thought you'd want to know."

West's ears perked up. "You spoke to Sage?"

I realized that West didn't know about Sage's altercation with Magnarella. It was probably for the best. The uncertainty would've distracted him from the fight.

"She's the one who called the pack and said you'd been taken in a white van. That's how we tracked you here."

I was relieved to know the fairy was unharmed. "Sage is something special, isn't she?"

"For a fairy," Anna replied. She glanced at the bloody pulp on the ground. "Is this him?"

West nodded.

Anna spat on the ground beside the lifeless body. "Good. Want me to help you get rid of it? We can dump it right in the lake. It can decompose right next to that three-headed monster."

"As much as I appreciate your willingness to dispose of a body for me, I'm going to drive the bodies back to Minnesota. I owe it to the pack to tell them what happened."

Anna flinched. "And then what? Will you stay there as alpha?"

West tilted his head. "Is that what you've been worried about this whole time? That I'd abandon Arrowhead?"

Anna lowered her gaze. "I knew if they found you, it would go one of two ways, and both outcomes involved you no longer being our alpha."

"So you tried to prevent the conflict from happening at all," West finished for her.

"That's why I didn't tell you. That's why I stole the

sketches. I just wanted this whole thing to go away." She squeezed her eyes shut. "I've lost enough people in my life. I'm tired, and I'd like it to stop."

Girl, you and me both.

West clapped her on the shoulder. "Fairhaven is my home, Anna, and Arrowhead is my pack. I have no intention of leaving."

"Then why bother going back? You don't owe those bastards anything."

"I owe the pack clarity—an explanation of what happened to their loved ones, and to advise them to choose a new alpha, so they don't wonder if I'm coming back."

"They could turn on you when they see the bodies," Anna warned. "Make you pay for what went down here tonight."

"I won't let that happen," a voice said.

I was startled to see Jax hobble out of the woods. His clothes were shredded, his hair was sticky with blood, and his left shoulder drooped, but he was otherwise intact.

West blew out a breath. "I thought you were dead."

Jax grinned. "Wishful thinking, brother. You can't get rid of me that easily, although that monster's tail has a mighty kick." His smile faded. "I'm sorry, West. About everything." His voice cracked. "I spent so much time cowering in Orson's company, I felt like my only option was to become him. If I'd been half the man you are, I would've stood up to him a long time ago." His gaze landed on the bodies of his pack. "I would've prevented this."

"Except I didn't stand up to him, Jax. I ran away to stay safe. I did what I had to do to survive, same as you."

Anna nodded at Jax's dislocated shoulder. "Can I reset that for you?"

"It's one of those strange things that brings her joy," West added. "I don't question it."

Jax angled his left side closer to her. Anna's smile widened at the satisfying popping sound as the arm bone shifted back into the shoulder socket.

"She cracks backs, too," West said.

Jax looked ready to be sick. "Maybe another time."

"What now?" Anna asked. "Back to the trailer park to get the truck?"

"We can take the van," Jax volunteered. "I'll park it as close as I can get and help you load the remains." He glanced at the lake. "The ones we can find anyway."

"I'm sorry," I told him.

Jax avoided my gaze. "It's the nature of battle. We knew the stakes."

"You get the van, and I'll meet you back here in thirty minutes," West said. "There's somewhere I need to go first."

I had a feeling that 'somewhere' was a cabin in the woods occupied by a certain fairy.

"Good luck in Minnesota," I said.

The sudden quiet of the forest was a blessing because I'd become acutely aware of an intense pain building behind my eyes. The sensation didn't surprise me. I'd expelled a lot of energy on the lake and my body was now relaxed enough to process it.

"Lorelei?"

I twisted to look over my shoulder. "Phaedra? What are you doing here?"

"It's midnight."

"We didn't agree to meet at midnight. I said we'd reschedule."

"I know, but I figured midnight would give me the most juice. I decided to break the curse on my own. My family. My responsibility." She took in the scene. "Looks like I'm too late. Sweet Hecate, what happened?"

"I'll tell you later, when I feel more talkative."

She held up her basket of ingredients. "Should I not bother?"

"You should definitely bother."

"What good will that do now?"

"Your family's curse is powerful enough to keep her spirit trapped here for eternity. All the spirits. You can change that."

Phaedra contemplated the slain body of the kulshedra. "It's the least I can do."

I was barely conscious of her movements and chanting. I reserved my remaining strength for my part—where I sent the spirits home.

"It's done," she said. "Or I hope it is."

"I'll let you know in a minute."

Phaedra gave me a curious look. "How will you know?"

"If I can help the spirits cross over, then it worked." Phaedra had demonstrated time and again that I could trust her. When I felt better, I'd tell her the full truth. It was time.

I pushed through the headache and guided the spirits out of the lake. The older spirits were first to go. They drifted skyward and broke into tiny brilliant specks of light as they crossed over. The werewolves were next. They seemed less certain of their surroundings. It was best to help them now, before they remembered too much. Less pain that way.

Last was the kulshedra. The demon's shade rose from the lake, illuminated by the moonlight. She looked just as incredible in spirit form as in life as it hovered above the surface of the water.

The throbbing in my head intensified. "Rest now, you magnificent creature. Be at peace."

The kulshedra's spirit broke apart and blended with the night.

"Rest now," I murmured.

"Lorelei?"

Phaedra's voice sounded like it came from a distant plane. I heard shouts and murmurs, but I couldn't understand the words.

The smell of sandalwood invaded my senses. I tried to see

the face hovering above mine, but my vision was too blurry. I breathed a little easier when Kane's rugged jawline eventually came into focus.

"Where were you?" I whispered.

"The opposite side of the lake. I thought I could attract the kulshedra in my monster form. I'm sorry it didn't work."

He'd tried to lure her away from the wolves to save her.

Tears pricked my eyes. "Thank you for trying."

"Do you need a healer?"

"No, just rest."

"That can be arranged." He scooped me into his arms. Feelings of peace and tranquility swept over me. Kane was starting to feel like much more than a dangerous attraction.

He was starting to feel like home.

CHAPTER 21

Bright sunlight pierced my eyelids. I forced them open and was relieved to note the pain was gone. Not only that, but I was tucked under the covers of my own bed.

I flipped aside the covers. Okay, I was in a bra and underpants, so Kane had stripped off my bodysuit and his jacket, which to be fair, were probably filthy. I hoped the vintage jacket was salvageable. My skin screamed for a hot shower, but my stomach gurgled for food.

My stomach always won.

I climbed out of bed and stretched my arms skyward. My muscles felt like they'd been slightly overworked and my ribs were on the mend albeit sore, but otherwise I felt fine.

I threw on a pair of sweatpants and a Chelsea Football Club T-shirt.

Downstairs there was no sign of Kane. I stepped onto the front porch to observe the street. No concept car. Only my truck.

Ray floated to the left of me. "If you're looking for Kane, he left once he was sure you were stable."

"And I undressed you," Nana Pratt added, appearing

beside Ray. "He seemed conflicted about it, but in the end, he asked me if I was capable. I think he wanted to preserve your dignity. That bodysuit was like a second skin."

"How did he know you were there?" I asked.

"Oh, he didn't. He wandered around, repeating his request. It was a good thing we came straight home from the gala like you told us. By the time he returned upstairs to check on you, I'd taken care of it."

I would've described her as flushed with pride if she were capable of gaining color in her cheeks.

"You were able to strip off my dirty clothes?" I had to admit, I was impressed.

"Lucky I was," she replied. "I'm sure they stunk to high heaven. I was tempted to throw them in the trash, but Ray told me to leave that decision to you."

"Thanks, Ray. I'll give them a good wash first and see what happens."

"Want to tell us what happened?" Ray asked.

A dashing figure at the gate caught my eye. "I will later, if that's okay."

I enjoyed the pleasant sensation of the ward as Kane passed through the gate, holding a pink box. When he noticed me on the porch, he cranked up his usual saunter to a brisk stride.

"I was hoping to find you awake," he said.

"You could've called."

"I didn't want to risk waking you with the phone."

"Do you think I would've slept through the ward?"

He stopped at the base of the porch step. "I didn't think it through. I only wanted to see you, to know that you're okay."

"I'm right as rain."

He held up the box. "I brought donuts." His gaze flicked to the door behind me. "May I come in?"

"Well, seeing that you brought donuts, I don't know how I can refuse." I paused. "Please tell me there's a Boston cream."

"As it happens, there is."

Thank the gods. I retreated into the house with Kane, leaving the ghosts on the porch.

"Shall I put these in the kitchen and brew the coffee?" he asked.

"That would be amazing. I'll meet you in the parlor room." I didn't want to admit I was still sore enough to need a comfortable chair.

I eased into the wingback chair and waited.

"I'll light the fire for you," Kane offered as he entered the room.

I resisted the urge to tell him he already did.

"Whatever you did last night took a lot out of you," he remarked.

"I'm a bit sore, especially my muscles. Other than that, I feel pretty good."

He held up his hands and wiggled his fingers. "I can help with the muscles. Just tell me where to put these hands." His eyes glinted with mischief.

"Are you sure? That's a lot of touching."

"You have advanced warning, and emotions aren't heightened." He eyed me closely. "Are they?"

I tapped the back of the chair. "Massage away."

He stood behind the chair and began to knead my shoulders.

Nice. I could get used to this.

"Nana Pratt said you asked her to undress me. You didn't want to do the honors?"

"Not under the circumstances, no." He leaned forward, his breath tickling my earlobe. "When I undress you, it's going to be under entirely different circumstances."

A pleasant shiver rattled my body. "You said 'when,' not 'if.'"

"I chose the right word."

"Someone's confident."

"You don't get to be a prince of hell without confidence."

"Are you sure you don't mean arrogance?"

He squeezed my shoulders.

"Gun's angry with me. He knows I kept things from him."

"He'll get over it."

I tilted my head back to observe him. "Do you really think so?"

"He adores you."

And I adored him. It was a mutual admiration society.

"I don't want everyone to be afraid of me."

"I'm not afraid of you."

I let myself get lost in his whisky-colored eyes. "I think that might be one of the reasons I'm drawn to you."

A lazy smile emerged. "You're drawn to me, are you?"

"Like a fly to a horse's ass."

He kissed the tip of my nose, and I straightened my head.

"I have no doubt your name will come up at the next guild meeting," he mused.

"Why?"

"Because you'll need to be recorded as an official threat. It's simple bureaucracy. Nothing to be concerned about."

"How am I a threat?"

"Every being in town with a certain level of power must be officially identified as a threat. It's in the by-laws."

"Are you on that list?"

"As a matter of fact, I am."

That made me feel slightly better. "Is Josie?"

"Josephine is ferocious in her own special way, but her power is limited to that of an ordinary vampire."

I smiled. "I'd like to hear you call Josie ordinary to her face."

"Unlike you, Lorelei, I have far too much sense for that." His knuckles dug into a knot in my shoulder, and I groaned. "How do you feel otherwise?"

"The headache is gone, which is a relief. Plenty of knots, though, as I think you can attest."

"I don't mean physically."

I closed my eyes as visions of last night appeared in my mind's eye. Dead werewolves. Dead demon. Ghosts. Gun.

"Guilty," I admitted.

"You shouldn't."

"I didn't mean for the wolves to die. I only wanted to protect the kulshedra. West was right about me. So was Pops. My powers are a danger to everyone around me."

His fingers continued to knead my skin. It felt better than I deserved.

"Why couldn't I have just let the wolves kill the kulshedra? She'd still be dead, but at least they'd be alive." And I wouldn't have their blood on my hands.

"Because you're a goddess in a human body that's hardwired with a fear response. You reacted to a genuine threat. It was instinct."

"But it wasn't a threat to me. I was defending someone else, and I managed to make the situation worse. Maybe you were right about me, Kane. Get too close and I'll drag you down with me."

His fingers danced along the sides of my neck. "Do you really not see?"

"See what?"

"The reason you couldn't let them kill the demon. In your mind, the kulshedra was you. That's why the attack felt like a threat to your life. By protecting her, you were protecting yourself."

"I'm not a demon, Kane. That's you."

He moved to kneel beside me. "The way you see yourself… Let's just say I understand it, but it isn't accurate."

"Since when? You're the one worried I'm going to drag you to the dark side. Didn't last night prove your point?"

"Quite the opposite, in fact."

I was confused. "How? I lost control. Death followed. You're right. I'm more like the kulshedra than I realized."

He sighed. "They were killing each other, and you are not a serpentine, three-headed killing machine."

I smiled. "If I were, would you still be interested?"

"Depends. Could you still fit in that dress you wore?"

"Magnarella did mention your kinks."

At the mention of the dead vampire, we both fell silent.

"The kulshedra had good taste," I finally said.

"Or bad taste, depending on your point of view."

"What will happen to his compound?" What would happen to Dr. Edmonds and the project?

Kane resumed his position behind the chair. "I'm sure his lawyers drafted a Last Will and Testament that spells out very specific instructions."

"What does this mean for us?"

"That we no longer need to be concerned about Magnarella or his elixir, obviously."

"Not him. Us."

His hands returned to my shoulders. "Are you still interested in an 'us?'"

A lump formed in my throat. "I share your concerns."

"But?" he prompted.

Here goes everything. "I'd like to see where this goes, and maybe even pick up the pace a little."

"I've seen where this goes many times over. I promise you'll enjoy it."

"There's a difference between fantasy and reality, Kane."

"And I very much look forward to bringing the two together."

I tapped his hand on my shoulder. "You're back where you started."

"Where would you like me to be?"

"We're picking up the pace, remember? A bit lower."

"So bossy," he said, but his hands obeyed, moving to cup my breasts. "Here?"

I closed my eyes and relaxed. "For now."

The ward activated, sending a surge of frenetic energy down my spine. I jerked to the side.

"Too fast for you?"

"It's the ward. As reluctant as I am to interrupt those hands of yours, I need to see who's here."

"Are you sure?"

Nope. Not at all. Maybe it was a child selling Girl Scout cookies door to door. I could ignore that. The image of a box of Tagalongs flashed in my mind. Who was I kidding? Peanut butter and chocolate trumped third base.

I rose to my feet.

"Spoilsport," he grumbled.

The doorbell rang. I very much wanted to get back to my massage. Those hands were headed in the right direction.

I peered through the window. What the hell?

Every fiber of my being warned me not to open the door.

"Open up! I see you standing there," she yelled.

Addison Gray a.k.a. Aite, goddess of mischief and ruin, was demanding to enter my home. My castle. No wonder the ward had jolted me.

"I will not let you in. Not by the hair on my chinny chin chin."

"No kidding. You really ought to do something about that. Has your face even met a laser?"

I opened the door a crack. "What do you want, Addison?"

"I need your help to harbor a fugitive. That's your thing, right? Helping those in need."

"The last time you were here, we nearly killed each other."

She flicked a dismissive finger. "Bygones. I barely remember knocking you into your moat."

I remembered every second of the bitter battle, and I wasn't keen to repeat it.

I looked past her to the gate but saw no one. "Who's the fugitive?"

Waving, she offered a meek smile. "Me."

Don't miss **Play Dead**, book 6 in the *Crossroads Queen* series.

To join my VIP list and download an extended scene from Kane's POV in Chapter 6 of *Dead to the World*, visit https://annabelchase.com/dead-to-the-world-offer.

Printed in Great Britain
by Amazon